1

I f she squinted just so, the flapping gray tarp in the passenger-side mirror looked exactly like a whale's tail. Raspberry Lynette Granby rolled down her window until the rain painted her face with imagined saltwater, then squeezed her squint tighter until she was looking out of the whale's mouth, searching the foggy, gray sea for an island where he might spit her out. It wasn't that she didn't appreciate the ride, but the smell of fish was...

"Xenomorph."

"Where?" Berry snapped out of her dream to look left then right, searching the mostly-hidden landscape for...something. "Wait, I don't know what that is."

Her father laughed and turned to look at his daughter. "It's not a real thing," he said.

"So you didn't see one, then."

"Nope.

She gently pinched his chin between her fingers and pointed his eyes back to the road, which faded in and out of view in rhythm with the windshield wipers. She had always loved his profile – especially the way his wild, long hair used to frame it with unpredictability. His hair was short now.

"Making things up is against the rules. Does it even start with

X?"

"I didn't know there were rules. But I didn't really make it up. It's from a movie."

"What movie?"

"Alien."

"Have I seen that one?"

"No. I'm saving it until you're old enough to be scared spitless."

"You mean scared sh…"

"Hey now…"

"I wasn't actually going to say it."

She rolled the window up and leaned against it, feeling the cool of the glass against her cheek, watching the forest blur by.

"So what's a xenomorph?" she asked.

"A really scary monster."

Berry shrugged. "It's too foggy to play," she said. "You won't punch me in the arm if I ask how much longer again, will you?"

"Maybe."

"How much longer?"

Her father's arm shot out toward her. She twisted her torso away from him, but he just grabbed her leg and gave it a squeeze. "A couple hours."

Berry groaned her disapproval. Leaving the home she'd known all her life – one day shy of a dozen years – for a new one she'd never seen was the second worst thing in the universe. The first, by a large margin, was her father's stomach cancer.

"Let's play a different game, then," her father said. He coughed as he often did, cleared his throat and let out a giant sigh. "Ah…I know. We'll go through the alphabet…"

"I'm so tired of alphabet games…"

"This is different."

"How so? Are we going to use the Greek alphabet?"

"You'd have to learn it first. No, I was thinking we could name

6

Stolen
Things

STEPHEN PAROLINI

STOLEN THINGS. Copyright © 2016 by Stephen Parolini.

Cover Photo by Kelly Sauer
Cover Font, Moon Flower, by Denise Bentulan
Origami illustrations by Abbie Parolini

ISBN: 978-0-9916212-2-4

 Renewable Angst Publishing
First Print Edition: May 2016

r.

an imaginary creature for each letter."

"Like unicorns."

Her father shook his head. "I have truly failed as a parent. Unicorns are real. I'm talking about creatures that don't *actually* exist."

"Like Penelope, then," she said. Berry turned to look directly at her father, gauging his reaction to the mention of her long absent mother.

"Berry..."

"Okay, fine. I'll go first then. Let's see...A..."

"Yes, that's the first letter."

"Shush, I'm thinking," said Berry. She leaned back against the window again, squinted at the darkening sky. She ran her index finger across the glass, drawing an invisible heart, then erased it with her palm. "Got it. My imaginary creature is...Aunt Annabelle. Double points."

Her father snorted. "I can see you really don't want to play."

"I'll play if you can convince me Aunt Annabelle is real. I don't know anything about her."

"What are you talking about? I've told you plenty."

"No," Berry interrupted, "you told me about when you were both kids. For all I know she could have been your imaginary friend."

"You spoke to her on the phone last week."

"I spoke to someone on the phone who *claimed* to be my aunt."

Her father sighed again. He was clearly an expert at sighs because this one sucked all the air out of the pickup truck.

"Well, you know Annabelle and I grew up on Granby hill, but it wasn't in the house that's there now. That one burned down. Only the garage survived. Your aunt designed the new house herself, but no one would mistake her for Frank Lloyd Wright. Well, maybe if the light is just right." He paused. Berry knew he was expecting a laugh or groan, but she had never seen a picture of Frank Lloyd Wright so she didn't know which to offer. He continued, undaunted. "But I wouldn't get your hopes up. It was built in 1980 and it's kind of a box."

"No secret rooms?"

"Not unless they're so secret no one knows about them."

"How old is she?"

"A few years older than I am."

"But she never left home?"

"She tried to once. But Granby Hill is hard to leave."

"You left," said Berry.

"I did. Right after high school."

"And now you're back."

"I am."

"Why haven't I met her before?"

"It's…complicated. Or was. We're fixing that."

"Why didn't Aunt Annabelle get married?"

"She nearly did. But then she didn't. You'll have to ask her about that. She tends to be a rather private person."

Berry scowled. "Great."

"Oh, but she loves you. Don't worry. It's going to be fine. I promise it's— "

A dark shape darted in front of them. Berry screamed and her father pulled hard right on the steering wheel to avoid it. They slid onto the shoulder and spat rocks and dirt, the truck shimmying as he tried to regain control. When he finally did, he slowed to a stop on the side of the highway. For a moment the only sound was the whisper of gentle rain on the roof of the cab. Then Berry noticed her father's raspy inhale and exhale. Breaths came in rapid chokes and lurches. Berry grabbed the water bottle by her feet, unscrewed the top and handed it to him. Her hands were shaking, but not nearly as much as his.

"That was too close," he said. He took a series of small sips from the water bottle.

"What was it?" Berry turned to look behind them. A small part of her wanted to see a monster lurking in the shadows. But only a very small part.

"Probably a deer."

"I think it was a bear."

"Too fast for a bear."

He was still breathing heavily. The look she hated most – the scared spit-less look – lingered in his pale blue eyes.

"Are you okay, Dad?"

He put his hand to his chest and held it there. "Just need another minute," he wheezed.

She matched her breathing to his, then started to slow her respiration until she was breathing normally again, hoping he would fall into synch with her. Just as he used to do for her when she was little.

He took a deep breath and let it out.

"What if it was a bear?" said Berry.

"It was a deer," he said. He reached for her hand and squeezed it, then grabbed the steering wheel and accelerated back onto the empty highway.

Berry held her breath and started counting to ten. *It was most certainly a bear.*

"Or maybe a Xenomorph," she said, exhaling the words.

Her father laughed a nervous laugh. "Let's hope not," he said.

They arrived just after nine. Berry walked into the box-shaped house and didn't know whether to be excited or disappointed. To the right of the small foyer was a walkway, a four-foot-wide landing that ended at a windowless wall. There were three doors on the right side of the landing. The one farthest away was Aunt Annabelle's room. The middle door led to a bathroom. The door closest to the entry foyer led to the second bedroom.

Two bedrooms. Three people.

To the left of the foyer was a brightly-lit kitchen. Straight ahead from the front door and down three stairs was the sunken great room. It was a high-ceilinged space that looked almost as empty as their last house after all the furniture had sold. Apart from a large couch, a few odd tables, and a TV so old it probably didn't even work, there was nothing in it. But there were two saving graces of the cavernous room: floor-to-ceiling windows and a sliding door along the back of the house, and a wall-to-wall bookshelf filled with books along one side.

Berry took everything in and filed all pending disappointments for later review.

Aunt Annabelle didn't look anything like Berry's father. Her hair was the kind of blonde that came from a bottle – and cut to a length somewhere between short and long and nowhere near flattering. She was tall, with big bones and big hands and pale, old skin. Not nearly as pale as her father's these days, but obviously the skin of an indoor person. She did have her father's nose, though.

It looked better on him.

Annabelle had smiled at Berry when they arrived. It was a smile that said, "You seem pleasant but I don't know you very well yet so this smile is subject to change depending on your behavior." The same smile teachers give on the first day of school.

"Good to see you, Kenny," said Annabelle.

Berry looked up through travel-tired eyes at her father. "Kenny?"

"She calls me all kinds of things, Berry. Ken. Kenneth. Kennebunk. Just you wait."

"You must be tired from the trip." Annabelle placed her hand on her brother's shoulder.

And from having cancer, added Berry in her head. After her aunt had given them the brief tour, she led them down to the great room, where she struggled to turn the couch into a bed.

"It's actually quite comfortable," said Annabelle as the bed frame finally plopped into position. It was made up with pink sheets and a floral comforter. Annabelle gathered a couple of pillows from behind the couch and tossed them onto the bed.

"So you've slept in it?" asked Berry. She looked over at her father. He was leaning against the walkway railing, shaking his head, a smile creeping onto his face.

"I've tested it. I don't think it's too bad."

"I'll let you know," said Berry. She immediately regretted her tone. "I'm sure it will be wonderful, Aunt Annabelle. Thank you."

It was long past midnight when Berry awoke. She sat up and struggled to make sense of her surroundings. Her breath caught at the sound of a muted snort. Once her brain recognized the noise, she exhaled.

Her father's snore.

She looked up at his closed door, barely able to make it out in the darkness.

Berry sighed and took seven measured breaths. Seven is a magic number, she thought. She slipped out of the "actually quite comfortable" sofa bed and onto the carpeted floor. She crept on silent feet to the sliding door and reached for the latch. It was already in the "up" position. She inched the door open, pausing for every little squeak, then squeezed through a too-small space onto the deck. The outside air was almost exactly the same temperature as the inside air, but tasted of the recent rain.

The forest her father had told her about was little more than a silhouette. Shadows butting up against shadows. Somewhere at the edge of her vision, she glimpsed a flickering light – the kind of glow that might come from a campfire. But when she stared right at it, the light disappeared.

She tried to imagine herself living here, in this strange hill house with her strange aunt, but when she looked directly at the thought, it too vanished.

A cool breeze blew up the hill from the forest, and with it, something like a song. Just the tease of a melody that curled around a single word, a question.

Home?

Berry shivered.

The melody morphed into a low rumble. A deep, resonant growl.

Berry held her breath and squeezed back through the door. She closed it a little too fast, interrupting the night with a thud, then flipped the latch down, adding a snap to her song of retreat. She scrambled back into bed and listened for her father's snore.

It was most certainly a bear.

2

The morning opened itself to her like an unexpected present. Berry climbed out of bed and stood at the sliding glass door to take in her new surroundings in daylight. The house was indeed set atop a high hill, close to the southern edge, like it was trying to escape the small town they had driven through the night before, a mile or so to the north at the end of a twisting gravel road.

The deck her feet had touched during the night ran the entire length of the house. Just a few feet beyond the deck, the grassy hill dove sharply down to a stone wall far below that seemed to go on forever in both directions. Beyond the wall was a thick green forest. A storybook forest. She was so high above it, looking down on the treetops was like looking across a rolling green ocean. She scanned the ocean for signs of life – a smoke trail, perhaps. But saw nothing.

After a breakfast of eggs and bacon and orange juice with far too much pulp, she helped her father unpack all their things into the second bedroom. Annabelle left around noon to go into town "just for a bit," so the two of them decided to relax on the back porch until she returned.

An orange cat sauntered up, giving Berry and her father no notice, then began scratching at the frame of the sliding door.

"That cat wants in," said Berry.

"I think she just does that to keep her claws sharp. For hunting." Her father was sitting in the leather recliner the two of them had wrestled out onto the deck.

"What does she hunt?" asked Berry.

"Xenomorphs." He smiled, staring off into the distance.

"Maybe she's thirsty. We should give her some milk."

"Check with your aunt when she's back. It might just be a stray." The cat rolled onto its back, wriggled against the weather beaten wood of the creaky porch.

"Nope. This cat lives here. I can tell. We're both redheads. I can read her mind."

Berry looked out across the forest. The wind was blowing the tops of the trees, rippling the leaves like waves. She thought of her gray whale and imagined him swimming below the surface.

"Is Aunt Annabelle getting me a birthday cake? Is that why she left for town?"

"Maybe."

"I don't need one."

"I said 'maybe.' But if she brings one, then you certainly do need one."

Berry nodded. She knew what he meant. *Be nice to your Aunt Annabelle.*

"Can I ask a stupid question?" she said.

"Sure."

"You're supposed to say 'there aren't any stupid questions,'" said Berry with a mock scowl.

"Oh, but there are," he said. "So far all of yours have been smart, though. I'll let you know if this is the first stupid one."

Berry sighed and shook her head. "It just might be."

"Well?" asked her father.

"You told me a long time ago that magic was real."

"It…is."

Berry paused, startled for the hundredth time by the broken sound of his voice. His words were fragile, like frightened dandelions expecting a stiff breeze. Maybe this wasn't the best time to ask a stupid question. She looked out across the green sea. The treetops waved to her, urging her on.

"Can forests talk?" she asked, her words as unsteady as his.

Berry's father scrunched his face into a thoughtful shape. A familiar shape. When he spoke again, he had found his other voice – his real one. "If they could, they'd have lots of interesting stories to tell." He smiled, clearly pleased with the words he'd found in answer to her stupid question.

"So they can't?"

"I think every forest has a voice. It might say something like 'come play' or 'stay away' or maybe 'don't bulldoze me.'"

"So forests *can* talk?"

"A forest speaks with the words we imagine for it."

"That's not the same thing."

"Nope."

"So you don't really know," said Berry.

"Not a clue," he said. He lifted his hand, and with a royal, sweeping motion, presented the forest below. "Ask the trees."

"I will," she said.

She inhaled through her nose, inviting the smells of a new place to register in her brain. She smelled the damp dirt and unnamable flowers and the tang of sweat that had redefined her father's scent. And she smelled something like history. It was a musty, dusty smell, with a hint of ashes. She looked down the steep hill, then back to her father. "What's the stone wall for?" she asked.

"To keep the monsters in and the children out," he said. He straightened up and set his magazine on the wobbly metal table beside him. "Should I prepare myself for one of your world-famous interrogations?"

"Probably."

"Okay," he said. "Ask away."

Berry paused and took a deep breath and looked down at her bare feet. A tiny ant was navigating around them, heading for wherever it is ants go.

"Does Penelope know you're sick?" she asked. She looked at her father, reading his face. There was the slightest of twitches in his left eye, but that could have been anything. The wind. The sun. A bug.

"You still don't want to call her 'Mom'," he said.

"She stopped being Mom when she left."

Her father pressed his lips together, opened them as if to speak, then closed them and nodded. Though far from what it should be, his hair was finally growing out from the ugly stubble that had served as a billboard advertising his illness. There were strands of gray hiding in the brown, but you could only see them if you knew what to look for. He had called the new color "distinguished," but she had called it "old." She wished she could take the word back.

"You still miss her," said Berry, pulling at the tangles in her own, shoulder-length hair.

"I do."

"What do you miss?"

He sighed. "Little things."

"Like what?" asked Berry.

"Her laugh. Her songs…"

"The way she smelled?" Cinnamon, thought Berry.

"Especially that," he said.

"I don't think those are little things," she said. "Aunt Annabelle hates her."

"What? She doesn't hate her. She's just…disappointed."

"I heard her say some mean things about Penelope. Last night after you went to bed. She was on the phone."

"I thought you were dog tired?"

"New house. New bed. Hard to sleep, you know?" Berry decided not to mention the middle-of-the-night excursion or the whispering forest or the deep, resonant growl.

"Yeah," he said.

"So do you want me to tell you?"

"Okay." Kenneth turned toward his daughter, sat up as straight as his lounge chair allowed.

"She said, 'I'm sorry, but that goddamn Penelope should have her head examined.' What did she mean by that?"

"It just means she wishes your mom had made...different decisions."

Berry decided not to press the issue.

Annabelle returned a little while later carrying a cake box and wearing an expression that was the opposite of birthdays. Berry and her father were sitting at the kitchen table, snacking on toast when she burst through the screen door. The red cat stole into the house between her legs, but Annabelle didn't seem to notice or care.

"That idiot Norwood screwed up the cake." She plopped the box down on the kitchen table and flipped it open. It was a small square cake with white frosting and multi-colored balloon candies scattered around the edges. The words, "Happy Berry Birthday," were written across the middle in a perfectly lovely script.

Berry smiled and her father laughed.

"I think that idiot Norwood got it righter than wrong," he said.

"I love it!" said Berry.

"It's supposed to say 'Happy Birthday Berry,'" said Annabelle.

"This is better," said Berry.

The cat rubbed up against her dangling feet and she reached down to pet it.

"Is this your cat?" she asked her aunt.

"Nobody owns cats," she said. "But this one and I get along just fine."

"Does she have a name?"

"I call her Red. I suspect she hates it that I don't know her real name, but so far that hasn't stopped her from eating my food."

Annabelle and Kenneth sang "Happy Birthday" loudly and off-key, the only way to sing "Happy Birthday" in Berry's opinion, but there were no candles on the cake. Annabelle had wrongly thought she already had a box of birthday candles, so instead Berry blew the flame out of a flip-top cigarette lighter that had been unearthed in the junk-drawer search.

"That looks old," said Berry. Her father turned the tarnished silver rectangle over in his fingers.

"It was grandfather's," said Annabelle. "Mom said he gave it to her as a wedding gift. Can you believe that? A lighter as a wedding gift? Did you know where I found it? In the ruins from the fire. Gotta love irony."

"Tell me again what irony is?"

Annabelle opened her mouth to answer, then closed it and turned toward her brother. Kenneth tilted his head to the side, the way he always did before teaching Berry something new.

"It means…something that's strange or funny because it's the opposite of what you might expect."

"The only thing that survived the fire was…something that starts fires?"

"Yes. Exactly. You are a smart little fruit."

"I'm twelve. Too old to be a fruit."

"Should we start calling you something different then?" Annabelle asked. Berry couldn't tell if she was being serious. Perhaps after a few more weeks in her house that would change.

"No. Berry is fine."

"Do you remember much about grandfather?" Kenneth handed the lighter to his sister.

"Not a thing. I was only four when he died."

"I don't remember Mom and Dad talking about him much."

Berry watched the interplay between her father and aunt with interest. She often wondered what it would be like to have a sibling. She would have preferred a sister. They seemed to get along fine, though they each had a different way of speaking. Annabelle spat her words out like they were sour candies. Her father's words floated out of his mouth like kites.

She liked the way her dad said things. He used interesting words that made her smile or made her think or both. He said he learned how to do that from Penelope. But Berry wasn't so sure about that.

The second night in Granby House came slowly, then suddenly. After the dark descended, Berry folded open her door to dreamland, turning a corner of her blanket and sheet down in a perfect isosceles triangle, then marched into the kitchen to get a drink of water. When she returned, there was a wrapped gift on her pillow. She looked toward her aunt's room, but the door was closed. The door to her father's room was cracked open, and a swath of light spilled through into the hallway and onto the pink-trimmed comforter that made the sofa bed seem a little less intimidating in the middle of the room. She smiled at the path of light, imagining it as an arm caught in the act of delivering a secret.

Her father's light clicked off and she slid under the covers through the dream doorway like he had taught her, then pulled them up to her chin. The package tipped and bounced as she settled in, then sat there, unopened, next to her on top of the mattress. She looked at it, seeing little more than a shadow against the dark night beyond the windowed wall.

The opening of a gift was a sacred thing.

"You don't just rip the paper off without imagining first," her father had said. "Sometimes the magic isn't in the gift at all, but in the thinking about it."

A scratching sound turned her head toward the kitchen.

Red, she thought. She wants in. Or out. Berry couldn't remember which.

The door to her aunt's room opened and Annabelle emerged wearing a robe with a high collar that made her look like a princess or a witch in a shadow play. She walked silently across the floor and into the kitchen. There was a hesitant squeak, then a thump and a click. Annabelle walked back to her room just as silently, not even acknowledging Berry as she walked along the north end of the great room to her bedroom door. She disappeared inside.

A minute later, Berry heard tiny footsteps across the hardwood floor, then a gentle thunk as Red leaped onto the sofa bed next to her. She sniffed at the flat package, then curled up next to it. Berry began to imagine what might be in the package to the accompaniment of purring.

When she looked to her right out the great window, she saw a sky full of stars. She knew about constellations, but didn't know how to identify them. She waited until she could hear her father's signature snore, then slipped out of bed and over to the sliding door. Her heart was beating fast when she carefully slid the door open just wide enough to step out onto the deck.

Berry had never seen so many stars. Red brushed between her bare legs, startling her. When she caught her breath, she turned again to the sky.

"Unicorn eating cake," she whispered, pointing upward. "It's a constellation I just invented," she said to the cat.

Home, the forest whispered again. But this time there was no deep, resonant growl.

Berry stepped back inside, locked the door, and climbed into bed. Red curled up next to her, but not before resting a paw on the gift.

To guard it from monsters.

3

"You still haven't opened your package."

Berry looked up, squinting, into her father's thin face. He was sitting on the bed next to her, already dressed in khakis and a t-shirt. He had lots of t-shirts; most of them with faded images of rock bands Berry had only known about because of the shirts. This one said "The Who."

"Who are you?" she asked, a sleepy morning smile pulling at her lips.

"I am Curious," he said. He lifted the package up off the floor. It must have fallen in the night. "And you?"

"I am Curious, Two," she said, holding up two fingers.

"Then open it." He handed her the package.

Berry scooted into a seated position, her back pressed against the couch, then straightened the blanket and sheet so they drew a straight line across her thighs. She lifted the box, held it to her ear, listening.

"There's no card," she said. "How do I know who it's from?"

"Maybe it's from the cat," said Kenneth.

"Doubtful," said Annabelle, walking with heavy footsteps into the room. She was balancing a cup of hot coffee or tea on a saucer. "She's been out all night."

Berry scrunched her forehead into a question, then let it go. She pulled at the wrapping paper gently at first, as if she might want to preserve it, then tore into it like a tiger, ripping the floral print into confetti. The box underneath was plain, white, like the kind a fancy store might use to wrap up a silk blouse or a scarf. She considered thanking her father for another box, but decided the joke was tired. She lifted the top off the box and peeled back pink tissue. Underneath was a neat, fat stack of paper. Thin, colorful, beautiful, perfect paper. Origami paper. And there was a book, too. "How to Fold Paper Into Magic," she read aloud. "It's perfect, Daddy. Just perfect."

She leaned over and gave him a big hug, forgetting about his cancer until he tensed up and gently pulled away. This made her sad again, but she kept her smile as bright as the yellow paper on the top of the pad.

"Do you know origami?" her aunt asked.

"A little. And now I'm going to know it even more." She patted her dad's hand that was pressed against the mattress, holding him upright. He grabbed it and squeezed. It was exactly the kind of moment she would write about if she hadn't lost her journal.

After breakfast, she helped Annabelle with the dishes, then sat down at the kitchen table to learn a new bit of magic. Her father had already gone down for a mid-morning nap, so it was just Berry and Annabelle until her aunt would have to leave for a half-day of work.

"Do you work at a zoo?" said Berry.

"A zoo? No, I don't work in…oh, you must have overheard your father and me talking. I work at a school, in the office – but I call it a zoo because it's loud and full of people squeaking and screeching and barking and bellowing. It's a middle school, so sometimes it kind of smells like a zoo, though."

Berry laughed. "I think I'd rather work in a real zoo." She opened her origami book to a page describing how to fold a penguin. She was thankful the little book was spiral bound because then she didn't have to hold the pages open while she studied the instructions. She sorted through the origami paper until she found a black square, then changed her mind and chose a pink one instead. She studied the instructions while Annabelle opened and closed cabinet doors in search of something.

"I like penguins," said Berry, "But not how they smell."

"They smell with their noses. Just like you."

"You know what I mean."

"Yes. I do."

"What are you looking for?"

"Something to fix for supper."

Berry started folding her pink paper, careful following the instructions. But by the time she got to Step 4, she could tell something was wrong. She unfolded the work in progress and started again, this time getting all the way to Step 6 before realizing her penguin was looking more like a dinosaur. She forged on ahead anyway and set the finished work on the table to see if she could figure out what went wrong.

"That's lovely," said Annabelle.

"It doesn't look much like a penguin."

"That's because it's out of context. Here," said Annabelle. "Let me see if I can make it work."

She walked over, lifted the top off the sugar bowl, and then carefully slid the pink almost-penguin hip-deep into the sugar so it stood there surrounded by white.

"You just needed Antarctica, that's all."

Berry smiled. "That helps." She nudged the almost-penguin a little so he tilted to the right. "Some things look better when they're crooked."

When her father woke up from his nap, Berry fixed grilled cheese sandwiches for lunch. Annabelle didn't have the cheese slices that came wrapped in plastic, so Berry carved some off of a big orange slab instead. She wasn't sure if grilled cheese helped or hurt his stomach, but it was the thing she made best. He nibbled at his while she took tentative bites of the slightly darker one. It wasn't exactly burnt, but it was next-door neighbor to burnt.

Another night came and went, and the next day her aunt left for work before Berry or her father were awake. They found each other in the kitchen just after nine.

"So what are we gonna do today?" Berry asked.

"I'm going to sit out on the deck and read and listen to your stories and warn you thirty-seven times to be careful and hope that I have enough energy left after all of that to go for a walk."

"How far can I go?"

"You mean on a walk?"

"No, I mean yes. I mean, what are my…boundaries."

"Well, you can roll all the way down to the bottom of the hill. You can walk down the front driveway until you get to the dirt road. And you can wander on either side of the house until you get to the place where the yard stops and the electric fences begin."

"There aren't electric fences here. Are there?"

"Probably not."

"So…what about the forest? Can I play there?"

"Have I ever told you the story of Hansel and Gretel?"

"Yes."

He set his half-eaten sandwich on the plastic plate and gave her one of his serious-but-not-really looks.

"I know your name sounds delicious, but I'd hate for you to be eaten by a witch."

"There's no such thing as witches."

"Tell that to the witches."

"So I can't play in the forest."

The deep, resonant growl.

"Well, let me talk to your aunt about it first. We need to respect her rules. That said, I have it on good authority that this an amazing forest. It has more than a few secrets."

"Secrets make things magical," said Berry.

"I've taught you well."

"Did you play in the forest a lot when you were little?"

"I did. But usually with friends."

"I don't have any friends here." Berry sighed a big sigh. A long, stretched out sigh. It was nowhere as good as her father's, but among her best so far.

"We'll have to get you some, then."

"What about the garage? Can I go exploring there?"

"That sounds reasonable. Do you like spiders?"

"Sometimes."

"When, exactly, do you like them?"

Berry took a long sip of water from her Minnie Mouse glass. "When they stay far, far away from me."

Kenneth laughed until he coughed, then regained his composure and sighed a big sigh much like Berry's. "Well, then. Let's hope they stay far, far away."

After Berry had cleaned up from lunch, they walked out to survey the garage. It was obviously old, but had been painted in recent years. All but one panel of siding, which looked as old as dirt to Berry. She noticed it had a row of neatly carved scratches in it. A tally of some kind.

"What was that for?" she asked.

"You'll never guess."

"That's why I'm asking, silly."

"A whole bunch of years ago, this used to be a really popular sledding hill. Every time it snowed, people would show up with their sleds and sneak out back and risk life and limb racing down to the stone wall. The trick was to fall off before you hit the wall. I think they used to put hay bales down there to make it slightly less deadly."

"What does that have to do with these notches?"

"That's the tally of broken bones."

Berry's eyes went wide. "Wow." She counted the marks. "Eleven broken bones."

"And probably a few they forgot to record."

Berry helped her father carry a folding chair from the back deck around to the front of the garage. He sat in it while Berry puzzled over how to open the garage. It had two wide doors that swung to either side. But wild grass had grown up in front of it, and gravity had pulled the doors into the earth and the hinges were rusted and resistant.

"I think we need a shovel," said Berry. "To dig away the dirt and grass. Do you think Aunt Annabelle has a shovel?"

"She probably keeps it in the garage."

Berry shook her head. "You're a goofball," she said.

They worked together at a slow pace – the only kind Kenneth was capable of – tugging at the doors for nearly an hour, edging them forward inch by inch. Finally, they managed to pull the doors wide, revealing a graveyard of rusted tools and broken machines and abandoned furniture and car parts. It was more like a small barn than the garage Berry knew from her old home. It was wide enough for two elephants, and tall enough for a baby giraffe. There was a loft across the back wall stacked high with boxes and crates and at least one old metal trunk. There were a few windows in the garage but they were so clouded by dirt that they barely registered as windows. There was a door on the western wall facing the house, but it looked like it hadn't been opened in decades.

Kenneth arranged his lounge chair to face the open garage and sat down. He was breathing heavily, but Berry was too. She collected a glass of water from the kitchen, then returned and handed it to her father.

"Thanks, Raspberry. So…where do we begin? What's the plan?"

"I don't know."

"You should probably speak to the spiders first. Let them know what you're doing."

"That's dumb," she said. "I don't know how to speak spider."

"Well then you'd better hope they speak English." He set his glass down on the rocky ground and stood up. Berry saw that he was moving extra slow, so she walked over and took his arm. Together, they stepped up to the open garage and stared into the cluttered, shadowy space. "Oh glorious arachnids…we beseech thee…" he began.

"Really Dad?" said Berry.

"Too much?"

"Yeah. Try normal English."

"Hey spiders, it's me, Kenneth. I used to live here a bunch of years ago. You know that one time when I used a sparkler to burn the spider nest under the front step? Well, I was kind of young then so I hope you'll forgive me…"

"I don't think that's helping."

"Hey, it's important to be honest with spiders. So…what I meant to say was, you know all those times I killed spiders with sparklers and hammers and shoes and fly swatters? I didn't mean anything by it. Honest. My daughter Berry and I would like to look around in there. To the best of my knowledge, she hasn't hurt a single spider. If my karmic math is correct, that should make up for all my errors. So, in summary, please don't freak us out or bite us or anything creepy like that. Okay?"

"I don't think they…"

"Shh…"

"But…"

"Shh…listen."

Berry rolled her eyes, then tilted her head to listen to the garage. All she could hear was the wind in the trees and a soft buzzing sound that came and went. A bee.

"Okay, well, thank you," said Kenneth. "I think that's a fair agreement."

"I didn't hear anything."

"That's because you don't speak spider. Perhaps I'll teach it to you sometime."

"What did they say?"

"They said they can't promise anything, but they'll do their best to stay out of the way. They did ask us to try not to disturb their webs. Those things take a lot of time to weave."

"But there are webs everywhere."

"I think they'll understand if we disturb one or two. So…where do you want to start?"

Berry pointed to the loft in the back of the garage. "I think we need to look in those boxes," she said.

"I agree. But this is a bigger adventure than we have time for today." Or energy, thought Berry, noting her father's hand on his stomach. "But that will be our goal. To make it to the boxes in the back."

"That one especially," said Berry. She was pointing to the metal trunk.

"Yes, that one especially."

Berry spent an hour and a half rearranging some of the tools at the front of the garage, trying to carve a path to the back wall, but gave up when she was surprised by a mouse running across the dirt floor. They decided to leave the doors open so Red could go hunting. And so the spiders could have a little fresh air, her father had added.

Berry leaned the folding chair against the garage and walked around to the back deck to sit with her father for a while. When he fell asleep, she returned to the garage and dug around through the junk until she found a wagon. It was old and rusty, but she cleared a path to it, then tugged until it came free. She whispered a small "sorry" to the spiders, then pulled it out of the garage and around to the back yard. She set it at the top of the hill, just at the edge of the incline, and imagined what it would be like to ride it all the way to the stone wall. Berry lay back on the grass and looked up at the clouds and thought about her friends back in Nashua. She thought about how strange and sad it was to no longer have a home there. Berry hoped that the new family liked her old house as much as she had. Especially the secret room at the back of her father's walk-in closet.

She wondered about Annabelle. Did she like living alone up here on the hill?

Then she thought of Penelope. As always, her thoughts of her mother were mostly sounds and smells and colors. Recalling them was like trying to look at the world through a scarf while wearing sunglasses.

Just as she began to nod off, there was a loud thud, then a squeak. She sat up and saw that Red had jumped into the wagon. It began to roll down the hill, trailing the black metal handle behind. She started after it, but the incline was too steep and she knew she would tumble down it.

"Red!" she yelled. "Jump off!"

Red didn't move, gripping the edge of the wagon and staring up at her. As the wagon picked up speed, the trailing handle bounced erratically from dirt to sky.

"You have to jump off!" she yelled again.

"What is it, Berry?" her father called down from the porch. She pointed at the wagon hurtling down the hill.

Just before the wagon smashed into the wall, Red leaped over the edge, landing on the other side as if she'd done this a hundred times before. The wagon slammed against the stone with a tinny "thunk," then flipped onto its end, resting against the wall like someone had just set it there.

Red meowed, jumped up onto the stone wall, sniffed at the wagon, looked up at Berry, then disappeared into the forest.

"Well, that was something to watch," said her father.

"I thought she was going to die."

"Cats have nine lives."

"Yeah, but what if she was already on number nine?"

"I see you found my old wagon."

"That was yours?"

"And my father's before me. Or maybe more my mother's than my dad's."

"I'm sorry I crashed it. I didn't mean to…" began Berry.

"We used to crash it all the time, my friends and I. We'd put toys in it and send it down the hill just to see it smash. It's remarkably resilient."

"Resilient?"

"Durable. Hard to break."

"Right. I knew that. Does it have a name?"

"No. But one of the sleds does."

"I saw those in the garage. Which one has a name?"

"The old one with the wooden steering handle," he said. "It's called Rosebud."

"It's kind of a silly name for a sled," said Berry.

"Not if you've seen *Citizen Kane*."

"I haven't seen that one either, have I?"

"Not yet." He smiled. "You will. Someday."

"Did you ever ride it down the hill?"

"The sled or the wagon?"

"Either."

He forced his expression into seriousness. "Why, that would be dangerous." A smile slipped out at the end of his sentence.

"I should go get the wagon."

"I hope you're not planning on riding it down the hill."

"I wasn't. I just don't think I should leave it there," said Berry.

"It's fine. We don't need a perfectly picked-up back yard around here."

"Because there's no one living behind us?"

Berry's father coughed, then groaned, then grimaced, then took a sip of water from a glass decorated with a fading picture of Donald Duck.

"Who says there's no one living behind us?" Then he smiled again, but it was a pained smile, the kind that took a lot of effort to seem effortless.

"Maybe I'll use the wagon when I go exploring in the forest."

"If your aunt and I say it's okay."

"I won't go far," she said.

"You'd leave a breadcrumb trail?"

"No. The birds would eat it."

"Then I really think you need to take someone with you. Anyone but that Hansel character."

She puzzled, then smiled, then paused, sorting her words in her head, considering her father's response and what it might cost. "Will you come?"

He started coughing again. He held up his hand like a stop sign and coughed some more. Berry started toward him, but he held his finger up, telling her "wait." When the coughing finally stopped, his voice was a hoarse whisper.

"Tomorrow, Berry," he said.

She smiled a pained smile, the kind that took a lot of effort to seem effortless.

"Okay, Daddy. Tomorrow."

4

Two more days came and went like cold syrup poured on day-old pancakes. Nothing more was said about the forest, and the forest itself had remained silent. Not a whisper. Not a growl. Then, on the fifth night since they'd moved in, Berry woke to the sounds of her aunt rummaging in the kitchen for a midnight snack. Soon after, her father trundled out of his room, and after a long visit in the bathroom, he joined Annabelle. They spoke in hushed whispers, but the sound carried right to Berry's ears as if they were standing at the end of the sofa bed.

"I waited too long," said her father. "I mistook a chronic stomachache for just another manifestation of heartache."

"I don't understand why you still pine for her," said Annabelle.

"I don't pine for her. I just miss her. There was no one like her."

"Thank God for that."

There was silence. The sipping of tea, thought Berry. Then her father spoke again.

"They said six months, Belle."

"Three months ago," she said.

"Or more. It could be more."

"It's not enough."

More silence.

"Berry wants to play in the forest. I think we should encourage that," said her father.

"Absolutely not!" said Annabelle. "Sorry. But I can't agree."

"Surely you don't still think there are monsters?"

"What? No. And yes. There are bears. And wolves."

"And lions and tigers and oh, my," laughed her father. "Seriously? Have there been reports of wild animals lately?"

"Well, no. But they were there once. They could be again."

Berry stifled a sneeze.

"Those were just stories, Anna. Never saw a bear or a wolf or anything scarier than a rabid squirrel when I explored the forest."

"Rabid squirrel? There are rabid squirrels?"

A gentle laugh floated into the great room. "Probably not any more."

"You told me scary stories, Ken. You scared me shitless when we were kids. That's why I never played in the forest."

"But you're a grown up now," said Kenneth. "You're not still afraid, are you?"

Another long pause. Berry wondered if somehow the house had stopped sending their voices her way. Finally, her aunt spoke.

"I don't know what to think. The kids in school still tell the old stories. I don't know how they even know them."

"You mean about the missing children."

"Yes."

"That was a hundred years ago," said Kenneth.

"Doesn't make the stories any less scary."

Berry couldn't hold back another sneeze. The voices in the kitchen stopped.

"It's late, Ken. We'll talk about this later."

Berry sorted through all the words and fell into a dream about rabid squirrels and missing children.

The next day, Berry looked down at the wagon at the bottom of the hill and practiced her sighing again. Her father had come down with a cold, so she stayed nearby. She watched old movies on Annabelle's ancient TV, folded a dozen paper swans, and brought her father water to sip and food to mostly ignore. And she read. She had only brought a few books of her own (she had given her best friend Meg the bulk of her collection), but the bookshelf was ripe with possibilities. Upon Annabelle's recommendation, she started *Anne of Green Gables*, but shelved it when she realized it was about an orphan girl.

Instead, she decided to tackle *Tender Is the Night*, by F. Scott Fitzgerald, even though it was clearly meant for adults. Her father had raised an eyebrow when she lifted the book from her perch on the deck stairs to show him, but he didn't say "no," so she pressed on, intent on figuring words out on her own as much as possible. She didn't get far before having to ask her father's help. Words like "deferential" and "façade" made her question her determination. But instead of giving up, she went back to the bookshelf and searched until she found a pocket dictionary. She carried it back to the deck, holding it for her father to see so he could figure out her plan. He gave her a thumbs-up.

Just a couple pages into the novel, she paused. "Dad," she said, just loud enough to see if he was awake, but not so loud as to wake him.

"Yes?" he rasped.

"Can I read you something from this book?"

"Of course."

She began reading, " 'However, one's eye moved on quickly to her daughter, who had magic in her pink palms and her cheeks lit to a lovely flame, like the thrilling flush of children after their cold baths in the evening.'" She looked up. Her father's eyes were closed, his lips pressed together. She couldn't tell if he was thinking or hurting. "That's really good, isn't it?" she said. "I mean, I can see the daughter in my head."

"It's brilliant. You picked a good book," he said, eyes still closed. Maybe it was the afternoon sun. "It's not an easy read, though. I don't want to spoil it for you, but…well, it's not the happiest of stories."

"That's okay. I'm okay, Dad. I want to try."

"Then good for you. And keep that dictionary handy. It's quite a bit above your reading level."

"I read above my reading level. Or however you say that. That's what my teacher said."

"She was right. But it's not just about the words. It's about what they say. It's a very adult story..." His voice trailed off.

"It's okay if I don't understand everything," she said.

"You're right, Berry," her father said. "You're so very right."

She smiled, feeling a quiet pride and an unquiet sadness.

Berry had rarely thought of reading as hard work, but this book was exactly that. She spent almost as much time in the dictionary as she did in the novel. It took her the rest of the day to get through two chapters. And then she went back to read them again, with the definitions of unfamiliar words fresh in her mind. It was still hard to understand, but there were some perfectly lovely sentences and that was enough for her to look forward to doing the same with the next chapter, and the next. Her summer had just taken a turn toward interesting.

That evening, after a supper of chicken soup – they ate a lot of soup, which Berry had previously thought was exclusively a winter food – Kenneth and Annabelle claimed the kitchen table to play a card game. There was still plenty of light before dusk, so Berry asked her father if she could go sit by the stone fence to read more of her book. He nodded. Annabelle retrieved a flashlight from the kitchen drawer that held a little of everything and handed it to her.

"I don't need a flashlight," said Berry, rolling her eyes the best she could. "It's still light out. And I know my way back to the house. It's...up."

"Oh, I know. But it's just always a good idea to have a flashlight, don't you agree Ken?"

"Yes. A flashlight is a good thing to always have." He said, mimicking her voice almost perfectly. Annabelle scowled at her brother and punched him in the shoulder. It was a gentle punch, but Berry saw a slight grimace under his smile.

"Okay," said Berry. She took the flashlight and turned it over in her hands. It was about the size of a toilet paper roll and cold to the touch. The metal casing was bright blue and shiny, like a jewel. When Berry clicked the black button on the end of it, the flashlight threw an intense beam right into her father's eyes.

"Oops, sorry about that," she said.

"Bright light," he said.

"Fright delight," said Annabelle.

"Night sight," added Berry.

The kitchen fell silent. One rhyme for each of them seemed...

"Just right!" Berry added suddenly, then spun on her heels to head out of the kitchen. She could hear her father and Annabelle laughing in her wake.

Climbing down a steep hill is harder than climbing up, Berry decided. She had pointed herself down the grassless dirt path that divided the hill – the sledding zone, her father had called it, but then moved a few feet to the left because falling on the hard dirt hurt more than falling on the thick wild grass. When she finally got to the bottom of the hill, she stepped up to the stone wall and set the plastic bag filled with her books and flashlight and a package of partially crushed peanut butter crackers on top of it next to the still-leaning wagon.

She ran her fingers across the top of the chest-high stone, then began walking left – east, she remembered, toward the ocean, though it was miles and miles away – feeling the softness of the stones with her right hand, and the cracks between them, brushing twigs and leaves and dirt as she went. The mortar that held them together was cracked and brittle, often little more than dust. Some of the stones were immovable, others wiggled or teetered as she ran her fingers across them. After a couple minutes, she stopped and turned around. The wagon seemed too small, too far away for such a brief walk. She looked up at the house, but all she could see was the low sun reflecting in the windows – orange lights hovering under a deep blue sky, like stars resting on the hill before returning to the heavens. Where had the time gone? She retraced her steps, this time letting her left hand explore the stones.

When she got to the wagon, she noticed the plastic bag was missing. She leaned over the wall to see if it had fallen on the other side. The flashlight and the books had spilled onto the mossy earth, but the bag and the crackers were gone. She looked up and caught the slightest flash of white disappearing into the forest. She traced a faint furrow in the earth from the forest back to the wall.

Something must have taken it. She thought first of Red, then of bears and wolves and rabid squirrels and finally, monsters. She carefully climbed over the wall and dropped to the other side. She picked up the books and flashlight and set them back on the top of the wall. She looked again into the forest, which was already dark as night.

A song blew through the trees to her ears. It was a child's song, like something she would have learned in Mrs. Jenkins' class in the third grade. The words were indistinct, but the melody sounded familiar. She tilted her head, bending her ear toward the forest to better hear the music.

Home, the forest whispered. Or was it *"Come"* this time? she wondered.

"Is someone out there?" she asked the trees.

Berry, came the voice again. But this time it blew down from the top of the hill. She spun around to look up at the house. The sun had nearly set, but she could see the shadow shapes of two people standing outside on the deck. "It's getting late," one of them called out.

She scurried over the wall, grabbed her books and the flashlight, and began climbing up the hill. Climbing up a steep hill is much harder than climbing down, she decided.

"Coming," she said.

Behind her, the forest song faded.

"Let me see your hands," said Annabelle.

Berry held them out, palms down.

"The other side."

She flipped them over. They were red and swollen.

"Poison ivy?" her father asked, taking one of her hands in his. He wasn't afraid of poison ivy.

"I don't think so."

"I didn't go into the forest," Berry said. "I was just walking along the wall."

Annabelle disappeared down the hall into her room, then returned a moment later with a tube of hand cream. She opened it and squeezed some onto her hands, then took Berry's hands, one at a time, rubbing them between hers to coat them back and front with the greasy stuff.

"What is this? It smells like a hospital…" began Berry.

"It's a magic potion," she spat, without even the tiniest bit of humor in her voice. It was almost as if she was angry at Berry for getting a rash, or maybe at the rash itself. When she'd finished with both hands, she started flapping her arms at her side like a bird attempting takeoff.

"Do this," she said. "Until they dry."

Her father bent his brow into a puzzle, then shrugged and started to flap his arms, too. Berry thought they both looked like lunatics, but it wasn't an altogether unpleasant look, so she joined them. Kenneth started to walk and flap around the living room and Berry followed him. Annabelle softened her scowl just a tad, but stayed in one place to flap.

A loud crash interrupted their dance.

"What was that?" asked Berry.

"Sounded like it came from the garage," said her father.

"I told you not to leave those doors open," said Annabelle.

"Probably just the cat getting into things."

Berry pondered that for a moment. Cats usually aren't clumsy. But her father might be right.

"Should we go see?" she asked. "I have a flashlight."

"I'll go," said Annabelle. She grabbed the blue flashlight from the sofa bed where Berry had set it, and marched like she meant business into the kitchen. There, she opened the cabinet where the glasses were, then reached up to the highest shelf and retrieved a gun. She looked back at her brother.

"Don't even think about lecturing me," she said. "I know what I need to know about guns. And I have a lockbox on order. It's not like I plan on leaving a loaded gun around with a child in the house.

"It's loaded?" he shouted. Berry hadn't seen her father angry often, she was more familiar with kind of intense disappointment. But his anger had a bite to it that scared her.

"I live in the woods, Ken. Alone. There are bad people in this world. Even in Maine."

Berry laughed at this, then felt bad for laughing when everyone else seemed intent on being serious.

"Sorry," she said. "But don't worry Dad. I know not to play with guns. I'm twelve, you know."

His expression softened.

"I'm getting a gun case," said Annabelle, as if she was in some other conversation.

"Just don't keep it loaded," said her father.

She grunted, then clicked on the flashlight and walked out the kitchen door.

"I want to see…" began Berry. But her father held her back and let the door swing closed.

A few minutes later, Annabelle returned.

"Must have been the cat. A box had been knocked off from the loft."

"Not the old trunk," said Berry. "Was it the old trunk?"

"Yes…it was. How did you…?"

"Red wants us to look inside," said Berry.

"Tomorrow," her father answered. We'll explore the trunk tomorrow. And Annabelle – keep that gun with you. Take it to your room. I don't like guns and I don't want to be anywhere near them."

His voice cracked at that last phrase, and the shake in her father's voice unsettled Berry.

"Tomorrow," he said again.

Berry rubbed her hands together. They were still moist, but not from the cream. They were sweaty. She couldn't remember a time when she'd ever had sweaty palms.

That night, as the house fell silent and the night bled into the living room, Berry said a prayer. She had only prayed once before, eight years earlier – the day her mother left. It hadn't done any good, but she figured she might have just said it wrong. So she tried again, whispering the words at the stars she watched through the wall of glass.

"Dear God," she said. "Could you please fix my dad? That's all." She closed her eyes, then opened them to the stars for a moment more. "That's not all. I think I'd like to see my mom again. Maybe you could fix her, too."

5

The next morning, Berry was awakened by the whir of a blender. She crawled out of bed and wandered, blurry-eyed, into the kitchen to see her father standing at the counter. He turned to look at her, a smile far too bright for such an early hour filling his thin face.

"Well, good morning Raspberry. You're just in time for a delicious smoothie."

His cold seemed to be gone. His voice was still hoarse, but there was life in it.

"Is it me-flavored? Or one of those gross ones with vegetables?"

"You won't even notice the vegetables."

"Yuck."

"Just try it. You'll see."

He poured a small amount into a juice glass, then held it out to Berry. She scrunched up her face into anticipatory disgust, then sighed and took the glass. She sniffed at it. It smelled like berries. She tipped it toward her mouth, letting the thick pink stuff brush against her lips. Then she took a tentative sip. All this time, she was watching her father, gauging his expression, wondering if her prayer had somehow worked. Was it that simple?

"It's okay," she said. "Better than chalk soup."

He laughed. It's something he had said to her once or twice, when she'd accompanied him to the hospital for one of his treatments.

"Then have some more," he said, filling her glass.

She drank it all down, and not like it was medicine, but like it was some kind of milkshake. It was good. She didn't want to know what vegetables had been blended in with the fruit.

"I know what that trunk in the garage is," her father said as she sucked on the last drops of the smoothie.

"You know what's in it?"

"No, I know what the trunk is."

"Well, duh. It's a box with stuff in it."

"So say you. I say it's something much more interesting."

"What?"

"A time machine."

"Really?"

"Really."

She knew what he meant – that it probably held old stuff and that seeing old stuff was kind of like being transported through time. But she held loosely to the slim possibility that it might actually be a real time machine. She would go back a few years. But then, would they still end up here? With her mother gone and her father sick? Maybe she wouldn't go back a few years.

"Hey Raspberry...you still in there?" he tapped lightly on her bedhead.

"Yeah. Just doing some time travel."

His smile retreated slightly.

"Where did you go?"

"It doesn't matter," she said. "I'm going to shower and get dressed. Then can we see what's in the trunk?"

"Yes."

She kissed her father's cheek as he bent down to collect her juice glass, then skipped out the kitchen, flapping her arms like they had the night before. His best laugh followed her into the living room and she marked that moment in case the trunk was really a time machine.

"You look like you're ready for an adventure," her father said when Berry finally returned from the bathroom. She was wearing the khakis that matched his, and a cream-colored button-down shirt over a black t-shirt Meg had given her. "All you need now is a hat," he added.

"Maybe we'll find one in the trunk."

They marched out the front door and around the forsythia bushes that lined the front of the house.

"Golden bells," her father said as he noticed her brushing her hands along the yellow flowers.

"I thought they were called forsythia."

"Yes. But some people call them golden bells," he said.

She smiled and nodded. "I want to be some people, then." She stopped, bent over and sniffed at the flowering bush. "Golden bells, happy smells."

When they got to the garage, they looked in. The morning light painted everything orange.

"If you squint, it could almost look like a treasure room," her father said, reading her thoughts.

Something was moving in the middle of the garage. Red popped up from behind the toppled trunk and landed on it, causing Berry to let out a surprised squeal.

"That's a new sound," her father said, putting his arm on her shoulder. She felt the heaviness of it as he steadied himself. When she turned to look up at him, she mostly saw his silhouette. He looked especially thin in silhouette.

"Just trying it out," she said, reaching up to place her hand on her father's. "Look, she's just as excited as we are to see what's inside."

"Mice, probably."

"Ew…really? Do you think it's full of mice?"

Her father started to answer, but his words turned into a cough. She had thought he was over his cold.

Berry edged her way to the back of the garage, then pulled at the handle on the end of the trunk, dragging it jerk by jerk across the dirt floor.

"I can help," her father said, clearing his throat. "It seems awfully heavy."

"It is awfully heavy. That's exactly the kind of heavy it is." She tugged at it again.

"Maybe it would be easier if it weren't upside-down?"

Berry let go of the handle, then together with her father, they righted the trunk.

"I got this," he said. He shooed Berry out of the way and dragged the trunk the rest of the way out of the garage and into the sunlight. He was breathing heavily.

"I'll get your chair." Berry walked over and grabbed the lounge chair that was still resting against the side of the garage. Her father was sitting on the trunk, bent over, catching his breath. She unfolded the chair and helped him into it.

"No more trunk moving for you," she said.

"I'm fine. Just out of breath."

Berry hated that phrase. When you're well and truly out of breath, you're dead. She stepped up to the trunk and reached down to the latch. She paused.

"Is there some kind of ceremony for this, too?" she asked. "I mean, like the way you talked to spiders before going into the garage?"

He coughed up a laugh. "A ceremony? For opening an old trunk? Let me think…"

She let him. She liked the kind of quiet her father radiated when he was thinking. It was like a giant bubble that surrounded them both until it grew big enough to hold his thoughts, then popped the moment he began to share them.

"Yes!" *Pop.* "But it's not so much a ceremony as a poem."

"Okay." She stood, put her hands on her hips. "So?"

"You'll have to say it," he said.

"Why me?"

"Because you're the one opening the trunk."

"But I don't know it."

"Repeat after me, then. Oh glorious trunk…"

She snorted. "Really?"

He ignored her. "Oh glorious trunk, be absent of junk…"

"Oh glorious trunk, be absent of junk…"

"And please play nice…"

"And please play nice…"

"No dead mice!"

She laughed her way through the last line. "No dead mice."

He pointed to the trunk.

"That's all there is? That's almost too small to call a poem."

"It's a small trunk."

It wasn't really, but she didn't correct him. She lifted the latch and bent it with some force until it rested against the lid. "Okay, here we go…" She pulled at the lid and it came open, then fell backward, snapping off at the hinge and falling into the grass.

"Well that was unexpected," her father said.

They looked inside. A folded, faded blue blanket covered whatever else was in the trunk. Berry reached in to grab it.

"Boo!" her father yelled. She jumped back, her heart racing.

"Hey, that's not fair."

"Oh, but it is. It's part of the poem. I'd just forgotten it."

She shook her head and folded her arms. "You're mean. And it can't be part of the poem because it doesn't rhyme with anything."

"Poems don't have to rhyme."

"Okay fine, but just this time." She stood there, arms still folded. "You can move the blanket." He bent forward in his chair. "Watch out for mice."

He gently took one edge of the blanket in his hand, and lifted it out of the trunk. He held it to his face, sniffing it. Then he set it on the grass. Under the blanket there was a battered, faded red game box. Checkers. He lifted that out gingerly, the checkers that hadn't escaped in the fall from the shelf rattling like bones, and rested it on the blanket. Under the box were other boxes, a few small metal cars, a baseball glove, a deflated football, the rest of the checkers, and a flat burgundy-colored leather case about the size of a placemat.

"Oh my," her father said. She looked up into his eyes. She had only seen her father cry a few times before. And almost all of those were from laughing too hard. He reached for the leather case, pulling it out from the trunk. He sat up in his chair and set the case on his lap.

"What's that?"

"I was wrong about the trunk."

"What?"

"The trunk isn't a time machine."

Berry bent her mouth into an exaggerated frown. To hide the real one.

"This…this, my little Raspberry, is our time machine."

She smiled.

"What is it?"

"Well," he said, then paused. "If we said the poem right…" He reached into the portfolio, then smiled. A single tear began to crawl down his cheek. Berry watched it travel across his face, noticing not for the first time how his cheeks had lost their shape and color. He pulled out a flat sheet of wood – like a shingle – and set it on top of the case. It was weathered and gray and otherwise rather unspectacular.

"It's a piece of wood," she said.

"Oh, it's more than that. This," he said, "was my most prized possession. I had no idea they'd saved it…" He gently grabbed the edges of the wood, and turned it over.

It was a map! Colorful splotches of green and blue and red filled the space, but mostly green, with black lines and neatly-printed words marking the locations of a tree house, a pond and a baseball field.

"I had almost forgotten about this," her father said. "My dad and I made it when…I think I was six."

"Your dad?" She hadn't heard many stories about her grandfather.

"He was gone a lot – business trips, selling stuff to people – but one afternoon he came home from being on the road and walked right up to me and said, 'We need to go on an adventure.' It was the first time he'd come to me to do something – usually it was me begging him to play." He cleared his throat. "We lifted the wagon over the stone wall, filled it with paints and brushes and a few pieces of old siding from the barn, then spent the rest of the day walking and mapmaking."

"Did you make more than one map?"

"What?"

"You said you brought a few pieces of wood."

"Well, sort of. We ended up using a pencil on one of the pieces of wood to sketch the map, then we climbed into the tree house – it was more of a tree platform, really – and together we painted this." He held it up again, letting the colors play off the light of the morning sun.

"It's a map of the forest, right?"

He lifted his hand and pointed to the back yard. "Yes."

She gasped. "Then we can be explorers, too!"

He seemed to be lost for a moment. She tapped him on his head.

"Yes. But not today," he said finally. He was still staring off into the distance, into some old memory, thought Berry.

A time machine.

"But today is the perfect day to go exploring."

"I'm just not up to it, Berrycicle."

"Well, maybe I'll go on my own then. Now that I have a map."

He turned to look her in the eye. "We weren't particularly accurate cartographers…"

"I'm not sure I know what that means, but I love the map. And I can use it, right? I can go exploring?"

He seemed to be torn in that moment. Or lost in it. She looked at the map again.

"I'll be careful with it," she said. "I'll keep it in the case until I need it. I promise I won't lose it or break it. I can tell it means a lot to you, like the adventure game we made when I was seven…" She tilted her head, trying to remember if they'd packed it.

He wiped the already-dry tear from his face, replacing it with a streak of dirt, and slid the wooden map back into the portfolio. He held it to his chest for one long breath, then presented it to her like a fancy tray.

"It's yours," he said.

That's not what she wanted to hear. She wanted to hear some resistance and maybe even a warning about how fragile it is. She wanted him to hold tight to it. She wanted him to fight for it, claim ownership and protection rights, like he did with his first edition of *The Hobbit* she'd pulled off the bookshelf the day he returned from his first hospital treatment.

But he just held it out to her, his hands shaking.

She reached for the leather satchel and took it.

After lunch, Berry began gathering supplies for her first forest adventure. A snack (more peanut butter crackers). A bottle of water (ice, mostly, but it would melt quickly). Her book and dictionary (because you can read anywhere but especially in tree houses). Her flashlight. The map, still in its leather portfolio.

She loaded it all up in her old school backpack – not the stupid one with the cartoon cat (she had given that one to Meg), but the navy blue canvas one with her name embroidered on the flap. "Raspberry." She ran her fingers across the pink threads and thought of Helen. The woman her father called "a friend from college." She'd only been a part of their world for a month when Berry was nine, then disappeared. Helen seemed nice enough, if a little boring. Berry *had* gotten a cool backpack out of the relationship. What had her father gotten? Absently, she ran her fingers across the cover of *Tender Is the Night.*

"You'll need one more thing," said her father, shuffling into the living room. He held out his hand. In it was a cell phone. An old one, by the looks of it.

"I thought you hated cell phones?"

"No, that's just what I tell you when you ask for one."

"That's not fair."

"I claim Parental Privilege."

She couldn't argue with that. Well, she could – and had – but there was no winning a Parental Privilege argument. Besides, if she won one of those arguments that would mean he could win the "I'm Just a Kid" arguments she often resorted to when trying to make up for some stupid decision or clumsy act. Could she still make those when she was 13?

"Okay, fine." She took the phone, flipped it open. "I like this. I thought you had a different kind…"

He reached into his pocket and pulled out a newer phone. An iPhone, she thought.

"I do."

"Then…what?" She held up the flip phone like a question.

"That's my…" he hesitated. "That's an old phone I keep around in case I need it. A backup. It works fine. I just wanted you to have it in case you get lost or something."

She looked at the battery life bar, and the one next to it…the signal strength?

"Does it work in the forest?"

He pointed to the screen. "It works here – there's a signal. Maybe not much of one. How about you call me once you're at the edge of the woods? We can check it out."

"What's your number?"

He laughs. "It's in the contact list…" He started to reach for the phone, but she'd already tapped the icon and opened the contact list. There were only two listings: "My other phone" and "Penny."

Penny.

Penelope.

Mom.

"You have…her number?" She felt a twinge of disappointment. Or was it betrayal?

"Your mother and I got our phones at the same time. I guess I just couldn't let go of this one. I don't know if she still has that number. I just…"

Berry flipped the phone closed and the click sounded very much like the period at the end of a sentence. "Okay. I'll try it at the edge of the forest."

"Berry…I…"

"I'm good. Sometimes you need to hold onto things for a while. I still have my stuffed tiger, right?"

He nodded.

"Okay, I'm off then. To the tree house."

"It might not be there anymore. Or the ladder might be broken. Watch out for rusty nails, okay?"

"I know. I'm always very careful."

Annabelle walked into the room at that moment. She had taken another morning off. She stared daggers at her brother, but softened when she turned to Berry. "Put these on," she said, handing Berry a pair of thin gloves. They had holes in them and were yellowed with age. "They'll protect your hands from…itchy things."

Berry laughed. "I'm not going to wear those. Those are for fancy people in old movies…"

Her father raised an eyebrow.

"Fine. I'll be a fancy adventurer, then." She slipped the gloves on. They were soft, silky. They fit surprisingly well. Berry looked over at her aunt's manly hands. These weren't her gloves.

"Thank you Aunt Annabelle," she said. "Maybe next time I'll bring tea on my adventure." She didn't mean it to sound like a dig at her backward aunt. She actually liked the way the gloves felt. And if it meant avoiding red, splotchy hands and awkward lotion dances, then fine. Well, maybe she'd miss the dancing.

"Don't mock tea in front of your aunt," said her father. "She thinks tea is the nectar of the gods."

Annabelle shook her head; a half-smile came to her lips. "No more so than you and your Mountain Dew. That stuff'll kill ya…"

A very small moment of uncertain silence fell on the room, then disappeared in her father's laugh. Annabelle had turned white, then just as quickly joined her father in laughing at a joke Berry thought wasn't even a little bit funny. But the way they laughed together was kind of contagious so she giggled, too.

"Mountain Dew isn't good for you," she said.

"But it tastes like heaven, yes it's true," said her father.

Berry slid the flip phone into the back pocket of her adventuring shorts and gathered up the backpack.

"Off I go, then," she said. Her father and aunt had stopped laughing and were looking at each other with quiet smiles.

"Don't go far," said her aunt.

"I have a map and a phone and a flashlight. Do you want to tie a string to me, too?"

She opened the heavy glass door and stepped out onto the deck. After slipping the backpack on her shoulders, she made her way down the hill. The backpack gave her better balance. She only slipped once. When she got to the stone wall, she carefully removed her backpack and set it on the other side. In a moment of grand inspiration, she lifted the wagon up and over the wall.

"Wheels are better," she said aloud to the nearest trees.

She climbed over the wall and dropped down onto the spongy, moss-covered dirt, gently placing her backpack into the wagon. She grabbed the handle and tugged the wagon behind her as she headed into the trees.

By the time she reached the first tree, she had forgotten about the phone in her back pocket.

6

Berry hadn't gone far when a howl pierced the whispering wind. She stopped and looked around. She could still just see the stone wall, but the branches of a dozen trees blocked her view of the hill and the house.

The howl again. *Was it animal or human?*

She spun in place, searching for the source of the noise. She wasn't afraid. Not yet. Not of a sound.

Again, the howl, but this time at her feet. She jumped back, startled, and bumped her elbow against the trunk of an old maple tree.

"Ow," she said. She rubbed her throbbing elbow and looked down at the wagon. Something furry was hiding behind it.

Red.

"Oh, it's you," said Berry. She stepped around the wagon and bent down to one knee. Red limped around to the opposite side, slithered under the wagon. "You don't have to be afraid. It's me. Raspberry." She reached out her hand to pet the cat. Red arched her back and started to hiss, but the hiss morphed into another yowl.

"What's the matter? Are you hurt?" Red looked up into Berry's eyes and nodded her furry little head. Berry was so sure of this she marked the moment in time.

"Let me see," said Berry. She got down on both knees and slowly moved the wagon out of the way. Red shuffled along behind it at first, then stopped and flopped down into the dirt. The fur around her rear right leg was matted and dark and wet.

Blood.

"Oh, Red. What happened to you?"

Another howl, but this one sounded tired, defeated.

"We need to get you to a doctor." Berry pulled her backpack out of the wagon and slipped it over her shoulders. "I'm going to put you in the wagon, okay? I'm going to take you back to the house. My dad will know what to do."

She slipped her hands under Red and began to lift her. The cat howled again and resisted. "Please Red. Let me help you." The howling stopped. Berry tried again, and this time was able to lift the big cat and set her in the wagon. She grabbed the handle and pulled it in a wide circle before heading back toward the stone wall. Red was resting on her left side, breathing heavily, her body rising and falling with each breath in a way that reminded Berry of the last days of her dog, Horatio.

"I can't pull the wagon up the hill with you in it," she said as she stared up at the house. She thought of leaving Red there, going for help. But what if she limped away while I was gone? she thought.

"I'm going to carry you, Red. I'm sorry if it hurts. I really am. Is it okay if I carry you?"

Red exhaled a sound like a sigh. She was barely moving now.

Berry lifted the cat out of the wagon and set her on the flat stones of the wall. She kept one of her hands on the cat, stroking her head as she climbed to the other side. Then she once again took Red into her arms.

The phone, she thought as she climbed the hill. I forgot to try out the phone.

Her father met her at the deck. She became aware he must have been watching them for a few minutes at least.

"I think she's been shot," he said, almost as out of breath as Berry. "A pellet gun, maybe." He had set Red on a towel atop the kitchen table. "We should take her to the vet." Right when he said this, Red howled again. Her first sounds since the forest.

"I don't think she wants to go to the vet," said Berry.

Her father was shaking his head. "I think that was just coincidence, Berry. She doesn't know what we're saying."

"What if she does?"

"Let me see what I can do," he said.

He disappeared into his room for a moment, then into Annabelle's room. Berry watched him come down the hall with an armful of supplies. First he cleaned the wound as gently as possible. Then he trimmed the fur away from the wound using tiny scissors and clippers that buzzed and startled Red. But she didn't try to escape. Berry thought this was some kind of miracle.

"Well, this is lucky," said her father. "The pellets didn't seem to puncture too deep. I think I can pull them out. This might be a good time to pet Red and tell her happy thoughts."

Berry hadn't stopped caressing Red's head the whole time, but bent down closer to speak softly. "Hey Red...I think this might hurt a little..."

"That's a happy thought?"

"No. It's called being truthful," she said. "You taught me that."

He laughed as his hands worked their magic with tweezers and a cotton swab. "Yes, I did."

"May I continue?" she asked.

"Of course."

Berry kissed the top of Red's head, tasting the forest in her fur. "It's the good kind of hurt, Red. The kind that means you're on the way to getting better." Berry forced a smile, remembering those words in her father's voice, remembering the tears that accompanied the pull of each splinter, remembering the empty seat where her mother should have been, arms stretched across the table holding Berry's hand.

A few moments passed. Red continued to be unusually compliant and free of complaint.

"There," Kenneth said. "I think that's all of them. Of course, we can't be too sure..."

"Is she going to be okay?"

"I don't know."

They didn't say another word as Kenneth cleaned the wound again, then bandaged it and wrapped the leg in gauze to keep the bandage in place. He taped off the gauze and sighed, slumping back into his chair.

"I still think she should see a vet..." he began.

Red meowed. A soft sound like a gentle "no thank you."

Berry looked up at her father. He offered a tired smile and shook his head. "This cat seems to think it's human," he said. His eyes were bloodshot, teary. She looked down at his hands. They were smeared with blood.

"Let's get her some water," he said.

"Milk," said Berry. "She wants milk."

Berry made a small bed for Red out of towels and a pillow and placed it in the corner of the living room, by the sliding door. "I think she wants to be close to the outside," she'd said aloud. Her father had already disappeared into his room to rest.

There would be no adventuring today, thought Berry. Except the kind you do in books.

She curled up in the corner of the sofa with *Tender Is the Night*, her eyes darting often from the words on the page to the cat in the corner, who seemed to be sleeping comfortably.

Berry continued her careful reading of the novel, looking up words she didn't know, re-reading a chapter after she'd been through it once. In chapter four, she paused at a phrase and tested it out loud. "...an endless succession of magnificent possibilities..." "That's what I want," she said to the sleeping cat. To the green ocean. To the big blue sky. To her resting father.

To her absent mother.

"An endless succession of magnificent possibilities," she said again, this time as a kind of prayer.

She fell asleep with her index finger between the pages of the novel, then awoke with a start when the front door opened.

"Aunt Annabelle," Berry said, through the haze of waking up. Her aunt was holding a bag of groceries and staring at the sliding door. No, next to it. At Red.

"What happened to the cat?" she asked.

Berry told her the story, noting a mild disgust in her aunt's expression when she went into detail about the improvised surgical procedure.

"We'll take her to a vet tomorrow," Annabelle stated after Berry had finished. It was almost as if she hadn't heard a word of Berry's tale. "I wonder how much that's gonna cost..." Those last words faded as Annabelle walked away into the kitchen.

Berry was disappointed Annabelle didn't see the magic of Red's rescue and repair.

After a quiet dinner and a ritual of watering all the indoor plants, they all sat on Berry's sofa to watch a movie. Her father chose *Forrest Gump*. Berry had heard about it, but had never seen it.

Annabelle hesitated. "It's not really for children..."

"Berry's twelve. And besides, she's not like most children." He tousled her hair, which usually brought a half-hearted complaint, but this time she leaned into his touch.

"Well, then we're going to need some popcorn," said Annabelle. She smiled and Berry saw a hint of her father's playfulness in that smile. A playfulness that had been harder to come by since he got sick.

A while later, just as Forrest was sitting at his dying mother's side, Red stood, stretched, and walked resolutely to the sliding door, staring out. She meowed her request, looking up at Berry in the evening light, her green eyes like jewels.

"Can she go out?"

"Sure," her father said. "Animals generally know when they're well enough to get back to normal."

"Really?"

"Your father doesn't know what he's talking about," said Annabelle. "We should keep her inside until we go to the vet…"

Red meowed again, louder.

"She really wants to go out," said Berry's father.

"Fine, then. But don't come crying to me if she never comes back."

"Anna!" he said. "Why would you say such a thing?"

"Because it could happen. That's why. We don't know what happened to her. Some stupid kids from town playing in the woods, maybe. Shooting at anything that moves. And that's another thing – I think it's pretty clear that Berry shouldn't play in the forest anymore."

Anymore? Thought Berry. I haven't played there *at all* yet.

"Because someone shot a cat?" her father said.

"Yes, because someone shot a cat. What if that had been Berry? What if whoever it was didn't notice his target was a little girl? What then?"

"It was a pellet gun. It's not like…"

"Not like what? That she couldn't be blinded? Or worse? We don't know what happened to the cat, and until we do, I just think it's a bad idea to send your precocious little daughter into the forest."

"Anna. She's right here. You're talking about her like she's not right here."

"I'm sorry, Berry. I don't mean to be rude. But the forest isn't safe. I mean, if someone thinks it's fun to shoot an innocent animal, what makes you think they wouldn't hesitate to shoot anything else? I'm going to have to claim 'house rules' on this one, Ken. We've had trouble in the forest over the years. But you didn't know about that. You weren't here. I do know about it. And if those assholes are out wreaking havoc again, I don't want Berry to be in their line of fire."

Annabelle looked over at Berry.

"Sorry. I shouldn't have used that word."

"What word?" asked Berry. "Precocious? Because I know what that means."

Her father stifled a laugh.

Berry looked up at him. His blue eyes were bright, intense. But he sighed and nodded.

"Fine," he said. "We'll place a moratorium on playing in the woods. Temporarily. You can ask all your gossipy church friends if they know anything about kids and pellet guns. I'm sure you'll learn plenty."

"I don't know that word, Dad. What's a moratorium?"

"A ban. It means – for now, anyway – the woods are off limits."

"But the map…"

"Only for a time. Your Aunt Annabelle will ask around to see if this is something we should be worried about. Okay?"

Berry scowled. "I don't have a vote, do I."

"Not this time."

"Fine."

Red meowed again.

"So can she go out or not?" Berry asked.

"I think she can," answered her father.

Berry climbed off of the couch and walked over to the sliding door. She flipped the little locking lever and pulled the door open wide. Red took a step out onto the deck, paused, looked up at Berry, then hobbled out into the coming night.

"I shouldn't have been so negative," said Annabelle. "She'll be back. She always comes back."

Berry climbed onto the sofa, wishing she had it all to herself. It was her bed, after all. But she didn't say anything. She settled back against a pillow.

"That Jenny sure does remind me of someone," said Annabelle, pointing to the TV.

"Anna, don't..."

"Don't tell me you can't see the resemblance. Except Penelope was born out of time. She should have lived through the actual sixties, instead of forcing you to endure a poor imitation of them."

"She didn't force me to do anything," said Kenneth. "I loved exactly who she was."

"The peasant shirts, the beads, the 'groovy' and the 'far out'? The unnatural love of the Stones?"

"All of it. Penny was one of a kind."

Jenny, Penny, rhymed Berry. But she didn't say it out loud.

7

"We're getting you out of the house." It was Annabelle's voice. Berry stopped brushing her teeth and listened through the thin bathroom door.

"I don't know if I'm up for..."

"Ken, you can't just wither away here. I'm not going to let you do that."

"Anna...Belle, I'm doing the best I can with what I have."

Annabelle started to laugh, then stopped. An accidental laugh, thought Berry.

"I'm sorry. It's just that phrase. Remember when you first said it?"

"We were kids. Playing some game...what was it?"

"You were a kid," she said. "I was nearly 16. And it was...what's the game with the miles..."

"Mille Bornes," her father said. It sounded like a foreign phrase.

"That's it."

Berry quickly rinsed her toothbrush and stepped to the door. She grabbed the handle, then released it, waiting.

"I think my tires are punctured, Belle. Today just isn't a..."

"Coup-fourré!" she practically shouted. That was definitely foreign.

"What...you can't..."

"I'm playing my 'puncture-proof tire' card. We're going out today. To lunch. I know the perfect place. You, my little brother, need some fried clams."

Berry decided then to open the door. She stepped onto the wooden walkway and leaned over the railing, looking down into the great room at her father and aunt. They turned to look at her.

"I need fried clams, too," she said.

Berry helped her father into the passenger seat of her aunt's sedan. He had offered to drive his truck, but Annabelle scolded him for even thinking of taking credit for this excursion.

"My treat, my car," she said.

They backed out of the parking square in front of the garage, then followed the long driveway to the winding road at the end of it. Within minutes they were passing a park, then turning up another street that followed the river. Houses started appearing on both sides, and then suddenly they were downtown. Berry had seen the downtown area on their arrival, but they hadn't stopped to explore the rows of small shops squeezed in between square modern buildings and the occasional two and three-story brick buildings that looked like they could have been in a movie about the old England, not just the New one.

"Damn," said Annabelle as she slowed in front what looked to be a small café. "Sorry, I meant 'darn.' I was hoping there'd be a parking place out front. I'll drop you two off here and find somewhere to park."

"You don't need to do that," said Berry's father.

"My excursion, my rules," she said. She pulled up next to a gap between a big black SUV and a shiny red VW Beetle convertible and stopped. "It's on the other side of that place," she said, pointing to the café. "You have to walk down the alley and go around back. It faces the river. Wait for me there."

"Does this place have a name?" he asked. "Am I supposed to remember it? Because things are so different…"

"You'll know it when you see it," she answered, cutting him off. "Now move or I'm going to get a ticket for blocking traffic."

There was no traffic. All the cars in town seemed to be parked along the street.

Berry climbed out and opened the door for her father. He smiled and took her hand and they walked between the cars, stepped up onto the curb, and made a beeline for the skinny alleyway between Walgreen's and an old, brick building called "Morrowton Mercantile." The sound of the river whispered through the alleyway, then began to murmur once they stepped beyond the end of the buildings onto a landing. To their left, the landing became a small loading dock. To their right, and down a couple steps, it was a patio overlooking the river. At least a dozen small tables occupied the space, all but one of them filled with people eating and chatting and smiling. Berry took the six steps two at a time, then paused, waiting for her father to climb down them slowly. She saw the muscles in his arm tense as he held the railing and descended like a hesitant groom heading to his wedding.

He laughed a hoarse laugh, then pointed to the backside of the building – which was the front of a small restaurant. The sign below the awning read, "You'll Know It When You See It."

Berry laughed, too. "That's the best name for a restaurant ever," she said.

A waitress wearing a bright blue, grease-stained apron nodded at them as she practically sprinted past, carrying three plates of fried food. "Just grab a table if you can find one," she called back.

They shuffled over to the only empty table, which was just outside one of the restaurant's two huge picture windows.

"Do you want to wait for one by the river?" her father asked.

"Next time," she said. "Because look." She pointed at the window. It offered a view not of the small dining room, but the kitchen. Inside a chef and his assistants were running around the small space like ants on a dropped Popsicle.

Berry sat facing the window, her father on the opposite side. A few minutes later, Annabelle came around the corner. They waved her over and she frowned, scanned the patio.

"We could wait for a table closer to the water."

"I can smell it just fine from here," said Berry. She was staring at a man in the window who seemed to be whispering something to a lobster before dropping it into a big pot.

The menu was printed right on the plastic table cloth in blue marker: clams, fish, shrimp (all of those broiled or fried), lobster (steamed, salad or roll), fat fries, skinny fries, vegetable of the day (unspecified), and just one dessert, something called "Blue Berry Tasty Crisp."

They ordered their food (fried) and sipped on iced tea and water while they waited. There was a long moment of silence that made Berry nervous, and she wasn't sure why. Then her father began talking. His first sentence sounded rehearsed.

"I think we should talk about the future," he said.

"Now?" said Annabelle. "You want to do this now?"

"It's not like we have all the time in the world."

"Stop it, Ken." Annabelle seemed to choke on her words. She turned away and reached into her purse, which was hanging on the back of her chair. She pulled out a tissue and blew her nose. Then she grabbed another one and pressed it to her teary eyes. "I'm sorry," she said, looking at Berry. "This isn't like me at all."

Berry didn't know if this made her feel better or worse.

"Raspberry-girl," her father began. Now he was starting to get weepy. "I'm not getting better..."

Berry stared through the window into the kitchen, willing this conversation to stop.

"We have to think about your future," continued Annabelle. "We need to have a plan..."

"There. He did it again," Berry said, pointing at the window. Annabelle looked where she was pointing, her father turned, too, but much more slowly.

"Did what?"

"That man is saying something to the lobster before he throws it in the pot. I'm sure of it. What do you think he's saying?"

She turned back to her father, he was looking right into her with kind, intense eyes.

"What do you think he's saying?" he asked, always one to turn the questions back on her.

"Berry, we need to talk about this…" began Annabelle.

"I think he's saying 'this might hurt a little,'" said Berry.

"Yes. And maybe something else, too," said her father. His voice was nearly gone, but it often was. "Maybe he's also saying 'it's going to be okay.'"

Berry thought that was the stupidest thing her father had ever said. Since when is getting boiled alive ever okay? She opened her mouth to argue, but the food arrived before she could find the right sort of words – the kind that were honest but respectful.

They ate in near silence, the conversation tabled until later. But Berry didn't need the conversation. She knew what they were thinking. Annabelle would care for her after her father was gone. If he died. When he died. If. *When.*

Her fried clams didn't taste as good as the idea of them. When she had first tried them two years before, she complained about the occasional grit that had found its way onto the plate.

"Sand," he father had explained.

"Who wants sand in their food?"

"It's from the ocean," he had answered.

The ocean on her plate, she thought, recalling the rest of the conversation. Who wouldn't want the ocean on their plate?

Berry declined the offer to share one of the Blue Berry Tasty Crisps.

"We'll plan for dessert next time," her father had said.

Plan for dessert. Berry stored that thought away in her head to think about later. When they passed Moose Run Park, she saw a family tossing a Frisbee around on the open grassy field along the road. She almost said, "I know what our next outing should be." But again her words caught in her throat. She wondered if this was the way her words were going to be from now on.

She didn't like it. Not at all.

That afternoon, Berry gathered up her growing collection of paper swans and carried them down the hill to the stone fence. It was a particularly calm, windless afternoon, the sky a bright blue. She lined up the swans along the top of the squat wall, spacing them a foot apart, arranging them by color. Red, orange, yellow, blue, green, purple, white. All 27 of them. She wasn't sure where to put the black one. She decided next to the white. Then she climbed part way up the hill and sat tall in the wild grass, a queen looking down upon her paper subjects. Or a god looking at her creation.

She lay back against the grass and felt something pressing against her left hip. She reached into the pocket and found the gloves her aunt had given her. She slipped them on, wondering if this was being ironic, then lay back down to stare into the sky. There were no clouds to turn into animals, and the stars would be hiding for another six or seven hours.

She felt an itch on her nose and brushed away a bee, liking the way the glove felt on her face. She wasn't scared of bees. Bees were good. But they were disappearing and that was bad. She had done a report on it.

She whispered to the bee. "Sorry. It's just that I don't want my nose tickled right now. I'm too angry to be tickled."

The bee circled around her head a few times, then darted off. She felt a tiny sting of sadness. It was only a stupid bee, she thought. And that's when everything hit her heart all at once. Her father was dying. He would soon be gone. There would be no "planning for dessert." No Frisbee tossing. No silly jokes or interrogation days. No proper tickling. When was the last time he tickled her?

She began to cry. What started as a whimper quickly morphed into an ugly, blubbering howl that reminded her of Red. Surely the forest heard her. Maybe the whole state of Maine. She didn't care.

"I don't want my daddy to die," she said to the perfectly blue sky. She had wanted to shout it, but she didn't have any shout in her. The wind picked up then, a sudden gust that poured down the hill. She sat up just in time to see her rainbow of swans lifted on the wind, spinning, diving, twirling, dancing through the air off into the forest. The white one stayed aloft the longest, climbing higher and higher on gust after gust, until it disappeared from view above the tree line.

The breeze continued, and brought her snippets of a conversation from the top of the hill. She turned but no one was outside.

They must be in the living room, she thought. She didn't even try to wipe her tears away. She lay back down against the hill and listened.

"I don't know if I can do this, Ken."

"Please don't say that..."

"...I'm not cut out...taking care of a girl..."

"She has nowhere else..."

"...better with someone else who can..."

For a moment, all Berry could hear was the wind. Then...

"No, Kenneth. She will just break Berry's heart all over again..."

"She's her mother..."

And then the wind stopped. But she'd heard enough. Berry stood up, walked back down the hill and climbed over the wall.

The wagon was missing. She took one long look up at the house, then turned and began to follow the faint dirt trail into the woods.

8

It was like tracking an animal. Berry studied the ground, looking for clues that the wagon had traveled this way or that, finding faint parallel stripes in the dirt, or flattened foliage that suggested the wagon's belly passing over.

Every few feet, she stopped to listen. The trees did have voices. Maybe that's what she'd been hearing all along. The tall ones with the wide trunks hummed old songs to the accompaniment of creaking bones, the smaller ones whistled aimless tunes. She imagined the big trees' frustration at the smaller trees' lack of melody. Once again she thought of her third grade teacher. She saw Mrs. Jenkins' jet-black hair and oversized glasses as she stood at the front of the room holding a small, rainbow-colored metal keyboard. No, a xylophone.

Someone had asked, "Why does the high note have to be blue? And why is the red note the lowest one?"

It was a stupid question, but Mrs. Jenkins didn't say so.

"The blue notes are like the sky – the red notes are like…"

"Like Berry's stupid hair!" said Becky Bloomberg. Stupid Becky Bloomberg with the perfectly straight blonde hair and the perfectly straight teeth and the perfectly annoying voice.

Mrs. Jenkins had paused then, looking right into Berry's eyes. "Like the earth," she had corrected. "Red and rich like the earth." She had nodded then, the very slightest of nods that Berry knew only she had seen. "Red and rich like the earth," she had repeated. But she wasn't only talking about musical notes.

Berry paused again to listen to the trees. There it was again, singing. But not tree song this time. She spun in place, looking around. She was far enough into the forest that she couldn't see the stone wall or the hill.

"Oh Dunderbeck, Oh Dunderbeck, how could you be so mean..."

The words were distinct. The voice, a child's. She spun back around and tried to follow the sound.

"Straight ahead," she said quietly, picturing the map her father had made. She had memorized it, then hidden it in a safe place among the books on the shelf. "Straight ahead until you reach a twisted tree." She knew she should turn back. That was the right thing to do. But she was tired of always doing the right thing. She wanted to know what it felt like to do the wrong thing.

She touched the most important trees as she passed, naming each one with her white-gloved fingers. "Bernice." "Buttercup." "Beanpole." "Snape." "Rosemary." "Fitzgerald." She named sixteen trees before she finally saw it. The twisted tree.

"Nicole," she said aloud. "Nicole Diver Tree."

Its thick trunk started out straight, then bent to the left, then the right before straightening out again. A lone pine in the middle of a sugar maple and oak forest. It was as if a bear had leaned up against it, pushing it out of shape. That would have to be a very big bear, she thought. Her heart raced. She began to feel every beat against her chest.

The song again. This time, a little louder.

"...the pussy cats and long-tailed rats, no more they will be seen..."

She stood there, frozen for a moment. She should go home. She should turn around and run home as fast as possible. What if it's the person who shot Red?

"Home," she said. It was both a sigh and a question.

A flash of sunlight near the twisted tree caught her eye. At first she thought it was a dragonfly, but it didn't move like a dragonfly. Then she thought it was a leaf, but it was too white for a leaf and leaves weren't supposed to fall in early summer. She continued

69

walking toward the twisted tree as the not-dragonfly, not-leaf floated to the ground at the base of the tree.

It was her white swan.

"Hello," she said. "You've come such a long way."

She picked up the swan and gently slipped it into the side pocket of her green camp shorts.

Turn right at the twisted tree, she thought. She walked up to its wide trunk. She thought she could make out an arrow carved into it, but the bark had grown around it like pursed lips. "Just a little farther," she said aloud to her pocketed swan.

The ground rose to her right, a gentle hill that was easy to climb. When she reached the crest, she looked down to discover a clearing where no trees grew. A baseball field, like the one where she and Meg played kickball with all of Meg's brothers and sisters.

The clearing was surprisingly flat and covered in thick wild grass that waved hello in a gentle breeze that had bent its way around the trees. She walked out into it, enjoying the sun on her face, and nearly tripped on something. She looked down. It was a perfectly square piece of wood. A piece of rotting gray siding. Just like her father's map. She wandered around the field, looking for more perfectly square pieces of rotting gray siding. And sure enough, there were three more. Kids had played baseball here. Her father had played here.

But a long, long time ago. The field was abandoned. Two of the bases were so rotten weeds had grown right up through them.

She walked over to what would have been home base and stood on it, imagining what it must have been like to play in this secret field. When she looked down the third base line, she saw a glint of something red hiding among the surrounding trees.

The wagon.

She started toward it.

"...they're all ground up for sausage meat in Dunderbeck's machine..."

The song was coming from the edge of the clearing. The red started moving toward her. Berry froze. She reached into her pocket to touch the paper swan. A girl in a red dress stepped out from behind a particularly wide maple.

"Hello," said the stranger, the wind stealing most of the second syllable. The stranger came toward Berry, stepping into the sun, pulling a red wagon behind her. She looked to be seven or eight. Maybe nine.

"Hello?" Berry answered back, surprised by the flat sound of her voice in the clearing.

The little girl continued her approach. "Did you like my song?" she asked.

"It's…it's not a very nice song."

"But it's fun to sing." The girl walked up to Berry and dropped the handle of the wagon. It was the very same kind of wagon as her father's, but this one was like brand new. Bright red.

"I've seen you before," the girl said.

"No you haven't."

"Yes I have."

"What are you doing here? Where do you live?" asked Berry.

"I live here," she said, spreading her arms out like she was blessing the forest.

"No you don't. Girls don't live in forests."

"They do if they want to."

"I don't believe you."

"You don't have to believe me for it to be true." She pointed deeper into the forest. "My house is that way."

"Do your parents know you're here?"

"My parents are dead," she said. Then she laughed, and the laugh sounded like a bear's growl. Berry took a step back.

"I should probably go," she said.

"Don't you want to see the tree house? You're so close to the tree house."

"Maybe next time." Berry turned and started back up the hill.

"My name is Antonia," the girl called after her. "I like your gloves."

Berry didn't respond. She just kept walking. When she crested the top of the hill, she briefly glanced back at the clearing, but the field was empty. She started walking faster, feeling every heartbeat again.

When she reached Nicole Diver Tree, she turned left and began to run. She was out of breath when she exited the forest, far west of where she had entered it. The wall here seemed older. The mortar was nearly all gone and nearly every stone wiggled when she brushed her fingers against them. She walked east along the wall, watching her feet as she went to make sure she didn't trip over a root or a fallen stone. The wind had stopped again and she felt sweat forming on her back. She looked along the wall and the scene before her stole her breath.

All her swans were lined up along the top of the wall. All but the white one.

She climbed over and quickly collected them all, then trudged up the hill to the deck as fast as her tired legs could take her. The house was silent.

"Dad?" she called as she walked in the sliding door. "Aunt Annabelle?"

She dumped the paper swans onto the couch and stepped up onto the walkway above the great room. Both her aunt and her father's bedroom doors were closed. She leaned her ear against her father's and listened. She could just make out his wheezing. Berry exhaled.

A tapping noise shook her from the moment's rest. She looked up to see Red pawing at the back door. She walked over and let her in. The cat followed Berry to the couch and jumped up onto her lap.

"I have had a very strange day," she said to Red. "An angry and sad and curious day." She began stroking the cat's fur. "You lost your bandage," she said. She studied Red's leg. The wounds seemed to have healed. Berry shook her head. "You are a mystery, Red. Like the forest." Then she began to sing softly.

"Oh Dunderbeck, oh Dunderbeck, how could you be so mean..." The cat hissed, and Berry laughed at the perfect timing. "You're right, Red. It's not a very nice song."

Red settled down on her lap.

"Antonia," Berry whispered to the quiet house.

Then she started to hum.

9

D ress nice," said Annabelle. They hadn't said another word about what would happen to Berry after her father died. Berry couldn't remember a quieter Saturday night supper. Hot dogs and baked beans. They didn't taste as good as usual because her father had soup instead. The only thing that made hot dogs and baked beans taste good was eating them together.

Everyone had gone to bed early. Berry tried to read more in *Tender Is the Night*, but gave up quickly, tired of the work it had become.

Then came Sunday morning. A day to sleep in, though all the days seemed to be sleep-in days lately. And here her aunt was telling her to dress up.

"Why?"

"I'm taking you to church."

"We don't go to church," said Berry, looking around the living room for evidence of her father.

"Your father is tired this morning. But he agreed that church would be a good idea."

Berry scowled. "That doesn't sound like something my dad would say."

"Maybe he's changed. People change." Annabelle's tone reminded Berry of the way classmates would reply to the teacher when they weren't entirely sure of the answer.

"I don't want to go to church."

"Please, Berry. There are some really nice people at my church. Of course there are some really snotty people there, too. But we'll try to avoid them."

Berry had already queued up another "no thank you" but her aunt's mention of the snotty people pressed pause on her response. She pictured a bunch of old ladies with runny noses and giggled to herself.

"Is it anything like the zoo?" Berry asked.

"Well, yes. I suppose it is, in a way." Annabelle reached over to tousle Berry's bedhead, but Berry slipped out of bed at that very moment and headed to the bathroom.

"I'll dress nice," she said.

The Morrowton United Methodist Church was the kind of church you'd find on Christmas cards. A small, standalone tissue box-shaped building with a tall roof and a taller steeple, it was as white as snow except for the doors, which were a bright red that reminded Berry of Antonia.

"Will you tell me which ones are the snotty ones?" whispered Berry as they walked up to the front of the church. Annabelle shushed her, but let a smile slip as she guided Berry toward the wide steps. Berry took a sudden detour and ran around to the right, following the wheelchair ramp instead. She met her aunt in front of the red doors.

"I was pretending I had wheels instead of feet," she said, by way of explanation. "Wheels are better."

They opened the door and walked into the foyer, a small space that was notable for the three brass signs along the top of the wall above the wide opening that led to the sanctuary. The middle sign noted the sanctuary's name. "Ronald J. Stephens Sanctuary." The sign to its right said "Sunday School Rooms This Way" and included a right-pointing arrow. The sign to its left said, "Bathrooms This Way" and included a left-pointing arrow. This made Berry smile, though she wasn't quite sure why.

Annabelle greeted a few other stragglers, then ushered Berry into the sanctuary. Berry and Annabelle sat in the fourth pew from the back, left side. She counted fifteen rows of pews in front of them. They were mostly empty, though the pews on the right side seemed marginally more popular.

"Summer is when we separate the fair weather Christians from the faithful," her aunt said.

"I don't understand. Isn't summer the fairest weather of all?"

Her aunt laughed, bringing a glare from the only other person in their pew – a creaky old woman wearing a pale blue dress and matching dress gloves.

"I'll explain later," she whispered to Berry.

All the men were old and wrinkly and wore suits and ties. All the women were old and wrinkly and wore dresses. It was a little like being at a wedding, but without the smiling. Berry had been to exactly one wedding – a friend's mother was re-marrying her original husband. Berry hadn't quite understood that, but the wedding ceremony was interesting and the cake afterward was the best she'd ever tasted.

Berry wished she had eaten more than a half piece of toast for breakfast. Her stomach growl brought another glare from the pale blue woman, but Berry detected the edge of a smile on the woman's lips and began to question if her perpetual glare was less a judgment and more of a physical ailment.

Piano music started playing. Annabelle stood and Berry mimicked her and helped her aunt hold an open book in front of her just low enough for Berry to see. A song book.

"What a friend we have in Jesus," the people began to sing. Berry didn't know the tune, but she read along quietly with the words, occasionally looking up at her aunt, who sang without a single glance at the songbook. When they got to the second verse, Berry closed her eyes and listened. The people's voices echoed around the small space, sounding twice as big as the numbers suggested. She heard warbling voices, sweet voices, broken voices and confident voices – like that of her aunt.

"Are we weak and heavy laden…" Berry nodded. Yes. She was feeling weak. And if "heavy laden" meant "sad," than she was that, too.

The song finished, and they sat again. After a few announcements, a special song (from one of the warbly singers) and a Bible passage read by a man so old and feeble, Berry thought he might turn to dust right there on the stage, the pastor stood up to speak. Berry tried to listen to his message, but the man's voice was deep and gentle and the rhythm of his words sounded like waves lapping a shore and instead she drifted in and out of sleep.

She was jarred awake when her aunt stood and began singing another song. Berry stood and helped to hold the song book, then smiled when her blurry eyes finally focused on the title of the song, "Be Thou My Vision."

"Well, what did you think?" Annabelle asked Berry as the service ended and they were scooting out of the pew into the aisle.

"Everything here is old. The people are old the sounds are old and the smells are old."

"Well…"

"But old isn't bad," she added.

Berry endured the handshaking and careful-not-to-break-any-aging-bones hugs that her aunt gave a half dozen or so of the people in the congregation, then followed her into the foyer, and off toward the Sunday School Rooms, where they turned once again and went down a long stairway to a basement she discovered included a big room filled with tables and folding chairs and a surprisingly bright kitchen complete with a buffet line of foods, some familiar, some frightening.

"Are all churches bigger on the inside?" asked Berry.

"Nope. Some are positively tiny on the inside."

Berry sniffed the air and the smell of chicken gracefully replaced the smell of must and dust.

"We won't stay long," said Annabelle. They stepped without hesitation into the line that was forming at one of the kitchen doors. "The fried chicken in the big blue bowl will be Lenora Stewart's. That's the good chicken." She bent down low to whisper in Berry's ear. "Don't eat the chicken in the flat pan. You'll be sick all afternoon. And don't even think about trying the potato salad."

"Which one?" Berry asked, noticing at least four bowls filled with it.

"Any of them."

"That won't be a problem. I can't stand the damn stuff."

Annabelle's eyes widened. "Do you often talk like that?"

Not often. She was testing a phrase she'd read in *Tender Is the Night*. "Just trying something new."

"Probably should keep the profanity to minimum when God's nearby." Then Annabelle elbowed Berry and pointed to a large woman wearing an apron who was guarding the food in the kitchen. "And by 'God' I mean Mrs. Murphy."

They filled their plates and sat at one of the long tables to eat. Berry smiled and nodded when Annabelle introduced her to strangers, most of who were much older than her aunt, but all of who brought out a gentle, thoughtful side of Annabelle. This Annabelle was much different than the one who lived by herself at the top of a hill. Well, not by herself so much now.

All the strangers smiled back at Berry, though they were sometimes difficult to understand with their cracked voices and strong Maine accents. A few offered Annabelle hugs that seemed like the kind you give to a person whose dog died. Berry dismissed that thought as soon as she'd had it.

Before they left the room Annabelle kept calling "Fellowship Hall," they collected a plate of food for Berry's father (the big blue bowl was empty, so they opted for ham and green beans and cobbler and mac and cheese, despite Annabelle's disagreement on the latter) and wrapped it in tin foil. The pastor whispered something to Annabelle on the way out of Fellowship Hall, then offered a too-friendly smile to Berry as she walked past him and up the stairs.

On the ride home, Annabelle started humming.

"Is that the song from the church service?" Berry asked.

"Yes. It's called a hymn. We only sing hymns, none of that praise and worship nonsense. Although some of the song choices are a little suspect. The pastor used to be Presbyterian."

"Your voice sounds different," said Berry.

"Does it?" She laughed. "Oh, I suppose when I get around my old friends, I start to sound more like them. I lost my accent when I moved to New York, and never really found it again."

"I didn't know you moved to New York."

"I did. For a time."

"But you don't sound like New York either."

"I suppose not."

When they got back to the house, Berry was disappointed to discover that her father was still sleeping. They put his plate of food in the refrigerator for later.

Berry walked out onto the deck and studied the forest below, trying to see if she could tell where the clearing was. But the rolling hills and valleys of the landscape made it impossible to discern. If only she had a balloon and a really long string. A red balloon. She would tie the string to a rock or a broken branch and set it in the middle of the field.

"Do you know where I could get a helium balloon?" she asked Annabelle.

"Oh, I suppose at a party supply place. There's one in Bangor, I think. Why, are you planning a party?"

"No. Just wondering."

"That's a pretty specific thing to wonder about."

"Specific things are the best kinds of things to wonder about."

Storm clouds were gathering to the west, so Berry decided to explore closer to home. She climbed off the deck and wandered around to the garage. The doors were still wide open, which meant Annabelle had decided not to press the issue with Berry's dad. He seemed to win most of the arguments, though it certainly wasn't because he was the tougher of the two.

Berry stood in the doorway and looked into the dark space, wishing it were brighter. She jogged back to the kitchen door and burst in with an idea.

"Aunt Annabelle? Where do you keep your window cleaning supplies?"

She helped Berry find them under the kitchen sink, then also helped Berry get the small step ladder out from the linen closet.

Berry spent the better part of the afternoon scrubbing away at the inside and outside of the three windows in the garage. Some of the dirt didn't come out at all, but by the end of her efforts, the light situation had definitely improved.

She sat down on the lawn chair in front of the open garage to admire her work, and to consider the monumental task ahead. She had decided to clean out the garage as much as possible, or at least organize it so it wasn't such a jumble. A shadow passed in front of her and she looked up to see her father's smiling face.

"Well, that's some pretty impressive work. Why weren't you this thorough when I asked you to clean your room back at the old house?"

She didn't want to tell him the truth. That this cleaning was more important somehow. She shrugged.

A moment later, Annabelle came out of the kitchen carrying a tray of iced tea and freshly-baked cookies.

"Wow," she said. "I don't know if those windows have ever been cleaner."

"They're still kind of dirty," said Berry. "But it's not the kind of dirt you can just scrub away. It's the kind that means the windows are old."

Berry offered the chair to her father, but he declined. She stood too, and the three of them stared into the garage while sipping tea and chewing warm chocolate chip cookies. The storm had done little more than threaten, but the wind had increased and was blowing up the hillside from the forest. Berry thought she could hear singing again, but when she looked at her father and her aunt, neither showed any signs that they heard it too.

That evening after dinner (Berry had most of a frozen pizza, Annabelle ate the rest of the baked beans, her father nibbled on the church plate, then swirled up a fruit and vegetable smoothie), they sat around the kitchen table playing old table games. Berry had been excited to play Monopoly (she hadn't played before), but got bored quickly so they moved to Parcheesi and then to dominos, which she won even though she had wrongly interpreted the rules at first.

"Beginner's luck," Annabelle had said.

"Oh no," corrected Berry's father. "Berry isn't lucky. She's smart."

"Beginner's smarts," said Berry.

"Bicycle parts," said her father.

"Delicious tarts," said Annabelle, who then laughed and opened the oven to surprise Berry and her father with...blueberry tarts. "How's that for timing?"

"And rhyming," added Kenneth.

"Whoa...now that was cool," said Berry. It felt a little like magic. They ate the warm tarts with a scoop of melty vanilla ice cream as the thunder finally announced its arrival, bringing with it buckets of rain and the promise of an early night.

10

I'm going down the hill to play," said Berry, calling back to her father as she slid the screen door closed. She didn't want to engage in a conversation that might reveal the fact that she was actually going exploring in the forest.

She scrabbled and slid down the hill, nearly losing her backpack once when she fell on her backside, then climbed over the stone wall and kept walking. She decided not to turn around, fearing she might see her father watching her with disappointment. She couldn't bear that look – she knew it as much by his posture as by the way his lips turned. Hmm...his lips turned nearly the same way when he was teaching her something. This seemed like an important thought, so she turned her own lips into teaching position and skipped the rest of the way into the forest.

She paused at Nicole Diver Tree to study her, to wonder again how she got so twisted. She must have grown around something that was no longer there. But what kind of something? Berry turned her ear in the direction of the clearing, listening. There was no song today, but there was another sound. A rhythmic squeak and squeal.

Berry climbed the hill and looked down into the clearing. Antonia, still wearing bright red, was pulling the wagon around the clearing, following the imagined base paths. Berry hesitated, wondering what kind of trouble a little girl could be, then walked down the hill with a manufactured confidence. Antonia didn't look up when Berry stepped into the clearing. She just kept dragging the wagon around the bases.

"Where are your gloves?" she asked.

Berry looked at her hands, then patted her back pocket. "I brought them."

Antonia stopped, somewhere between third base and home. She looked up at Berry.

"Can I wear them?"

"They're really old and have holes in them."

"I don't mind."

Berry shrugged and pulled the gloves out of her pocket and took them over to Antonia. Antonia's eyes were a kind of green Berry hadn't seen before.

Antonia slipped the gloves on, admiring them like she'd just discovered her hands. Berry looked at the wagon.

"I had a wagon just like that. But someone took it."

Antonia furrowed her brow. "This is my wagon. This has always been my wagon. Somebody took my wagon too but now I have it back and it's mine."

"I'm sorry…I didn't mean to make you upset. It's just that the wagon I lost was my dad's, and before that his dad's. It's kind of special to him. My dad, I mean. My grandpa is dead."

"You should check with the neighbors. Neighbors are always stealing things."

"Maybe I will."

"You want to see the tree house?" asked Antonia.

"Okay."

"This way," she said. She started toward the opposite edge of the clearing. Berry followed a few steps behind, ever more curious about this girl who seemed perfectly at home among the trees. She watched the wagon as it rolled and bounced on the hard ground. It sure looked like her father's wagon. It even sounded like it.

They climbed up a gentle slope on the far side of the clearing, then down into a valley, and up one more hill before Antonia stopped suddenly. She turned and looked right into Berry's eyes.

"Stealing is wrong," she said. Her eyes flashed like emeralds in a trickle of sunlight that slanted through the trees, then she turned and continued down the other side of the hill. East, thought Berry. We're heading east. When they reached the bottom, Antonia stopped again and pointed to a big tree in front of them. Its trunk must have been at least five feet across. Berry had never seen such a tree.

She looked up, following the line of the trunk straight into the sky.

"I don't see a tree house."

"This isn't the tree house tree. It's the permission tree. You have to get permission from this tree before going any further."

Berry thought of her father's spider poem.

"Why?" she asked.

Antonia huffed. "Because if you don't get permission you're stealing. And stealing is wrong."

"You're a very weird girl," said Berry.

"Who says I'm a girl?" Antonia laughed another bear-like laugh. "Do what I do," she said. It wasn't a request. Berry thought she looked older than nine today.

Antonia walked up to the tree, curtsied, then gave it a big hug and held tight for a very long time. Then she backed up, curtsied again, and turned toward Berry, folding her arms in front of her. Berry walked up to the tree and curtsied the best she could in shorts and a t-shirt. She heard a not-very-well-stifled laugh from Antonia. Then Berry walked up and wrapped her arms around the trunk. The bark was deeply grooved, full of secrets, but cool and soft. She didn't want to let go. But after counting to ten in her head, she did, then stepped back.

"Well?" said Antonia.

"Well what?"

"Did the tree give you permission?"

"How would I know?"

Antonia huffed again. "Were you even listening?"

"Look, I don't know what I'm supposed to do. And you're being kind of mean."

"Sorry," she said. And suddenly she was back to being a little girl, her voice light and airy, her smile one of innocence. "I was just kidding about the permission tree."

"No you weren't."

"Maybe I was."

Berry had had enough. She turned and started walking back the way they'd come.

"Wait," Antonia called to her. "I really am sorry. It's been a while since I had a friend. I guess I'm not doing it right."

Berry stopped. "Be nicer. That's how you're supposed to do it."

"Okay."

She turned and followed Antonia past the permission tree. When they got to the top of the next hill, she saw it. The tree house. It was much more than the platform her father had told her about. It was a small cottage situated about twenty or twenty-five feet in the air, stuffed in the space between two diverging boughs, as if it had fallen from the sky and split the tree down the middle. The siding was painted a dull blue, the shingles were a dark gray, and the door was red.

Wagon red.

"I've been fixing it up," said Antonia.

"You took my father's wagon," said Berry. "You took it and you painted it to look new."

"It's *my* wagon," she growled.

"Lying is just as wrong as stealing," said Berry under her breath.

"What?"

"Never mind." Berry walked around the forked tree, looking for a way up. "How do you get up there?"

Antonia brightened. "With magic," she said. She walked right up to the tree trunk and pulled at a bent nail that Berry hadn't seen until then. A plug of bark and tree pulled away and revealed a gouge in the trunk just about big enough for a foot. Antonia slid her left foot in the space, then reached up to another bent nail. That's when Berry noticed a succession of bent nails that went all the way up to what looked like a trap door in the tree house. She waited until Antonia had revealed all of the secret hand holds and was peering down from the open trap door of the tree house before following up after her. Halfway up, she looked down at the dozen plugs Antonia had pulled from the tree and thought how painful it would be to fall onto them, rusty bent nails and all. She wondered about how much work it must be putting them back in place.

Berry climbed higher, until she poked her head into the small tree house. Antonia was sitting on a small step stool, hands folded in front of her, smiling under a stream of light that filtered in through a small square window and painted her face with the shadow of a cross. She pulled herself up and onto the tree house floor, then closed the trap door.

"Wow." It was rustic, in sharp contrast to the exterior. The interior walls were a patchwork of plywood and siding and shingles. It was a surprisingly big space. Berry could stand in the middle of the room and there was still another foot above her head before the peak of the roof, which also was pieced together, but with two-by-fours nailed together into a web of questionable structural integrity. Aside from the footstool Antonia sat on, the only other piece of furniture was a long wooden box along the back wall that appeared to have been built into the tree house. A neatly-folded brown blanket rested upon it.

"Sit," said Antonia.

Berry sat on the blanket.

There were two windows in the tree house, the square one divided into quarters by small strips of wood, and a round one with a brass frame – a porthole – awkwardly fitted into a mostly-square space. Light spilled in around the porthole as much as

86

through its grimy surface. The red door she'd seen from below opened to a small deck, no more than three feet wide, where she imagined one might sit and dangle feet in honor of gravity or direct challenge to a fear of heights.

"What's in your bag?" asked Antonia.

"My bag?"

"The bag you carry on your back."

"My backpack."

Antonia's eyebrows furrowed. "I can call it a bag if I want to."

Berry shrugged. "A flashlight. Snacks. My book."

"Snacks?"

"Berry set the backpack on the plywood floor and unzipped it. She pulled out a bottle of water and two packages of peanut butter crackers. Antonia scooped up both packages and began tearing into them.

"Hey, it's not polite to grab…"

"I'm hungry," Antonia mumbled, cracker crumbs spitting out as she spoke.

"Don't your parents feed you?"

"Told you. They're dead." Antonia tilted her head in a question, pointed to the water bottle.

"Go ahead, take it."

She seemed momentarily puzzled by the twist-off top, but once solved, began to guzzle the water.

"What's your real story?" asked Berry when Antonia had finally pressed pause on her snack attack.

"You like stories?"

"That's not what I mean…"

"I know lots of stories. Wanna hear one?"

Berry sighed. This wasn't exactly the kind of day she'd expected. But then she smiled. Expected days could be pretty boring. She gathered up the plastic wrappers from the crackers and stuffed them into a pocket on her backpack.

"Once upon a time there was a monster…" Antonia began.

"Really? That's how you're going to start the story? Once upon a time? Lame."

"It's not lame. It's the way all stories start."

"Fine. Go on."

Antonia had reached down and was playing with the backpack straps, running her white-gloved fingers across them like she was inspecting fine linen.

"Once upon a time there was a monster who lived in the forest. This forest. He had…green eyes and long claws and teeth like knives."

Antonia stopped and sat up straighter.

"That's it? That's your story?" asked Berry.

"And he collected children," she added.

Berry shivered. The tree house began to move ever so slightly in the breeze. Berry wondered how a tree house so securely stuffed between giant branches could move at all. Perhaps the whole tree was moving.

"That's not much of a story," said Berry.

"A story doesn't need to be long and boring."

"No."

"Then it's a good story." There seemed to be a question at the end of her statement.

"It's not a good story if nothing happens in it."

"The monster. Collects. Children," Antonia said. "Children!"

"Fine. It's a great story then. Best one ever."

"Better than the one in your book?" Antonia reached over to the backpack, but Berry pulled it close.

"I don't know yet. I haven't finished that one."

They sat in silence for a long time, listening to the wind in the trees and the creak of the tree house. Berry watched the cross-shaped shadow slide from Antonia's face to the back of the red door.

"Want to sit outside?" Antonia stood and opened the door. It swung open and slammed against the outside of the tree house. She ducked through the space and sat on the narrow deck. Berry stood up, but her legs stuck to the blanket and it came with her, lifting the lid of the bench seat slightly. She brushed the blanket away from her and turned back toward the box. She slipped her fingers under the lip of the lid and began to lift.

"Now look who's not being polite!" Antonia's foot slammed down on the box. Berry pulled her fingers away just in time.

"I just wanted to see what's in the box, that's all. Geez."

"Don't say 'Geez.' That's a swear word. Swear words are bad."

"Sorry."

They stood like that for a moment; Berry bent forward with her fingers just next to the box, Antonia with her right foot pressed against the lid.

"May I please see what's in the box?" Berry asked.

"No."

"Fine, then. I'm leaving." Berry held her hands out and pointed to the gloves on Antonia's hands. She reluctantly pulled them off and Berry stuffed them into her backpack. Then she slid her arms into the backpack straps and hefted it up onto her shoulders. She felt something press against her back. The cell phone.

"Don't go…" said Antonia.

Berry lifted the trapdoor and let it drop to the tree house floor. She squeezed herself through the space, careful to find the nearest foothold with her left foot, then the next one with her right. When she had climbed down to the last foothold, she jumped away from the tree to avoid landing on the rusty nails.

"Goodbye Antonia. Try being nicer next time."

Antonia looked down at Berry through the trap door. Her shoulder-length hair spilled down around her small face, hiding all but her green eyes.

"Next time?" Antonia asked.

"Only if you promise to be nicer."

"I will."

"Promise?"

"Cross my heart and hope to die."

"Okay."

"Will you bring more snacks?"

Berry nodded, then felt a drop of rain land on her upturned face. No, not rain. Was Antonia crying?

"I'll bring snacks."

Berry walked away. She stopped just once to look back at the tree house. Antonia was sitting on the deck swinging her feet, waving her hands in the air like she was directing an orchestra.

Her white-gloved hands.

11

W here were you?" Her father's voice had an unusual edge to it.

"Just exploring."

"I looked all over for you, Berry." Had he climbed down the hill? Surely not.

"You know those bushes in the..." She paused, picturing the map, pointed. "...southeast corner of the yard at the bottom of the hill?"

He looked over her shoulder, even though he wouldn't be able to see that far from here, then nodded.

"I've adopted those bushes as my secret fort. Only now it's not a very good secret anymore."

He laughed a hesitant laugh. "Where did you learn to talk like an adult?"

"From you, of course. And books."

"I'm sorry, Berry. I didn't mean to get upset. I just...Your aunt thinks the forest isn't safe. She's overthinking it, but it never hurts to be cautious. She wants you to...we need you to stay on this side of the stone wall. Can you do that?"

Berry sighed. She hoped it was a convincing sigh, but most of hers usually were. "Okay. Just don't tell anyone about my secret fort."

"I won't."

"Promise?"

"Cross my heart and hope to die."

Berry suddenly felt sick to her stomach. She excused herself and ran into the house, then up the steps and down the hall into the bathroom. She plopped onto the floor next to the toilet, fighting the urge to throw up.

A few long minutes later, there was a knock on the door.

"You okay in there?"

Berry swallowed once. Twice. Sipped the air until she was sure she wouldn't puke. "Yeah."

"Are you sure?" He coughed and then cleared his throat for so long Berry nearly asked the same question.

"Fine. Must have been too much sun or something."

"I'll get you some water."

She waited until his slow steps faded into the distance, then stood, washed her face, and went to the kitchen to meet him. He was sitting at the table, his head in his hands. He pointed vaguely to a Mickey Mouse glass on the table already beading with condensation.

"I think you need to stay closer to the house," he wheezed. "You might be coming down with something."

Can you catch something from lying? she wondered. "Okay."

She sipped the water, then pressed the cold glass to her forehead. She really did feel a bit hot after all.

"I think you're sicker than I am," she said. She reached over and placed her hand on his shoulder. He dropped his hands from his face and turned toward her, yet another tired smile on his lips.

"I am," he said. Then, after another long coughing spell, during which his face contorted into all kinds of unfamiliar expressions, he pushed away from the table and began to stand. "I need to go lie down." He faltered a bit as he took his first step, but Berry jumped up from her seat and put her arm around him.

"I'll help you," she said.

Together, they hobbled down the hall to his room. Berry helped him onto his bed, troubled by how easily she was able to steady him. He had lost so much weight. She asked if he needed anything.

"More time," he said. It was the saddest his voice had ever been.

Berry left his bedroom, closing the door quietly behind her, then ran down the hall, through the kitchen door, and out to the garage. She dropped onto the dirt floor there between a stack of boxes and an overturned wheelbarrow.

"It's not fair!" she shouted to the dust and the spiders and probably to God, too. "He's the best man in the whole world."

She curled up into a ball on the garage floor and cried until she had no more tears left. She knew her face was a dirt-streaked mess, but she didn't care. When her breathing finally calmed, she looked up and saw Red sitting on one of the boxes. She tilted her furry head, then meowed. Berry reached up to Red and she leaped down beside her, rubbing her body against Berry's outstretched hand.

"There has to be a way to fix him. There has to."

She fell asleep to the thrum of a purring cat and the scatter of mice in the loft above her.

"Berry?"

She stirred and looked up to see the shadow of her aunt silhouetted against the garage door opening.

"Aunt Annabelle."

"Oh, Berry, you're a mess. Let me take you inside and get you washed up."

Berry looked around but Red had disappeared. "I dreamed Dad could fly," she slurred in her best half-awake voice. "He was a kite."

"Perhaps he is," Annabelle answered. She helped Berry to stand and together they walked back into the house. Berry paused next to her father's bedroom door to listen for his wheeze but was surprised to hear his snore instead.

"He's sleeping. I checked on him after I got back from work. But you...you're a hard one to keep track of." Annabelle started filling the tub.

"I can do that by myself," she said.

"I know. You can do lots of things by yourself." She poured in a capful of bubble bath, looked over at Berry, then poured in two more. "I still can't believe how grown up you are."

"I'm not *that* grown up, Aunt Annabelle." Without thinking, she wrapped her arms around her aunt and hugged her tight. After a brief moment of surprise, her aunt hugged back and they stayed in that humble pose nearly long enough for the tub to overflow.

"I'll leave you to it," Annabelle said, turning off the faucets. "Sometimes it's just good to soak for a while."

"Until you're a raisin?" said Berry.

"Yes, until you're a raisin."

"I don't really like raisins."

"It's either that or a prune," Annabelle said as she stepped into the hallway.

"Fine. A raisin then."

The door closed and Berry peeled off her clothes and stepped into the tub, settling gingerly into the hot water.

She whispered, "Thank you Aunt Annabelle" to the bubbles that had climbed as high as her shoulders, then slid the rest of the way down until only her head was above water.

She imagined herself among the clouds, floating like a kite as her father had in the dream. *Is this what heaven is like?* she wondered.

The next morning, Berry awoke to see her father looking down at her.

"What's that on your face?" he asked.

She thought he was kidding and for a moment felt relief that he was back to being himself again. She brushed at her cheek, expecting to find nothing, but instead touched rough, bumpy skin. She looked down at her the back of her hands, her arms. She was covered with spots – little bumps that looked like bug bites. She crawled out from under the rumpled sheets and stood next to the sofa bed in her pajamas.

"Looks like an allergic reaction to something," said Annabelle, who was standing in the kitchen doorway.

"Or an army of spiders attacked her last night," said her father.

"Kenneth! Don't scare the poor girl," said Annabelle.

"Yeah. Don't scare the poor girl," said Berry. She smiled despite the discomfort she was suddenly starting to feel.

Annabelle came closer, lifted Berry's arm and studied the spots. "I don't think it's Poison Ivy. Or Poison Oak for that matter."

Her father lifted her other arm and mimicked Annabelle's scrutiny. "Yep. Spider army."

Berry pulled both arms back and wrapped them around her chest. "Must have been the bath last night. Maybe I'm allergic to soap."

Her father laughed. "Well, that came on suddenly. How on earth are we going to keep you clean now?"

"Not *all* soap. Just the kind in the bath."

Annabelle disappeared into the bathroom, then returned holding the bubble bath bottle. "Never been a problem before."

"Well, whatever it is, it's itchy," said Berry.

"I'll leave a bottle of lotion on the bathroom counter. Then I need to go. I'm late for work."

Berry wondered not for the first time what kind of work a school administrator did in the summer. Annabelle answered her unspoken question as she opened the front door.

"Summer school sucks," she said, then the door closed behind her.

She looked at her father. He was shaking his head and smiling.

"You're feeling better today," Berry said.

"Yes. I am."

"Better enough to go to that park we passed on the way here?"

"Moose Run Park?"

Berry nodded. "Was it here when you were little?"

"Yes, but it wasn't called that then."

"What was it called?"

"Big grassy field where people go to play."

"Very funny." Berry paused. "Do you think we could fly kites?"

"We'll see. Maybe we can make a kite at least. But you probably should bathe in lotion first so those spider bites don't itch."

"They're not spider bites." She scratched at her arm and started to walk toward the bathroom, then stopped and spun around on one foot. It was a perfect 180 and she didn't even feel dizzy when she stopped. She walked up to her father who was leaning against the arm of the couch and gave him a hug. Not too tight, of course. And only for a moment. She didn't like the way his rib felt against her arms.

"Spider bite," he whispered. She slapped at him playfully and started walking away.

"Make a kite," she called back.

"Damn right," he said. She laughed and closed the bathroom door.

They had managed to make a single kite out of balsa wood and pink sheeting Berry had unearthed in the garage. It was nearly as tall as Berry, and twice as wide. They couldn't find any string, so Berry added that to the grocery list on the refrigerator.

Kenneth picked up the kite and carried it out into the front yard.

"It still needs a tail," he said.

"And we can't fly it until we get string," she said as she caught up to him on the grass.

"No, but we can teach it about the wind."

"Why would we do that?"

"So it knows how to fly when it has a tail and we have string. Duh."

Berry rolled her eyes. "You can't teach a kite..."

Just then a gust snapped the kite to attention. It lifted her father's arm up into the sky. "Fast learner!" he said, struggling to keep hold of the crossbeam. Berry began to giggle. She was still laughing when her father finally tamed the beast and safely returned it to the kitchen counter.

She stopped laughing when her father started coughing. She filled the Goofy glass with water and handed it to him. He nodded his thanks and sipped until the coughing had finally stopped.

"Maybe tomorrow we can go to the park," he said. "Besides, we need that string. Really strong string. This one's got a lot of energy."

"I thought the wind was the energy," said Berry. She furrowed her brow and folded her arms as if to scold him for his silliness.

He coughed again. "Oh, how I have failed in the education of my daughter." Another cough. "Remind me later to teach you about the particular pluck of persnickety kites."

"I will," she said. "But first I'll have to look up some of those words."

She helped him down the hall to his room.

That afternoon, Berry decided to take a different approach to reading *Tender Is the Night*. Stopping to look up every word was turning the reading experience into a school assignment. Instead, she would plow through it without pausing. Then, when she was done, she'd read it again. She would read it over and over until it made sense. However many times it took.

She finished the first read-through just before bedtime. Over the next few stormy days, she read it three more times.

"I don't know why you love that book so much," said Berry to her father the following Sunday morning. He was leaning against the bathroom sink, running a comb through his thinning hair.

"What book?"

"*Tender Is the Night.*"

He smiled. "Well..."

"I mean, no one in it is happy," Berry interrupted. "At. All. I mean, they think they're happy sometimes, or they do things they think will make them happy. But they're not."

"How many times have you read it now?"

"Four."

"I think it took me five times before I started to see the beauty in that book."

"I'm not sure I can endure it again."

Her father laughed. "You sound just like Mrs. Diver."

"No I don't."

"Okay, okay. Then Rosemary."

"Nope. Not even Rosemary." Berry saw her father falter as he started to walk out of the bathroom. She grabbed him by the elbow and helped him to the railing overlooking the great room.

"Did you like how it was written?" he asked as they shuffled down toward the kitchen.

"Yes."

"That's one of the things I love about the book. I'm smitten by beautiful language."

"But it was so sad."

Kenneth lifted his hand from the railing and ruffled it through Berry's hair.

"Even sad things can be beautiful."

Berry decided she would give the book one more chance.

Annabelle drove them to church in her car. The truck that had brought them to Maine continued to gather dust at the end of the driveway. Berry watched it disappear in the rear view mirror and felt a twinge in her stomach.

They arrived late again, just as the congregation was standing to sing a hymn. Annabelle took her brother's arm and led him down the center aisle to the second-to-last pew on the left side. Berry thought she was walking too fast, but her father kept up without complaint. The old lady Berry had seen the previous week stood in her same spot, two rows in front of them, as if she hadn't moved at all. She turned her head to see Berry and nodded a slight "good morning" without breaking stride in her singing, then turned back to sing to the pastor or the big cross at the front of the church. Or God, maybe.

When they all settled down to endure the sermon, Berry felt a tap on her leg. Her father handed her a big envelope. She hadn't seen him carrying it and looked up with a question on her face. He winked and went back to singing, or probably just mouthing the words. Berry opened the envelope to find some of her origami paper. At least a dozen perfect squares in black and white and blue and green.

She removed a book from the rack on the back of the pew in front of her and set it on her lap. When she realized it was a Bible, she almost put it back. But it made a perfect table for her folding, so she kept it. Surely God wouldn't mind, she reasoned.

She slid all the papers but the blue one back into the envelope and set it beside her. When she looked down, she saw her father's hand gripping the edge of the pew. She glanced sideways at his face and expected to see him grimacing, but he appeared relaxed and calm. He looked down and smiled at her.

Some of the pastor's words filtered into her consciousness as she folded the blue paper along familiar lines.

"…I find it fascinating that Jesus asked the man, 'Do you want to get well?' I think I would have responded rather curtly, were I in that man's shoes. Or should I say sandals…"

A few scattered laughs echoed throughout the room. Was it okay to laugh at church? Berry filed that question away to ask later.

"…There he was, obviously a very sick man, so sick that he couldn't even make his way to the healing pool. And here was Jesus asking 'Do you want to get better?'…"

Berry finished the final fold and held the blue swan between her forefinger and thumb, but she wasn't thinking about origami anymore.

"The healing pool," she whispered to herself. She started listening to the sermon, but the pastor quickly moved on to another story and she lost interest. She made three more swans, then skimmed through the Bible a bit, finding it even more confusing than *Tender Is the Night*. And then the service was over. She stuffed the Bible back into the rack, and balanced the blue swan on top of it.

Once again, everyone poured themselves through the small hallway and down the stairs into the fellowship hall. Berry walked beside her father, noticing the smiles from all the old people were different than they had been the week before. They tilted their heads as they smiled, and their smiles were often accompanied by nodding. Berry knew that look. That was the "so sorry for your loss" look. She'd seen it plenty at school when her father was in the hospital.

There was a palpable excitement in the air as they queued up at the first kitchen door.

"Lobster rolls," whispered Annabelle. "Someone's gone and brought lobster rolls."

"For the whole church?" asked Berry.

"Just for the lucky ones at the front of the line, I'm afraid."

And sure enough, when their turn came, the lobster rolls had already been cleaned out. All that remained was a small chunk of lobster meat, lying in wait on a big glass tray for anyone bold enough to sneak it onto their plate. It was still there when they had rounded the food-filled counter and exited the kitchen.

They sat down at an empty table that quickly filled up with smiling, talky people who were in the middle of conversations that might have begun minutes or decades before. Berry lifted her drumstick to her mouth and took a bite, hoping she'd chosen the right chicken. She felt a tap on her shoulder and turned around. It was the old lady from two rows in front of her. She offered Berry a plate, a single lobster roll balanced in the middle.

"You have to be fast to get the good stuff," the woman said, then set the plate in front of Berry. Berry finished chewing her chicken and mumbled a "thank you." The woman just smiled and walked away.

"That was unexpected," said Annabelle.

"Well, aren't you special now," her father added.

"I'm not special," she said.

"Oh, but you are Berry. If only you knew just how much…" her father's voice trailed off.

"Mrs. Howard must like you," said Annabelle. "Maybe you remind her of her granddaughter."

Berry didn't ask for clarification. She just grabbed her knife and cut the lobster roll into three pieces and, despite their objections, gave one each to her father and her aunt.

Before they left to go home, Berry wound her way through the maze of tables and scramble of chairs to find Mrs. Howard. She was sitting at the back of the room, next to a man in a wheelchair who was hooked up to an oxygen tank. He lifted his head when Berry approached, but didn't register recognition. Berry tapped Mrs. Howard on her shoulder, the same way she had tapped on Berry's.

"Thank you for the lobster roll," Berry said.

"I thought you might like that," she said.

"I shared it with my dad and my aunt."

"I wouldn't have expected anything less."

Berry looked over at the man in the wheelchair again, listened to his rhythmic wheezing, then turned back to look at Mrs. Howard. The woman's skin was nearly translucent. There was something both frightening and beautiful about the way it gathered up against her bones.

"I like the way you sing," Berry said. Then she reached into the right pocket of her skirt and drew out one of her swans. A white one. She held it out to Mrs. Howard, who received it into her bony, wrinkled hand like she was being given a diamond.

"A swan from a swan," Mrs. Howard said. "How perfectly lovely."

On the drive back to Granby house, Berry watched the trees and houses blur by, wondering about what it is that draws people to church week after week to sit on uncomfortable benches and sing cobwebby songs and listen to a man talk on and on and on about someone who lived hundreds of years ago. Maybe they came for the food.

"Is there such a thing as a healing pool?" Berry asked.

Her aunt huffed, but her father answered.

"I can't imagine why not."

"Really?"

"Oh Kenneth, don't mislead the girl. Of course there's no such thing."

"I guess I'm not as certain as you are about what does and doesn't exist." Her father's tone was light and friendly, but Berry heard a hint of sadness underneath the words. Or maybe it was disappointment. Sometimes she couldn't tell the difference. "And I thought you were the religious one," he added.

"What? Oh, I see where you're going with this," Annabelle said. She laughed. "You think because I go to church that I believe everything I hear there? Not a chance. Some of it is absolute…excuse the expression…bullcrap."

"Then why do you go?" asked Berry.

"Oh, I don't know. Because I have friends there. Because it's a good thing to do. Because I've always gone…"

"And because of the fried chicken?" asked Berry.

"And because of *Lenora Stewart's* fried chicken."

"So what do you believe, then, sis? About God."

Annabelle took a deep breath and let it out slowly. She flicked her turn signal lever up, then merged onto the dirt road that led up the hill to Granby House.

"I believe God exists, but that he's been absent for a while."

"Where's he been?" Berry asked.

"Anywhere but here," she answered.

That silenced her father.

They spent the rest of the day napping and watching old movies and listening to the thunder of a distant storm. Annabelle insisted on applying another layer of cooling cream to Berry's spotted skin before bed. But instead of making Berry feel better, it just made her feel greasy. Like her fingers after Lenora Stewart's chicken. After tossing and turning for an hour, she got up and went to the bathroom to rub all the lotion off with a towel.

Red was outside the sliding door looking in, the moonlight painting her fur a deep burgundy.

She let Red in, then climbed back into bed. The cat leaped onto the mattress and sidled up next to Berry, purring. She dreamed of kites and swimming pools.

12

B erry!"
      She slid to a stop halfway down the hill, dropped her backpack and looked up at her father. He was standing on the grass at the bottom of the deck stairs, humming a vaguely familiar tune. The Dunderbeck song? wondered Berry. *Surely not.*

"What day is it?" he asked.

"Have you forgotten the days of the week?"

"Well, they do sort of blend together here, don't they," he said.

"Yeah. It's Wednesday."

"Ah yes, hump day." He tilted his head in his thoughtful way.

"What does 'hump day' really mean?" she asked, squinting against the sun.

"It's the middle of the work week – the hump of the week. Once you're past Wednesday, you're 'over the hump,' so to speak."

"Oh," said Berry. "I thought it had something to do with a camel."

"Maybe camels like Wednesdays."

"Maybe so." She started down the hill again, then paused. She looked up at her father, who was still standing there, looking down to her.

"I wish I could come with you," he said.

"You mean to my hideout in the bushes on *this side* of the stone wall?" She rolled her eyes.

He laughed. "Yes. To the hideout in the bushes on *this side* of the stone wall. Well, that, and maybe the tree house."

"I'm not going to the…"

He took a step forward. Too close to the edge of the hill, thought Berry.

"You are being careful, aren't you?" he asked.

"I..." Berry sighed. "I'm sorry, Dad. I know I wasn't supposed to go into the forest. But...how can I *not* go?"

"Don't worry, Raspberry. I won't tell your aunt." He sat down on the grass and leaned back on his thin arms. "So, tell me. Is it still there? What's it like?"

"Yes! It's still there. And also I've been to the twisted tree and the baseball field and the permission tree..."

"The permission tree?"

"You need permission to visit the tree house, silly."

"Tell me about the tree house."

"It's not a boring old platform at all. And there's...someone must have fixed it up since you were here last. It has walls and windows and a roof and windows..."

"Really? Huh. Well, now I really want to see it."

Berry started back up the hill. "So come with me, then."

He stood and took a tentative step onto the slope.

"Wait for me. I'll help you..." But before she could take another step, her father slipped and began to fall. He rolled, then slid down the hill for a few yards before his left leg was able to dig into the dirt and wild grass to stop his descent. Berry climbed the rest of the way to meet him. A sound she had never heard him make spilled from his lips.

"Oh...that wasn't such a good idea," he said. "I think..." he tried to sit up, but groaned again in pain. "I think I might have broken my leg. Roll up my right pant leg...gently...tell me what you see."

Berry fought tears as she carefully rolled up his right pant leg. There was an unnatural bump pressing up in the middle of his shin. It made her want to vomit, but she kept her composure.

"I don't think it's supposed to look like that," she said. "Does it hurt?" The knees on his khakis were torn and bloody.

"Yes. It does. A lot. I think you probably should call someone to help," he said.

"I'll call Aunt Annabelle…"

"So she can yell at me for being stupid? Um…how about you just call the hospital. The number is on the fridge…"

"I'll call 911…"

"It's not an emergency, Berry." He groaned again. "Okay…no…you're right. Call 911. Do you know our address?"

She nodded, then climbed the rest of the way up the hill to the kitchen. The house phone was hanging on the wall above the trash can. She lifted the handset to her ear but didn't hear a dial tone. She tried pressing 911.

Nothing.

"The cell phone!" she said. She ran to her father's room and found her father's iPhone on the nightstand. She quickly dialed the number again.

After the paramedics lifted her father into the ambulance, Berry climbed in and sat on the bench near him. He smiled and held out his hand for her to hold.

"It's just a broken leg. Nothing too serious," he said. "I'll be fine."

Berry started crying.

"I promise, Berry. I'll be just fine. At least until your aunt finds out what I've done." His speech was slurred, but he managed a crooked smile and reached over to tussle her hair for the millionth time.

Annabelle met them in the recovery room at the hospital. She didn't say a word for a long time. When she finally spoke, her voice was unusually quiet.

"Can I get you anything?" she asked.

"An adamantium skeleton?"

"A what?"

"Never mind. A glass of water would be just perfect."

She handed him the plastic cup with a straw. He took a long sip.

"No more skiing, okay Ken?" Annabelle took the cup from her brother and set it on the tray, then took her hand in his.

"I suppose that goes for hang gliding, too."

"Yep."

"Is running with the bulls out?"

"Most certainly."

"Hemingway will be disappointed. What about my dream of playing professional baseball..."

"Oh Kenneth...you are incorrigible." Annabelle sniffled and rubbed a stray tear away from her face, then smiled at Berry. She reached over and brushed a wayward strand of Berry's red hair from her face.

"It's uncanny how much you look like her sometimes," she said. "Except for your hair color..."

"Like who?" Berry asked.

"Like your mother," answered her father. He was staring at her with glassy eyes.

Berry wished she could see herself through their eyes. She stood up and walked to the window. It looked out across a lower section of the building – the entrance, she guessed, and beyond that, a small park.

"You're going to have to heal fast," she said, tracing the movement of a red-shirted boy in the park across the window pane like she was drawing his path on a touch screen.

"Oh, I will. You can count on that."

He didn't sound very convincing.

"Aren't you going to ask me why?" she asked.

"I am now. Why?"

She drew a line from the red-shirted boy up into the clouds.

"Rhymes with…um…light crying," she said.

"Hmm…fight buying?" her father rasped.

"No, try again."

"Blight drying?"

Berry smiled and drew a long line on the window from left to right and back again. "No! And what's a blight anyway?"

"It's a disease plants get," said Annabelle.

"Then it's definitely not blight drying. You get one more guess."

"Is it kite flying?"

"Yes!"

Berry thought she heard her aunt whimper. She turned from the window to see Annabelle running her fingers through her father's hair. Berry felt an unexpected twist in her stomach. She had been getting lots of those lately.

A nurse entered the room with two doctors.

"Could we have a word alone with our clumsy patient?" She was speaking to Annabelle, but looking at Berry.

"I think I'd like to stay," Annabelle said to the nurse. Berry watched a wordless conversation between the nurse and Annabelle.

"It's okay, Anna," said her father. "Take Berry down to the cafeteria for ice cream. I promise I'll spill all the secrets when you return." He smiled at Berry, then looked up at his sister and she nodded.

13

I hate it," said Berry. She stood with folded arms as the last of the medical personnel left through the front door. "I hate it I hate it I hate it I hate it!"

"It's only temporary, Raspberry," said Annabelle.

"No it's not," said Berry. She walked over to the sofa, which had been pushed up against the bookshelves, blocking access to the bottom two shelves, and plopped down on it, pulling her pillow to her chest. The hospital bed was out of place in the living room. The wheels were all wrong. The chrome safety bars were all wrong. The IV was all wrong. The perfectly white sheets were all wrong.

"I want you to take it all back," she said.

"We can't take it back, Berry," began Annabelle. "Your father needs it…"

"No! Take it back! Take everything back!" She spun around on the couch and buried her face in her pillow and screamed.

"Berry…"

"It's okay, Anna," said her father. "It's okay."

"But it's not okay, Ken," she said. "It's not fucking okay." She began to cry a blubbering cry.

Berry leaped off the couch, whipped her pillow across the landing into what used to be her father's room, then stormed outside, slamming the sliding door behind her. She ignored the muted call of her aunt and scrambled down the hill, tumbling and scraping her knees at least three times before she came to the stone wall. She climbed over it, curled into a ball, and leaned against the cool stones.

"It's not fucking okay," she yelled to the wind. She felt a twinge of guilt for using profanity, but it quickly faded. "Stupid cancer."

She felt something brush against her arm and jumped, then realized it was only Red. The cat sidled up next to Berry and curled into her own ball.

"Don't even think of purring," said Berry. But Red didn't listen and purred anyway. Berry stayed there for the longest time, battling with her thoughts and fears, scratching at her spots until her skin ached so much she had to move. She climbed back over the wall and up the hill and into the house, barely glancing at her father lying in the bed with his arm hooked up to a tube dripping liquid into his veins, his right leg in a cast atop a pillow. She walked into the second bedroom to grab her backpack, then stomped her way into the kitchen to collect as many snack foods as she could fit into the big compartment. Her aunt stood by her father's side and watched, her mouth half-open, not in puzzlement, thought Berry, but because her father had stopped her from saying something in the middle of a word.

"I am going to the tree house," Berry said as she walked back through the living room and out the sliding door. This time she closed it more carefully. Red met her at the stone wall and followed her into the forest.

"They didn't even try to stop me," said Berry.

They passed all the trees she'd named and she greeted each one, pausing to hug Rosemary because they both needed it, then made their way into the clearing. Red stopped there and wouldn't move.

"Stop being such a scaredy-cat," said Berry. The cat meowed, then followed Berry up the other side of the hill to the permission tree. Berry wrapped her arms around it.

"I don't know if permission trees are a real thing, but just in case...is it okay if I go to the tree house?"

She waited, listening to the wind and the birds. Then she heard it. A low rumble like thunder that morphed into a hum like a billion bees. It started in the ground beneath her feet, then climbed up the thick tree trunk. Berry felt it roll against her chest and arms. She leaned her cheek against the rough bark and the vibration tingled like electricity.

She wasn't afraid. God wasn't someone to be afraid of, was he?

"Rasp Berry!" Antonia's voice came flittering through the forest. She sounded far away and right next to her at the same time.

Berry let go of the tree and took a step back.

"It was just my imagination, wasn't it," she said to Red. But Red was nowhere to be seen.

Antonia climbed up ahead. Berry watched her feet disappear through the trap door. She was wearing black lace-up shoes that looked like props from an old movie and long red and white striped socks that reminded Berry of Pippi Longstocking and a heavy white dress with long sleeves. Berry climbed up after her, sat down on the bench, and slipped out of her backpack.

"Aren't you too hot in that dress?" Berry asked.

"I'm too hot in everything." Antonia's green eyes were lit by a stripe of waning sunlight that poured through the porthole.

"Yes, I brought snacks," said Berry. She pulled three packages of peanut butter crackers and an apple out of her backpack and set them on the floor in front of Antonia. Antonia cupped her hands around them and pulled them close, then lifted the apple to study it before taking a big, loud bite.

"Mmm..."

"You're welcome."

"Mmm-hmm."

"You really don't know what good manners are, do you."

"I guess not." Antonia ripped open a package of crackers. "Why do you have spots?"

"What?"

111

"On your skin. You're all spotted."

Berry had nearly forgotten about the red splotches, but the moment Antonia mentioned them, her whole body began to itch. "I don't know. Poison oak or something, probably."

"We should go for a swim!"

"What? Where?"

"At the pond."

Berry tried to picture her father's map. There was a swimming hole, wasn't there? "I don't feel like swimming." She dug around in her backpack for the second apple. Her fingers brushed against her father's old cell phone, paused there for a second, then wrapped around the apple. She pulled it out and took a bite. Antonia scrunched her face into a pout.

"What? I can't have one too?" asked Berry.

"Of course you can," said Antonia. "I'm just sad about the pond. It's been a long time since I had someone to swim with."

"How long?"

"Oh, years," she said.

"Fine. How far is it?"

"Not far."

"I'll need to go get my swimsuit…"

"It's not a swimsuit kind of pond," said Antonia. She took another bite of the apple.

"I don't skinny dip," said Berry.

"I don't know what that is."

"It means I don't swim naked."

"Oh. Then you will swim in your underwear."

Antonia finished the apple, tossed the core down the trap door, then stuffed the rest of the cracker into her mouth. She started climbing down the tree ladder.

"You're coming, right?"

"Yeah." Berry stood up, then waited until Antonia was halfway down before risking a peek into the storage chest.

"Don't be slow!" called out Antonia.

The storage chest was filled with dirty clothes and dolls' heads and something long and metal and shiny.

"Coming…"

Berry reached for the metal object and lifted it up through the pile of clothes. It was a rifle. A pellet gun?

"You better not be going through my stuff," called Antonia.

Berry closed the lid quietly and stepped through the trap door into the first foothold.

"Antonia, why do you have a gun?"

"I told you not to go through my stuff!"

Berry climbed down another step, and another. She looked down at Antonia. Her arms were folded tightly around her chest.

"It was an accident. My backpack snagged on the lid." She climbed down another step.

"My gun is my business."

"You're too young to have a gun," said Berry. Just two more steps and she could leap off away from the nail-studded plugs that were scattered below.

"I'm older than you think," she said.

Berry jumped down from the second foothold and landed awkwardly on one of the plugs. Her ankle twisted and scraped on the rusty nail.

"Ouch!" she yelled.

"Didn't jump far enough," said Antonia. "This way." She started off deeper into the forest. Berry picked at the broken skin on her ankle, then rubbed off the blood with the strap of her backpack. It didn't look too serious, but it stung.

Berry hobbled after Antonia, certain she was making a bad decision but unable to make a different one. The day was quickly getting away from her, and she knew her father and aunt would start to worry about her before long.

"How much farther?" she called out. But Antonia didn't answer. The shadows had begun to grow longer and darker when Berry finally followed Antonia out into a small clearing. It wasn't much bigger than a football field, and a glassy pond filled almost the entire space.

"Why is there a pond in the middle of the forest?" asked Berry.

Antonia was already untying her shoes. "Why is anything anything?" she said in response.

Berry just shook her head.

"Are you sure it's safe to swim in?"

"Why are you so worried about what things are safe?"

It was a very good question. Berry filed it away to think about later, then noted that the "later" file was getting rather full. She slipped out of her shoes and ankle socks, then pulled off her shorts and shirt. She stood at the water's edge in her underwear and dipped her toe into the black water. It was nearly the same temperature as the air.

She looked up to see Antonia standing on big flat rock that was half in the water, half out. A natural diving board. Antonia was completely naked. Her tiny body looked unusually old and wrinkled. But before Berry could rule it out as a trick of the dappled twilight, Antonia jumped into the pond with a loud splash. She disappeared under the surface for a long minute, then reappeared in the middle of the pond.

"It's best to jump in," she called to Berry.

"Okay."

Berry stepped carefully along the shoreline, avoiding rocks and sticks and muddy pools and climbed up onto the diving rock. She walked to the edge and looked down. It wasn't more than a four foot drop, but it seemed farther now that she was standing there, shivering under the setting sun.

"How deep is it?"

"Deep enough," said Antonia.

Berry took a step back, then rocked forward and leaped into the water. She sliced through the surface and went underwater, the wetness enveloping her like a summer rain. This pond shouldn't be here, she thought.

Her chest felt like it was about to burst, so she kicked her way to the surface. When she broke through the sky was dark. A full moon shone overhead and stirred below in reflection.

"I wondered when you'd come back up," said Antonia. She was fully clothed, sitting on the diving rock and swinging her feet over the edge.

"What? How?"

"How what?"

Berry felt a chill and it wasn't from the water. She swam back to the rock and hoisted herself up onto it.

"What time is it?"

"Time to eat more snacks," said Antonia. She was going through Berry's backpack.

"But I just dove in...and...my Dad is going to be worried about me. I need to get back right away!" She grabbed the backpack from Antonia and stumbled her way around the shore until she came to her clothes, still hanging on a tree branch where she'd left them. She put them on as quickly as her wet skin would allow, then slid her feet into shoes. She threw her socks into the pack and rooted around until she found her flashlight. She started back through the forest.

"That's not the right way," said Antonia.

"Then show me the right way."

After a long slow walk through the unfamiliar part of the forest, they came to the tree house. Berry paused at the base and turned around to look at Antonia. Her dress was waterlogged and her hair was slicked back. She looked almost like a boy.

"Antonia, what happened at the pond?"

"You swam. I swam. We played. We had fun."

"Then why don't I remember it?"

"Sometimes people forget things," said Antonia. "I've forgotten thousands of things."

Berry looked up at the tree house.

"Why do you have a gun?"

"Because there be monsters in these, here woods." Antonia's voice was that bear growl again. But then Antonia laughed. "Check your spots," she said, then skipped away into the deeper forest.

Berry looked down at her arms and legs, but in the darkness of night, she couldn't tell if the spots were still there. She flicked on the flashlight and ran back through the forest as fast as she could, nodding a silent thank-you to the permission tree as she passed, and wishing all the other trees a good night. She climbed over the rock wall and looked up to the house at the top of the hill. The lights were on and she could just make out someone standing by the sliding door. She made the now-familiar climb back to the deck and walked up to the door. Annabelle slid it open to let her in.

"What happened to you?" she said. Her voice was too tired to be angry.

"I fell in a pond." She said. Lying was easy when you weren't sure what the truth was.

"Berry...your skin!"

"What?"

"It's...your skin is perfect!" Berry looked down at her arms and legs again in the bright light of the living room. Sure enough, all her spots were gone. She didn't feel the least bit itchy either.

"Guess it was a magic pond," her father said from his hospital bed.

She looked over at him. His eyes were sunken and red like he'd been crying. She ran over to him and leaned down to hug him. He grunted at her sudden hug, but she just held tight anyway. Just then, the power went out. Annabelle swore under her breath and shuffled off to the kitchen. Berry climbed up onto the bed and lay down next to him, her head against his shoulder. She was careful not to bump the leg cast.

In the absence of electricity, the moonlight painted the room in a cool gray, drawing striped shadows across the sheets in the shape of a cross. Berry reached up and tousled her father's hair, then curled back up next to him and fell asleep to the rhythmic rattle of his labored breathing.

14

Berry woke up the next morning in the second bedroom. She was wearing her pink and gray polka dot pajamas. She jumped out of the bed and raced out into the great room, leaning over the railing to look down at her father. He was sitting up in his bed.

"Good morning, Raspberry Lynette Granby." She could tell by his voice that he was smiling.

"Are you…better?" she asked.

"A little," he said. "Enough for today."

"Berry, I need to head into work for a while," said Annabelle as she peeked around the corner from the kitchen. "Usually Fridays are half days, but it might take me a bit longer to put things in order so I can take…extended time off. The nurse was already here to check on the IV. It's just saline and water now. She'll be back later to take care of the catheter bag."

"What's a catheter bag?"

"Your dad will explain it. I need to go."

"Okay."

Annabelle paused for a moment to look at Berry, then offered a forced but kind smile and disappeared out the front door.

Berry looked at her father and tilted her head. "Is a catheter bag what I think it is?"

"Well, that depends. Are you thinking 'pee bag'?"

An embarrassed giggle escaped Berry's mouth. "Well, I am *now*. Thanks Dad."

"Glad I could help. But don't worry. I'm not planning on keeping it for long. I'd rather crawl to the bathroom dragging my broken leg than pee into a tube."

"Um, gross, Dad. I don't want to hear you talk about bathroom stuff."

"Sorry. How about I talk about other stuff, then?"

"What kind of stuff?"

"Important stuff."

Berry shook her head decisively. "Nope. I don't want to talk about that either."

"Another time, then."

"If you say so," she said.

After a breakfast of cereal and toast, Berry got dressed and grabbed her book and settled into the couch.

"I can't see you back there," said her father. "Maybe you can swing this bed around so I'm parallel with the couch."

"I can try." She set the book on the cushion and hopped off the couch. With careful instruction from her father ("release the brakes first, then make sure the IV and the power cord don't get tangled as you whip the head of the bed around toward the landing"), she managed to reorient her father's bed. She went back to the couch and settled in along the arm nearest the wall of windows so he could see her without turning his head.

"How's the reading experiment going?" he asked.

"Good. I think I understand it pretty well now. Mostly, anyway. There are a few things I still don't get."

"Adult things, I suppose," he said. There was a gentle whirring and grinding sound as her father's bed settled down into a reclining position. "I suppose I could explain those things if you insist, but I'm not sure I want to. I warned you it's a pretty adult book."

"You mean because of the cheating and sex and lying, right?"

"Well, yeah," he said. He coughed. "And maybe the sad parts."

Berry shifted her position to look directly at her father.

"I understand those parts. Besides, I already know plenty about lying," she said.

"Is this your way of introducing a new topic of conversation?"

"Sort of. Yeah." She looked out the window at the forest far below. "I didn't fall into a pond. I dove into it. I went swimming."

"You found the swimming hole? It's still there? That's really far away. How did you…?"

"Well, the map of course." Sigh. Another lie. "And yeah, it's still there."

"It's a spring-fed pond, I think."

"What does that mean?"

"It means you're less likely to get typhoid from swimming in it. Why didn't you answer my phone calls?"

She furrowed her brow. "What phone calls?"

"After you'd been gone a while, I called the old cell phone. The one I gave you. Did you remember to keep it in your backpack?"

"Yeah, I had it. Maybe it was turned off? I don't know. But I didn't hear it. I'm sorry." She paused, looked down at her bare feet. "Can I ask you something?"

"Of course."

"Have you ever lost track of time?"

"Sure."

"I mean like a lot of time. Like one minute you're diving into a pond and the next you're coming up for air and it's hours later."

He tilted his head. "Well…not exactly like that, no. But I've lost track of loads of time. Kinda wish I could find out where it went. Maybe I should check under the fridge…"

Berry laughed. "Yeah. That's probably where it is."

Kenneth pressed a button and bent himself into a sitting position. "We were worried about you, Berrycicle, running off into the forest like that. Annabelle was beside herself."

"What does that actually mean, anyway?" asked Berry. "How can you be beside yourself? I mean, unless there are two of you and then you have other problems to deal with."

Her father started laughing. "Oh Raspberry, don't ever change."

She took a deep breath, then exhaled. "I think I already have."

"I'm sorry you have to grow up so fast."

"It's not your fault."

"Whom shall we blame then?"

Berry opened her mouth to speak and the sound of a doorbell came out.

"Hey, how'd you do that?" her father asked.

She rolled her eyes. "It wasn't me. It was the door."

"Well, go see who it is. We might have won the Publisher's Clearing House contest. I certainly entered it enough times."

"They'd give it to Aunt Annabelle. It's her house."

"Well, then we'd better hope she's feeling generous."

Berry was already at the door. She opened it. A sweat-drenched woman wearing a navy blue business suit stood there with a briefcase in hand. No, not a briefcase – a suitcase. She had a pale, freckled complexion and strawberry blonde hair pulled back in a bun so tight it lifted her eyebrows. And her eyes were…her eyes…

"Oh my god…Raspberry?" said the woman.

15

Penelope stood at the foot of the hospital bed, studying her ex-husband.

"When I heard, I…" her voice caught. "Well, I got on the first flight I could."

"How did you…"

"Oh, now that's a story. I got the oddest call yesterday. He, or maybe it was a woman – I couldn't really tell – said he was calling on your behalf, but wouldn't give a name. All he said was that you were…sick. Really sick. I tried calling the number back but no one would answer. It took at least a dozen calls before I finally tracked down where you were. Your boss…former boss, I guess…didn't want to say. But I was insistent. Then I…well, I dropped everything and…here I am."

Berry was standing by her father's side, holding his hand. This was not her mother. This was a businesswoman who had stolen her mother's eyes.

"Go get the cell phone, Berry," said her father.

"Wait…the phone number. It was your old number?" said Penelope. "Was it you?"

"No. It wasn't. Bring me the phone, Berry," said Kenneth.

Berry didn't want to leave her father's side, but she obeyed and walked over to the landing and down the hallway to the second bedroom. She rifled through the backpack, but the phone wasn't there. She checked the floor, under the bed, the folds of the bedspread.

"It's not here," she said as she walked out onto the landing. She leaned against the railing, looking across the length of her father's bedridden body to her mother standing at the foot of the bed. A few strands of hair had escaped the severe bun and floated above her head like tiny flames.

"Why are you here, Penelope?" her father asked. Berry hadn't heard that edge in his voice in a long time. This is what he sounded like just before he proved himself capable of real anger.

"Because you're...because..." and then she broke into tears. Berry had never seen such a train wreck of a breakdown in all her life. Not even on TV. Penelope nearly folded over as she cried, then staggered to the couch and fell back onto it, bending down toward her knees, crying and sniffling and saying words that didn't have any shape but ache. Berry tried to feel sorry for her, but mostly she just felt embarrassed. She grabbed a box of tissues from the TV stand and handed it to her mother.

Through the mumbling storm of pain, Berry managed to make out a few words like "sorry" and "stupid" and what sounded like "selfish." Berry looked up at her father's face, expecting to see the growing anger in his bent brows, the way he held his mouth. But his anger had been replaced by an expression she couldn't read.

Penelope calmed down and proceeded to blow her nose. It was a loud, trumpet-like sound that first shocked Berry, then sent her back in time. Six years back. Berry felt a bit like crying. But she had cried too many tears lately and knew she would have to cry again, so she saved them.

"Oh, Raspberry," Penelope whimpered. "You must think me a monster."

Berry choked down her memories. "I actually hadn't thought much about you at all," she lied. Her mother recoiled. She took a deep breath, then started nodding.

"I deserved that," she said, still nodding. More hair fell from her now nearly useless bun.

"I don't think Berry was intentionally punishing you, Penny," said Berry's father. His voice was calm, confident.

"Maybe I was," said Berry. "But it's also true. You went away and then you never came back." She looked at her father. He

123

opened his mouth, then closed it, but she knew the words he held back. *Never hasn't happened yet.*

"I don't have any good excuses for what I did. I don't expect I'll ever be able to atone for my sins."

Berry looked up at her father again. He nodded toward Penelope.

"What does that mean?"

"It means...I'll never be able to make up for all I've done to hurt you and your father."

"Oh." Berry pondered that for a long, quiet moment. She looked again at her father. His lips were dry and his cheekbones were far too pronounced, poking through his shrinking skin like they were preparing to leave. But his eyes smiled.

"Never hasn't happened yet," she said, and she saw her father swallow hard.

They spent another in a series of long, quiet moments listening to the uncertain air between them. Berry queued up a hundred questions in the silence, then stored them away for another time.

"You two should talk about things," she said, her voice piercing the stillness like the snap of a branch in a graveyard.

"Berry, you don't need to leave," said her father.

"I know. But I have things to think about and you have things to talk about." She walked over to her mother who was still seated on the couch. "I'm not here for a hug," she said. She pointed to the bookshelf behind the couch. "I just need my book."

Penelope twisted around and grabbed the paperback that was balanced on the shelf next to an old family photo – one Berry knew was of her father and aunt as young children standing in front of the old Granby house.

"This one?" she said, studying it before handing it to Berry."

"Yes."

"Really?" Penelope looked over at Kenneth.

124

"She asked if she could read it," he said.

"It's my dad's favorite," said Berry. The words tumbled awkwardly out of her mouth.

"Is it? Still?" Penelope asked. The edges around her eyes softened. Kenneth nodded.

"Do you know it?" asked Berry.

"Do I? It's my absolute favorite book of all time," she said. A half-smile appeared on her makeup-smeared face.

"Are you just saying that because my dad and I like it?"

"No. I've loved it forever. Isn't that right, Ken."

Her father shrugged. "I can't vouch for forever, but you were the one who told me about it."

Berry scrunched her face into doubt, then shook off the expression. "Okay." She walked over to the sliding door, picked up her backpack, stuffed the book inside and slid the door open. "I'm going to the forest, Dad. To the tree house. To think and stuff. And to look for the cell phone."

"Don't lose your way," said her father.

"Don't you either," she said, and then she left.

Red was waiting for Berry as she climbed over the wall. The top stone wiggled when she slid across, like it might fall. Berry turned around and re-seated it, noticing that more of the stuff that held them together had turned to dust and spilled down onto the ground.

"Nothing lasts forever," she said to Red, then walked resolutely into the woods. She didn't bother to greet the trees by name, and didn't even pause at the permission tree. The footholds were plugged at the tree house, so she pulled them out, one by one, until she'd climbed up through the trap door. She walked to the red door and pushed it open, then sat on the small deck, her back against the outer wall.

Red meowed and Berry looked down to see her hiding behind a tree just across the way.

"Why are you so skittish, kittesh?" Berry tried to smile at her rhyme, but failed.

"She doesn't like me much," came a voice from behind her. Berry turned suddenly, nearly losing her balance on the deck. Antonia was halfway through the trap door.

"How do you do that?" asked Berry. Her heart was racing. She looked down and Red had disappeared.

"Do what?"

"Sneak up on me."

"I'm very good at being quiet." Antonia began rifling through Berry's backpack.

"Hey, what did I tell you about manners?"

"You said I should get some. Maybe they're in here?" Antonia pulled out the book, looked at it, then set it aside. "No snacks today?" She frowned.

"This wasn't a planned escape."

"But you're here."

"Yes."

"Because you're upset about something."

Berry felt a chill on her bare arms. "Why would you think that?"

"I know things."

"That's not an answer."

"Of course it's an answer." Antonia tossed the backpack into the corner of the small room and picked up the book. She held it up to the light spilling into the tree house from the square window. "What's this about?"

"Screwed-up people," said Berry. She turned back to face the forest, started swinging her legs.

"You're not supposed to say 'screwed.'"

"And you're *still* not supposed to go through other people's things."

Antonia climbed through the open door and sat on the deck next to Berry. She thumbed through the pages like she looking for the moving pictures in a flip book.

Berry reached for it. "It's not for kids," she said. Antonia pulled it away.

"I told you a long time ago I'm not a kid."

"Of course you're a kid," said Berry.

"Would a kid be able to do this?" Antonia scooted forward so she was just barely balancing on the edge of the deck.

"Be careful…"

But before she could say another word, Antonia had pushed herself off the deck and was falling to the earth. Just before she hit, she curled into a ball. She landed with a much-too-quiet thud, then rolled a few feet before coming to a stop in the shadow of a giant oak.

"Antonia!" Berry scrambled back through the door and down the tree, leaping to the ground from four footholds up and nearly twisting her ankle again.

Antonia was still curled into a ball, but her right hand started to snake out from under her. It was holding the book. Two of her fingers had been bent backwards at right angles. Berry felt like throwing up.

"Antonia. Are you okay?" she mumbled through clenched teeth.

A stirring, and then the ball unfurled into Antonia.

"Your fingers," Berry said. She pointed.

"Oh," said Antonia. She dropped the book, then pulled at the twisted fingers with her left hand. They popped into place with a sound that Berry knew she'd never be able to forget. She only barely managed to turn away before throwing up. When the waves had subsided, she turned to look at Antonia.

"How did you do that?" Berry said.

"It's not so bad if you don't think about it first," she said, rubbing the properly-bent fingers.

"Shouldn't you go see a doctor?"

"Me? Nope. I'm fine."

"I thought you were dead."

She sighed. "Not yet."

Berry suddenly felt as angry as she did scared and confused so she poured all of that anger into her voice. "Don't you ever do something like that again! Do you hear me? Never, ever, ever!"

Antonia laughed. "I'll do whatever I want."

"Then I'm never coming back."

"Why do you keep using that word?"

"What word?"

"Never."

Berry sighed. "Shut up."

"That's not very nice," said Antonia.

"You are…exasperating."

"What does that word mean?"

"I don't know," said Berry. "But it's what you are. And you're also a thief. I want my gloves back. And my dad's wagon."

"I didn't take your stupid gloves. And I told you…that's my wagon. I'm going to the pond now. You coming?"

"What, now? No. I mean, maybe. I don't know." Berry grunted her frustration and shook her head.

"Well, I'm going," said Antonia. She started walking away.

"Hey, wait. Have you seen a cell phone? Mine…my dad's…is missing."

"Are you saying I stole that too?"

"No, I'm not saying that." She brushed the dirt off the book, bent a dog-eared corner back into place. "Did you?"

"No. Maybe you dropped it at the pond."

128

Berry kicked some dirt over the puddle of puke and nearly felt like puking again.

"Okay, I'll come with you. But just to look for the phone. I'm not swimming. The last time creeped me out."

"You said you loved it."

"No I didn't."

Antonia started skipping through the forest. "Whatever." A few minutes later, she spoke again. "I've decided something."

"What?" Berry jogged to catch up.

"You can have *my* gloves."

Without looking back or slowing down, Antonia tossed two gloves over her head. They rose on a wisp of wind, then floated to the ground like butterflies landing on lavender. Berry picked them up and dusted them off. They were the same gloves her aunt had given her, but whiter, like they had been bleached. She slipped them into her backpack. She would get the stolen wagon back, too.

Berry searched the ground as she approached the pond, looking for any signs of the cell phone. She looked up to see Antonia sitting on the diving rock, swinging her feet over the water.

"Your spots are gone," Antonia said. "Told you."

Berry looked at her skin under the noonday sun. "Was it the pond?"

"Don't ask me. Ask the pond," said Antonia.

"That's a stupid thing to say."

Antonia shrugged and stood up, then shuffled to the edge of the flat rock, the toes of her scuffed white shoes hovering over the water. Her frilly yellow dress floated in the gentle breeze as she raised her arms to her sides and leaned her head back into the sun. The sunlight dancing off the pond lit her from behind. Berry thought she looked like a painting.

"What's she like?" Antonia asked. She sat back down on the rock.

"Who?"

"Your mother."

"How do you know…have you been spying on my house?"

"*Your* house?"

"Fine. My aunt's house."

"I don't spy on people. Spying is bad. Want to hear a story about spying?" asked Antonia.

"No. Your stories are boring."

Antonia folded her arms and huffed. Berry nearly laughed, but caught herself in time to hide the laugh in a cough.

"So…what's she like, then?" Antonia finally asked.

"I don't know yet." That's all Berry was going to say. It was the truth. "What's *your* mom like?"

Antonia laughed her guttural bear laugh. "I told you, my parents are dead."

"Well, what *was* she like, then?"

"She was…kind. She made soup. She was good at stories. At least I think so. It was a long time ago."

Berry finished searching the shore, slipped off her backpack, and walked over to the rock to sit next to Antonia. "When did she die?"

Antonia turned to look at Berry. The intensity in her green eyes frightened Berry.

"I don't know. Probably a hundred years ago," she said without even the hint of a smile.

"Ex-ass-per-a-ting," said Berry.

"You still haven't asked the pond," said Antonia.

"What am I supposed to ask?"

"Ask if it's a magical pond."

"I came to the forest to have quiet time to think about things. I didn't come here to listen to you talk about crazy stuff."

"Then why did you follow me?"

"Because…because I was looking for the cell phone." Berry stood up.

"Ask the pond." Antonia's voice was different. Deeper. Insistent.

"Fine," said Berry. "Pond, are you magical or what?"

She looked at the pond's surface, caught between hoping that nothing would change and that everything would change. There were a few bubbles here and there, but there were always bubbles here and there.

"That's not how you ask." Antonia reached over and grabbed Berry's leg, tugged at it. Berry lost her balance and started to fall backward. In an instant, Antonia was behind her, stopping her fall. Then she pushed Berry off the rock.

Berry landed with a splash that was much too quiet. She swallowed a gulp of water and sank into the pond. She opened her eyes to see the sunlight painting diagonal stripes in the emerald green water. The surface seemed a million miles away, but she wasn't scared. She felt at peace. Content. Happy, even. Her reverie was broken when a strong hand grabbed her arm and pulled her back to the surface, then dragged her to the shore. Berry coughed up pond water and rubbed her eyes and looked up to see a giant shadow blocking the sun. She rubbed at her eyes again. Antonia was standing in the shallows, soaking wet.

"Why did you do that?" asked Berry.

"Which part? Pushing you in or saving your life?"

Berry stood up slowly to fight the dizziness. "I think I need to get back home." She walked over to her backpack, grabbed it by the straps and started back through the woods as quickly as she could.

Antonia shouted after her. "What did the pond tell you?"

Berry didn't answer. She was still trying to hear its voice.

16

You're soaking wet!"

Penelope stood at the top of the hill, arms out to Berry. She had changed out of her business suit and was wearing a plain white t-shirt and navy blue shorts. She had given up on the bun and her long blonde hair was flying wildly around her face in the suddenly breezy air. Berry grabbed her mother's hands. Penelope helped Berry up the two steps onto the deck.

Berry slipped out of her muddy sneakers, stripped off her soggy socks, then followed her mother into the house. Her father was sleeping in the way that most scared Berry – with his mouth half open.

"He's fine," said Penelope, as if reading Berry's mind. "Talking tires him out."

"And listening."

"Listening too."

Berry changed out of her wet clothes, then grabbed a snack from the kitchen and looked around for her mother. She was outside on the deck, wrapped in a blanket, curled up on her father's chair. She looked small.

"Did you have some time to think?" Penelope asked when Berry had settled into the plastic deck chair.

"Not enough." She ripped the tiny package open and bit down on a cheese and peanut butter cracker. She didn't understand Antonia. Something was seriously wrong with that girl.

"Berry...I'm not going to try and explain myself. There are no excuses for what I did. But I want to let you know that you can ask anything you want and I promise to tell you the truth."

"Even if I ask hard questions?"

"Especially then."

"There is no 'especially' with the truth," said Berry.

"No. Of course not."

They sat in silence, listening to the wind play through the trees below, then the rumble of thunder as a storm crawled toward them from the west. Rain began to fall like it was testing gravity, just a few drops at a time. Berry listened to each tiny slap against the roof, counting the drops until they began to fall more urgently. In a matter of seconds, the hesitant storm had become a confident drenching. Berry and her mother scrambled back into the house as the wind whipped the rain across the deck. Berry started to slide the heavy glass door closed behind them, but Penelope stopped her.

"Let's just listen to it for a while," she said. Berry gave her a curious look, then helped her carry a couple of kitchen chairs into the living room. They set them on the wet tile entryway in front of the open door and sat, watching as the downpour blurred the outside world.

"I think it sounds like a train," said Penelope after a long stretch of silence.

"Really? A train?" said Berry. "More like a rushing river."

"Well, sure. It is water, after all. But listen to how the wind whips the rain against the house – there's a rhythm to it."

Berry scowled, then shook her head, not at her mother, but at her own scowl. She tilted her head slightly to the right, then the left. She looked over at Penelope, nearly laughed at her comically-high raised eyebrows. Then she shrugged.

"That's not a train rhythm..." she began. Penelope opened her mouth to speak. Berry put up her index finger to stop her. "...but...I do hear an army of giants running through a forest."

Penelope closed her mouth.

They went back to watching the storm. Its intensity grew minute by minute.

"Did you ever think of me?" Berry spoke just above a whisper, but her words cut through the white noise like a knife.

"Oh, Raspberry. Yes. Of course I did. All the time."

"I don't think that's a very good answer."

"What? Why do you say that…"

"Because it means the thought of me wasn't enough to bring you home." Berry still didn't want to cry, so she swallowed hard and concentrated on the river that was pouring down the sledding path like an anxious waterfall.

"How did you get to be so smart?" Penelope used the back of her hand to wipe away yet another tear from an apparently endless supply.

"I'll take some credit for that." It was her father's voice. They turned to look at him. He pressed a button and the bed slowly bent him into a sitting position. He grimaced, then pushed another button and the bed fell back a bit into a slightly less severe angle.

"You're awake," said Penelope.

"Duh," said her father. That brought an eye roll from Penelope. Berry smiled, but she wasn't sure if it was because of her father's response or her mother's facial expression. "So what have I missed?"

"Only a rainstorm of apocalyptic proportion," said Penelope.

"Well, why didn't you wake me? You know I don't want to sleep through the apocalypse." *How would she know that*, Berry wondered. A crack of thunder shook the house and the lights flickered and then went out. *Again.*

"This house has stupid electricity," said Berry. It was as dark as night in the house, and nearly as dark outside.

No one spoke for a while. Berry listened for her father's rasp, but couldn't hear it above the rain. She strained to see the forest, but could barely see the first row of trees through the downpour.

"Guess it's a good thing we live on a hill," said Penelope, breaking the silence. Berry didn't correct her mistake, but the word "we" hung heavily in the air for a long time before her father brushed it aside with a coughing fit.

Penelope jumped a little too quickly from her chair, sending it sliding toward the screen, and rushed to Kenneth's side. She reached for the bed adjustment buttons and pressed the "up" button once, then twice, then over and over again like she could pummel it into agreeing to work.

"Power's out, remember?" said Berry.

Penelope grabbed a pillow from the couch – Berry's pillow – then stuffed it behind Kenneth to prop him up. The coughing subsided.

"Thanks," he said.

The front door opened. Berry turned to see the shadow of Annabelle shaking off a dripping umbrella. In the dark, it looked like she was threatening a would-be attacker with a weapon. The lights flickered on and Annabelle stared into the living room, first at Berry, then at the hospital bed. Penelope was standing next to it, holding her ex-husband's hand. She quickly pulled her hand back.

"Penelope," said Annabelle. Her voice was calm, measured. Berry looked at her mother.

"Annabelle."

"Been a while," said Annabelle. She hooked the umbrella onto the coat rack and slipped out of her soaking wet jacket. Berry watched the umbrella swing back and forth like a pendulum until it stopped.

"I had to come," said Penelope.

More thunder. More lightning.

"Guilt finally got to you, did it?"

Annabelle walked down the hall to her room, went inside and closed the door. She was gone for a few minutes, during which no one spoke. When she finally returned, she was wearing dry clothes. It was the first time Berry had seen her in jeans and a t-shirt. She looked ten years younger.

"Berry…" began her father.

"I know, I know. This would be a good time for me to go to my room. Except it's not my room. It's not even your room. And this isn't our house." She grabbed her backpack from the tile floor and dragged it behind her through the living room, up the two steps to the landing, then down the hall to the guest bedroom. She wanted to slam the door to make a point, but she wasn't sure what point she'd be making, so she closed it gently, leaving it open just a crack. She pulled *Tender Is the Night* from the backpack and plopped down on the bed. She opened it randomly and read the first thing that she saw. It was a line from a song.

"A woman never knows
What a man she's got
Till after she turns him down…"

She closed the book.

17

B erry opened her eyes, momentarily disoriented. She was on the living room couch, a blanket wrapped around her. She looked over at the hospital bed. It was empty. She ripped the covers off and jumped down onto the carpeted floor.

"Dad?" she said, tentatively at first. "Dad?"

"He's in the bathroom," said Annabelle. She was standing in the doorway to the kitchen, a look of measured skepticism on her face.

"Does that mean he's doing better?"

"Well..."

The hallway bathroom door opened and Penelope walked out slowly, Berry's father, in peacock blue pajamas, leaning heavily against her. He grabbed the railing of the landing and hobbled down the hall balancing his cast in the air. Penelope was stuck to his left side like a remora.

"Good morning, sunshine," he said, pausing at the top of the stairs that led down into the living room.

"Are you supposed to be up?"

"I had a pretty good reason," he said. Penelope switched to his right side at the bottom of the stairs and helped him back to the hospital bed. He waved her off when she tried to lift his right leg, then made a show of swinging it up onto the mattress. "Ah, nothing quite like the morning constitutional."

"I don't know what that means and I don't think I want to," said Berry. She felt a tiny surge of happiness. Her father looked almost human. The IV pole had been rolled off to the side. Berry noted the bandage on his arm and wondered if he'd pulled the needle out himself. The pee bag was nowhere to be seen. Had the nurse stopped by?

"Look outside," he said, a big smile on his face. He pointed at the sliding door. "I think you're going to be impressed."

Berry walked over to the door and looked through the screen. She slid it open, slowly, staring at the bottom of the hill. A wide portion of the stone wall had been washed away at the end of the dirt path that was now a deep, muddy rut. Some of the smaller stones had been pushed nearly as far as the forest. She looked along the wall to the left and right, but this was the only place where it had been damaged.

"It takes an epic storm to wash away a wall that's been standing for a hundred years," said her father.

"It didn't wash the whole wall away."

"Nope. But just think – next winter you can sled all the way into the forest."

Next winter, thought Berry. *Next winter.*

Annabelle called out from the kitchen. "Breakfast is ready for anyone who wants some."

Berry went to get a plate of food for her father, but Annabelle was already carrying one to him. Scrambled eggs and bacon and hash browns. Penelope waited until Berry had filled her plate, then followed her into the living room. The two of them sat on the couch and set their plates on tray tables Annabelle had brought in from the kitchen. They were rickety metal trays with fading floral prints and raised edges. Berry thought they looked ancient.

Annabelle joined them a few minutes later, sitting on a kitchen chair and balancing her plate on her lap.

"Because of all the flooding," she said, answering a question no one had asked.

"Because of all the flooding, what?" asked Penelope.

"I was explaining to Berry why you're still here," she answered. Her words were matter-of-fact, but her eyes weren't.

"You're staying here?" asked Berry.

"For the moment," she answered.

"Someone moved me to the couch after I was asleep," said Berry.

"Yes," said Penelope. She didn't say any more, but Berry didn't need her to. She could still smell her mother's cinnamon scent on her pajamas.

She looked over at her father, who was picking at his food. At least he was eating, she thought.

"So, what does your husband think of you coming to see Kenneth?" Annabelle pointed her empty fork at Penelope.

Penelope shifted her position, folding one leg under her on the couch. She was wearing jeans that were too tight, and a fluttery, off-white blouse with an intricate embroidered pattern decorating the neckline and the three-quarter sleeves. When she moved, the material shimmered in the morning light. Silk, thought Berry.

"Why does that matter?" she answered.

"You did tell him, didn't you?" asked Kenneth.

"I left him a message."

"A message," said Annabelle.

"It's how we communicate." She took a bite of the scrambled eggs and nodded what appeared to be a "thanks for breakfast" to Annabelle. Annabelle smirked and shook her head ever so slightly, but enough for Berry to notice.

Berry listened to the chewing and the sipping of coffee and the tick of a clock that she hadn't heard before. She looked around the room. There was no clock that she could see.

"We're dealing with some things," said Penelope after a particularly long sip of her coffee.

"That doesn't surprise me one bit," said Annabelle, not even trying to hide her disgust.

"Look, Annabelle," began Penelope. "I know you don't like me. I wouldn't like me either if I were in your shoes. But I think it would be easier on…everyone…if we could at least pretend to get along."

"Uh oh…" said Kenneth. Berry noticed a half-smile on his face. It seemed like the wrong kind of expression to have at that moment.

"Pretend?" said Annabelle. "I'm not very good at pretend. But I'm a black belt at brutal honesty."

"There's no such thing as brutal honesty," said Berry. "There's only honesty."

"Wow," said Penelope. She looked over at Kenneth. "That come from you?"

"Probably."

"I'm right here!" said Berry. "Stop talking like I'm not right here."

"I'm sorry," said Penelope and Annabelle at the same time.

"I think we need to all tell the truth. Right now. Pretending is for children," said Berry. She knew exactly how this would be received by all three of the other people in the room. But she said it anyway.

"But you're just a…" began Annabelle.

"Don't say it!" said Berry. "I'm not a little kid. Or maybe I am. But I'm big enough to know you're all being stupid." She slammed her plate onto the tray in front of her and it collapsed, spilling eggs and uneaten bacon across the carpet. Then she kicked at the sideways tray table and sent it toward the sliding door. It came to a stop with a screech on the tile.

"Berry…" began her father. He didn't continue.

"I'm not storming out of the room this time," said Berry. "Talk to each other. Stop being so mad about things and just talk." Her words were directed mostly at her aunt, but Berry looked at all three of them in succession. After a long, awkward silence, Annabelle finally spoke. Her voice was calm, but her words didn't hide their bite.

"Penelope," she began. "I'm angry at you. I think it was downright evil of you to leave Berry in the first place – and then to never even reach out once after that – and I certainly don't think it's right for you to show up now. Why are you here really? Guilt? Or do you honestly think you have any right to be a part of this family? You gave up that right when you walked away."

"Annabelle. I'm sorry. I don't know how many times I'll have to say that for the truth of my apology to matter. But I am truly sorry for what I did all those years ago..."

"And every damn day since..." interrupted Annabelle.

Kenneth cleared his throat. Annabelle backed down.

"And," continued Penelope, "I'm sorry for showing up unannounced. But I am not sorry to be here now."

Berry looked at her father. He nodded at his daughter.

"My turn." She turned to look at her mother. "I don't know what to think yet. I hated you as soon as I knew what hate was. Then I think I felt sorry for you. And you know what? You're right here and I still miss my mother." She looked at Annabelle. "I don't know if I like the idea of living with you after Dad is gone. I know that's what you're both planning, though you sure do have a hard time talking with me about it and yes that's partly my fault because I keep avoiding it, but you're the adults and you can do whatever you have to do. And I know you're trying really hard to be my friend or whatever, but you don't like kids..."

"Berry, that's not true..."

"If you did, you'd have one or two."

"I work at a school full of kids..."

"In the office! People in the office don't like kids. Sheesh, didn't you ever go to school?" She took a deep breath. "So I'm kind of angry at you, too, for pretending to be someone you aren't. And isn't that...what's the word, ironic? I think that's it. I mean you just said you don't know how to pretend but obviously..."

"Berry, I..." she attempted again.

141

"I'm not finished yet! I don't think you like kids…but I do think you're starting to like me. And I'm starting to like you."

Annabelle looked as if she was about to cry.

Berry folded her arms.

"Is that it?" her father asked.

"No," she said. She shifted on the couch so her whole body was facing her mother. "I don't have to like you at all…Penelope." Berry took a deep breath. "But I'm going to be…what's the word? Dad? The one that starts with an 'm'? It means generous. Mag…something…"

"Magnanimous?" His eyes were wide, but he had a big smile on his face.

"Yes. Magnanimous. I'm going to give you a chance to…I don't know, be someone I could like someday."

Now it was Penelope's turn to tear up.

"Oh, and one more thing," said Berry, nearly choking on her words. "There's way too much crying around here. I mean, look at the hill. It's practically been washed away by tears." She was surprised by her own words, but in the best sort of way. Annabelle's whimper quieted. Penelope smiled through her sobs.

"God cried enough for all of us," her father said. "I mean, if you believe in that sort of thing."

18

There were a least a half dozen puddles in the driveway, most of them between the parked truck and the garage. Berry stepped right into the middle of the biggest one. It wasn't very deep, but her sandaled feet felt every drop of the standing rain. It was warm.

"Do you step in puddles a lot?" her mother asked.

"As much as possible," said Berry.

"You really do take after your father." She stepped into puddle next to the one where Berry stood, kicked at the water.

"Not like I had much choice," said Berry. She continued on into the garage.

Penelope didn't move. After a long stretch of awkward silence, she finally spoke. Her voice was quiet, broken.

"I followed your dad through every puddle."

"And then you didn't."

"Berry, I..."

"I don't want to talk about this right now," said Berry. She pointed to the lone chair at the front of the garage. The ground around it was wet, but not too muddy. "You can sit there if you want. I saw another trunk I wanted to explore."

Penelope didn't sit down, but instead followed Berry through the maze of machinery to the back of the garage. Berry looked up at the loft.

"That one," she said, pointing.

"Oh, that looks old. And heavy."

Berry dragged the ladder from the side wall over to lean it up against the loft edge, then climbed up, feeling the water-soaked sandals squish against her feet with every rung. She pulled at the trunk, dragging it to the edge, then paused.

"I think it's too heavy," she said. "I could just look through it up here?"

"Oh, but I'm curious too. Maybe we could lower it with a rope?"

It didn't take long for Berry to discover a long rope hanging along the eastern wall of the garage. It was carefully looped and hanging behind one of the old sleds. She looped it over her shoulder and climbed the ladder, then stood next to the trunk, trying to figure out how to attach it. A moment later, Penelope joined her. Together they figured out a way to wrap the rope crossways around the trunk and knot it in the middle so it could be lowered. Two feet from the ground, it slipped out of the rope sling and landed on its side with a thud that stirred up a cloud of dust.

They climbed down the ladder and stood in front of the trunk. The lock had snapped and was hanging open. Penelope pushed the trunk upright, grunting as she did. Berry was impressed by how strong she appeared to be.

"Your face is a mess," said Berry, pointing. "It's all mud and dust."

"Yours is perfect." Penelope dipped her finger in the dirt and ran it down the bridge of Berry's nose before she could react. "Well, now it is."

They scooted around to the front of the trunk. Gold light from the side window splayed across it.

"We should ask permission first," said Penelope.

Berry shot a look at her. "What?"

"Opening someone's trunk is a sacred act. It's only polite to ask, first."

"Yes," said Berry. She was trying to read the expression on her mother's face. It was a respectful look. And polite. But curious, too. "How about a little poem then?"

"Oh, that's a perfect idea. I'll start." She held her hands out to the trunk, palms up. "Oh ancient lovely trunk…" She paused, nodded to Berry.

"You landed with 'kerplunk…"

"We've been in a kind of funk…"

Berry searched through all the words she could find that rhymed with trunk, then found one she liked.

"May we explore your junk?"

Penelope snorted a laugh. "Perfect," she said. She flipped the latch and lifted the lid, spinning a flurry of dust mites into the light. Berry studied her. She looked like a fairy surrounded by a thousand tiny diamonds. Berry had always remembered her as pretty, but this moment far exceeded anything she could have imagined. Her mother was beautiful – even the sprinkle of freckles on her neck. Especially those.

"Well, let's see what treasures we have here…"

"I hope none of them were breakable," said Berry.

Penelope lifted out two pieces of a very old bowling trophy. "This one was, I'm afraid."

Berry peeked into the chest and they both started rooting through it, removing old clothes and books and a uniform and a football helmet around in search of something more interesting.

"Oh, now this could be good," said Penelope. She lifted up a bundle of envelopes for Berry to see.

"Letters?"

"I think so. People used to send these to each other. All the time."

"I never get letters from anyone. Not even relatives," said Berry. It was the truth.

"They're pretty old…" she studied the top envelope, then carefully pulled at the string, slipping the letters out of the bundle.

Berry held out her hand and Penelope handed her half of the letters. "They're all to a Reginald Granby. Was that…I think that's my grandpa."

"This must be all his stuff. Your father never said much about his dad. The dates on the postmarks seem about right. I think he died in the sixties." She skimmed through all the envelopes. Berry counted at least twenty. "The last one is dated 1966."

"Should we read them?" asked Berry. "What if they're really personal? That would be like looking in someone's diary."

"Oh, but it could be so…informative, don't you think?"

"I don't know…"

"Tell you what. Let's just read one, okay?"

"Isn't it a little like stealing?" asked Berry.

"To read someone's mail?"

"Yeah."

"I like to think of it more as time travel."

Berry sighed.

"But you're probably right," continued Penelope. She gathered up all the envelopes and started to tie the string around them, but it was so old and brittle, it disintegrated. "Do you think that's a sign?"

"No, I think it's just a really old string."

She set the pile of envelopes inside the upturned football helmet next to the chest, tossed the broken string aside, and went back to sifting through its contents.

Berry reached over and stopped her. "Maybe just one letter," she said. Penelope giggled like a little girl.

She lifted the letters out of the football helmet, then flipped it around and placed it on her head. "Which one?"

Berry laughed. "You look ridiculous!"

"You're right. I'm not really an autumn. More of a summer. I wonder if there's a baseball cap in there." She removed the helmet.

"Pick one from the middle," said Berry, pointing to the letters.

She did, then set the rest on a football uniform with the number 73 on it, except the 3 had been mostly eaten by moths or mice, leaving only the memory of it on the purple cloth.

Penelope held the envelope to her chest, then stood up, brushed the dust from her jeans and cleared her throat.

"Wait," said Berry. "There's a permission tree in the forest."

"A what?"

"I was thinking about asking the trunk permission and wondering if we needed to ask the letter permission and that reminded me of the tree in the forest."

"What does the permission tree grant? Wishes?"

"I wish. No. It gives you permission to visit the tree house."

"And what if it doesn't give you permission?"

"I don't know. It hasn't said 'no' yet."

Penelope's contemplative look reminded Berry of her father's thoughtful expression, except she tilted her head the opposite direction. She imagined them side by side, tilting their heads toward each other in deep thought. Or away from each other.

Penelope handed Berry the envelope.

"I think you should be the one to read it."

Berry stood up and held the envelope at arms length, whispered a "sorry" to whomever might object, then pulled out the letter. It was a single sheet of stationery with an "R" written in fancy lettering at the top and both sides were filled with fancy script handwriting that Berry thought was one of the most beautiful things she'd ever seen. Penelope stepped behind Berry to look over her shoulder. Berry could feel her mother's warm breath on the top of her head, her hand on Berry's shoulder.

"Oh, that's calligraphy," Penelope said. "Good calligraphy, I might add. Whoever wrote this was quite talented. See?" She pointed to the letter, waving her finger down the text like she was searching for her name in a word search puzzle. "Not a single drop of wayward ink. I'll bet whoever wrote it…" she took it from

Berry, gently. "May I?" she asked. Berry nodded. Penelope sat back down and motioned for Berry to do the same. Penelope turned the letter over. "...Benjamin...huh..." She paused, flipped it back to the front again.

"What? Who's Benjamin?" Berry scooted closer to her mother. Their knees touched and Berry didn't mind.

"Hang on a second..." said Penelope. Berry looked up at her mother and counted four distinct expressions on her mother's face as she read silently. Puzzlement, surprise, concern, and finally something that looked just a little like sadness.

"Well?"

"It's...oh, I don't know if I should say."

"Why not? Is it bad?" Berry held her hand out for the letter.

"No, it's actually rather extraordinary." Penelope set the letter down on her lap turned to face Berry. "This is kind of awkward," she began, and she certainly was proving that to be true by the way she fidgeted. "It's...well, it's a love letter."

"Really?" Berry picked it up. "From a girl named Benjamin?"

"Um...well..."

"Ohhh..." said Berry. "Oh," she said again, and one more time, "Oh."

Penelope raised her eyebrow.

"Benjamin wasn't a girl, was she. I mean he," said Berry.

"I don't think so."

"Are all the letters from Benjamin?"

Penelope nodded. "I think so." She reached for the pile and sorted through them. "Yep."

"Do you think Dad knows about this?"

"I don't know."

Berry bent forward to look inside the half-empty trunk. "Let's keep looking," said Berry. "There might be more surprises."

Penelope lifted out a couple of sweaters, also moth-eaten. Then she reached both hands in and pulled out a long box nearly the size of the trunk. "I think I know what this is." She lifted the top of the box.

"A wedding dress!" said Berry.

"Yes. Your Grandmother's?" Penelope seemed perplexed. She dug a little further and pulled out a knit cap for an infant, and some tiny baby clothes. There was a small cedar box as well.

"Open it," said Berry.

"I think it's your turn to find a surprise," said Penelope. She handed it to Berry. Berry held it in her hands for a moment, examining the simple, unadorned container. It had a single front flip latch that stayed closed as she observed it from every angle.

"Well, aren't you going to open it?"

"I think it's empty. I can't hear anything moving around." She shook it.

"Open it."

Berry pried the latch open and tipped the lid back. It had just one item in it – a faded black and white photograph slightly bigger than the interior of the box so that it bowed inward like a shallow paper bowl. Berry pried it free with her fingernail, then set the empty box on the ground next to her.

"It's really old," she said. The photograph was of a couple and their young daughter. The man wore a striped suit and tie and a really tall hat and was holding a toddler in his arms. The woman wore a layered dress and a hat with a bonnet and white gloves and appeared to be quite pregnant. There was a big tent behind them.

"Check the other side," said Penelope. Berry turned it over. There was some lettering there, but it was a kind of cursive that Berry couldn't read.

"It's too fancy," she said, and handed the photograph to her mother.

"More beautiful handwriting. I guess that means I'm to blame if yours is crappy." She smiled at Berry. " 'Opening Day, June, 1916.' This is nearly a hundred years old."

"Could it be my great grandfather?" asked Berry.

"I think it might be. Your father said he emigrated from Romania – and doesn't he look Romanian?"

"I don't know what Romanian looks like," said Berry.

"That toddler must be your grandmother. Doesn't she look like your dad?"

Berry didn't see the resemblance.

"But I didn't know Kenny's mother had any siblings and this woman is obviously pregnant." Penelope paused, then held the photograph to her chest. "Maybe they lost the baby," she said. The quiet that followed was the heavy kind that adults would often use for thinking about hard things, so Berry let it sit there a while before speaking again.

"Looks like we found another surprise, then," she finally said.

"Yes." Penelope held the photograph to her chest for a moment more, then set it on the letters and began sifting through the remaining clothing in the bottom of the trunk. She tugged at something that seemed to be quite heavy. "Oh, this is very interesting," she said as she removed a thick, heavy cloth that had been folded into a bulky square. "I think it's a banner. Let's take it outside and unwrap it."

"Just a minute," said Berry. She stood up and put everything back into the chest, except for the letter and the photograph. She thought about keeping the broken bowling trophy out as well because it seemed important, but decided against it.

They walked out into the sun and, together, carefully unfolded the cloth into a long banner. There were sharp lines from the folds in the fading image, but otherwise the banner was in amazing condition. Large red and gray letters across the top announced the "Tatarescu Traveling Circus Show." Below, painted in the shape of a smile were the blue and yellow words, "Featuring Tonne, The World's Biggest Dancing Bear." Two matching cartoon images of a brown bear in a pink tutu danced on either end of the ten-foot-long banner.

"Your great grandfather was in the circus!" said Penelope. "I think it might have been his very own circus. Look at that photograph again."

Berry held it out and they looked at it together. A cartoon bear like the one on the ends of the banner could just be seen on a partially obscured poster behind the man and his family. The more Berry looked at the man's expression – a big, toothy smile, the more she was sure that he was Mr. Tatarescu – a name that rang with vague familiarity – and that he indeed was the owner of a circus. Or at least a very important person in the circus.

"Now that's what I call a fun surprise," said Penelope.

"We should hang the banner."

"Where?"

Berry thought for a moment. "Probably in the garage," she said. "I don't know if Aunt Annabelle would like it hanging across the front of her house."

Penelope laughed. "Probably not. But wouldn't it be fun to see her expression?"

Berry smiled and then felt a little bad for smiling.

They spent the next few minutes searching for something to tie it up with, settling on a spool of rusty wire that they threaded through the grommets on either side of the banner. They hung it across the bottom of the loft. It bowed a little in the middle and brushed against a cluster of garden tools that stuck out from a barrel like dead flowers, but Berry thought that just made it look better. "Circuses aren't meant to be perfect," she said. "I'm not supposed to like them, according to Janelle Stevenson. And I guess I don't really. Janelle says they don't treat the animals very well."

"Who is Janelle Stevenson?"

"Some girl in my class last year."

"I tend to agree with Janelle. But the banner...that's really cool, don't you think?"

"Very cool." Berry looked up at the banner again. "What kind of name is Tonne?" she asked.

"It's just a British word for 'ton,' I think. The weight, I mean."

"It's a silly name for a bear."

"Unless it weighed a ton," said Penelope.

"Hmm...then I'm changing my name to Sixty-Two Pounds."

Penelope laughed again. "I'm not telling you what I'd have to change my name to."

Berry would have guessed "One Hundred Pounds," if she'd been given the chance. They started to head back to the house. "What *did* you change your name to?" she asked as they opened the door and walked into to the kitchen.

"My name is still...oh, you mean my last name. Parker."

"Really?"

"Really. I'm Penny Parker."

"I like Penelope Granby better."

Penelope sighed and ran her fingers through Berry's tangled hair. "Let's show this stuff to your dad."

They sat down at the kitchen table a moment later. Kenneth was already sitting there, his right leg resting on a pillow set on an empty chair. He was peeling the charred edges away from a piece of dark toast. Crumbs fell to the table like black snow.

"What do you have there?" Kenneth asked. He looked the healthiest Berry had seen in days. He crunched a bite of toast.

"We were looking through an old trunk in the garage and found a whole bunch of cool stuff."

Berry held out the picture. "Is this your mom's parents?"

He studied the picture. "Yes. I think it is. That's her." He pointed to the toddler, then slid his finger over to the image of his grandmother and held it there on her pregnant belly. He sighed. "Your great-grandpa was a circus man. He actually brought his circus – well, whatever he could bring anyway – from Romania and tried to make it work in New England. But then the war began and things fell apart for a bunch of reasons. I think he still had family back in Romania. After he gave up the circus, he got into banking, of all things. At least that's what my mother told me. She didn't say very much about him. You must have found my mom's trunk of keepsakes…"

"Your mom's trunk?" asked Penelope. "I thought it must have been your father's…"

"Why, what else did you find?"

Berry held up the letter. "Your dad's name was Reginald, right?"

"Yes."

"I think you should read it," said Penelope.

Berry handed him the letter. She and Penelope waited patiently as he read the letter front and back.

Her father paled and looked momentarily unsteady when he was finished, but then he sighed and shook his head and leaned back into his chair. "Well, I'll be damned," he said. There was a tear in his eye. He wiped it away. "Are there more of these?"

"Yes," said Penelope. "Would you like to see them?"

He lifted the letter up to his forehead and tapped it there while in thought. "Yes. But not right now."

Without another word, he scooted his chair back, stood, and limped out of the kitchen, carrying the letter in his hand.

"Probably shouldn't mention Grandpa Reggie's bowling trophy," whispered Penelope after he was out of earshot.

"Why, because we broke it?" asked Berry.

"Well, maybe. Or what if he never took your father bowling? It might not be a happy memory, you know?"

Berry thought back to the dozen or so times her dad had taken her bowling. She thought about the chicken fingers and the greasy French fries and the ice-cold Cokes and the smell of beer and cigarettes and how her father cheered for her not only when she bowled a strike but when she rolled a gutter ball too.

Penelope had never taken her bowling.

"Yeah," she said. "Probably shouldn't."

19

Y ou're sure you don't mind?"
Penelope had given up all pretense of looking professional and perfect. Her unwashed, wild blonde hair, torn jeans (probably a designer brand), and oversized t-shirt said as much. She didn't even seem to be wearing makeup. Having another woman with naked freckles in the house made Berry feel slightly less alone.

"I like sleeping here," said Berry. She turned to face the bookcase, ran her fingertips along the book spines like she was playing a harp. "There's something about being close to books that makes me feel safe and unsafe at the same time."

"Maybe we could move the hospital bed so there's room for the sofa-bed..."

"No, I sleep on it fine this way," said Berry. "The cushions are really comfy."

Penelope tilted her head and gave Berry a thoughtful look. Then she sighed, shook her head and leaned back against the hospital bed. "Well, if you want to sleep in the bedroom, you're welcome to join me. I don't think I snore..."

Her father snorted.

"What? I don't snore, do I?"

"I don't know about now, but back in the day, the neighbors were always complaining about the noise. And that was when we lived in a house."

Penelope swatted her ex-husband on the arm. He didn't flinch. He even looked a little sad after she pulled her hand back and folded her arms again. Berry noted the look and added it to her growing list of "Expressions I Haven't Seen Dad Use Before."

"Well, I'm going to call it a night, then," said Penelope. "I think this might be the earliest I've gone to bed in years. This place is just so quiet."

Annabelle appeared from the kitchen, clearing her throat and walking with loud footfalls across the landing toward her room. Berry and her father started to giggle. She stopped and leaned over the railing.

"What's so funny?"

"Nothing," said Berry. "Goodnight Aunt Annabelle."

"Goodnight Raspberry." She nodded at her brother and Penelope, then continued down the hall, disappearing into her room.

"I think she's starting to hate me a little less," said Penelope once the door had closed.

"Why do you say that?" asked Berry's father.

"Her sneer wasn't quite so distinct."

"I'm starting to hate you a little less, too," said Berry. She had meant it to sound funny, but the word "hate" seemed to flash a little too much like a neon sign.

"I'll take it," she said.

Berry hopped down off of the couch. "I'm going to get ready for bed. You should too because we're all going to church with Aunt Annabelle tomorrow."

"Oh we are?" asked Penelope.

"Yes. It has been decreed. And you can't ignore decrees, can you Dad."

He shrugged. "I wouldn't advise it." He reached out to grab Berry's arm as she passed by his hospital bed. "Since when did you become so responsible?"

She fought the urge to pull away from his cold, bony fingers, and instead used her other hand to rub the back of his like she was petting a cat. "Oh, five minutes ago, maybe?"

Penelope laughed and Berry added the sound, pending further review, to her list of favorite things.

Berry rolled onto her back and pulled the sheet and quilt up to her chin. She kicked at both until she was able to line their edges up perfectly, then scowled at herself for untucking them from the couch cushions in the process. By the sound of his breathing, her father was in a deep sleep, the kind he needed most of all. She looked across the darkened room through the floor-to-ceiling windows into the middle of the night. She couldn't see a single star.

A gentle scratching noise drew her attention to the base of the sliding door. She sat up, still holding the sheet and quilt tight against her, and looked at the door.

"Red? Is that you?" she whispered, knowing full well that she couldn't hear her. Berry looked over at her father. A soft white light glowed from the remote device hanging from his bedside, casting eerie shadows from the bed frame and wheels across the carpet.

The scratching began again, this time in earnest. She squinted, but could only see the hint of movement in the dark beyond the door. A muffled snort caught her by surprise and she turned to look up at the closed door where her mother was sleeping.

"Okay, Red," she whispered. She climbed out from under the rumpled covers and walked quietly to the back door. She knelt down and stared at the deck, but couldn't see the cat. She considered turning on the outside light, but knew that might wake up her father, so instead she walked back to the couch, rummaged through her backpack, and removed her flashlight. She walked up to the sliding door, her bare feet cold against the small square of tile, then flicked on the light, pointing it onto the deck. There was no cat. She moved the light back and forth, searching for Red. Still nothing.

Had she been dreaming?

Just as she clicked the flashlight off, a shadow passed in front of the deck. A shadow much bigger than a cat's. She fumbled for her flashlight, but it slipped out of her hands, landed on the tile floor and snapped into two pieces, the back section spinning away like a bottle cap, the batteries rolling toward the far wall. She looked back toward her father's bed. He was sitting up straight, his shadow like a tombstone.

"Dad…" she whispered.

He didn't answer.

"You awake Dad?"

Still nothing. Then, a sudden and bloodcurdling screech. She spun around to see a giant shadow cross in front of the deck again.

"Dad," she whispered again, but louder. She turned around and he was lying down. "Something's out there. Dad?" Her voice cracked this time. He stirred.

"Berry?"

"Dad…there's something out there." She turned to look at him again, then back at the shadowy deck.

Her father pulled the remote up from the side of the bed like he was raising an anchor. He pressed a button and the grinding of gears bent him up into a sitting position.

"What is it?" he asked.

"I don't know. I thought I heard Red. But then I saw shadows."

"Turn on the porch light."

She crawled to the side of the door and reached up to the switch, then paused. "I'm afraid."

"What are you afraid of, Berry?"

"Monsters."

Her father kicked his left foot over the edge of the bed and slowly slid his cast-heavy right leg along side it. He dropped down onto the floor with a pained grunt, balancing himself against the side of the bed before standing tall. Berry watched as his shadow limped over to her. She shivered when his hand brushed against her cheek.

"Stand up." She did. He wrapped an arm around her, as much for his own support as for her comfort. "Okay, I'm going to flick the light switch on. You ready?"

"No."

"How about now?"

"No, but okay."

His left hand banged against the sliding door, making Berry jump, then found its way to the light switch. He clicked it on.

"I don't see anything," she said.

"Wait…" he said. They stood still, staring out into the yellow-tinged night.

"Maybe I dreamed it…"

"Look there." Her father lifted her hand and pointed with it toward the edge of the hill.

Just where the light began to fade Berry saw fur disappear down the hill.

"What was that?" said Berry after her heart had stopped racing.

"I don't think it was Red."

"Maybe a dog?"

"Maybe. Or something a bit wilder."

"Like a raccoon?"

"Or a bear," said her father. He sounded almost as if he was smiling.

"Are there bears in the woods?"

"We used to pretend there were. My best friend and I…what was his name? Jimmy? No, Jeremy. Jeremy and I battled an army of imaginary bears the summer we turned twelve."

"Then what happened?"

"We grew up, I guess."

Berry was silent for a while, staring out into the strangely-lit yard. The hill dropped so sharply just a few yards from the house it looked like the edge of the world.

"Do you think Red's safe?" she finally asked.

"She seems like a smart cat. I think she'll be fine."

"I hope so."

"Tomorrow...er...later today I guess, I'll ask around about wild animals roaming our little forest."

"Dad?"

"Yes, Berry?"

"Is the forest really ours?"

"It used to be. A hundred years ago, when your great-grandfather moved his family here from Romania. They bought acres of land out in the middle of nowhere."

"You mean here."

"Yes. But they didn't develop the property. They moved to Portland and settled there."

"Is that where the circus was? Portland?"

"I think it traveled all over. Most circuses did. Do. Are there still circuses? Anyway, when my father found out about the hill with the forest behind it, he took over the land and built the first Granby house. Of course, that house burned down. Your aunt built this one."

He had already told her that.

"I'm confused. Who owns the forest?"

"Honestly, I don't know. Maybe the forest is like a cat – can anyone really own a forest?"

"Someone has to."

"Let's ask at church."

"Okay."

Berry flicked off the porch light, then started to walk back to the couch. When she saw that her father wasn't following her, she paused.

"Do you need me to help you back to the bed?"

"No, Berry. I'll be fine. I just wanted to look out at the world for a while longer."

"But it's so dark. You can't see anything."

"Sometimes it's easier to see with the lights off."

STEPHEN PAROLINI

20

There's no food," said Berry, peering into the fellowship hall kitchen.

"What do you mean? Look at all those cookies," said her father. She pushed him in through the doorway toward the counter. They had been given preferential treatment, thanks to her father's wheelchair.

"I mean no *real* food."

"No pot-luck today, I'm afraid." Annabelle squeezed past them and grabbed a plate, then filled it with a variety of store bought cookies. Berry thought they looked like the kinds of cookies old people didn't know they had in their pantries until someone came around to visit. And there was no punch – just coffee and tea.

Berry managed to steer her father around the counter and back into the fellowship hall. They parked the wheelchair at the far table – the one by the mostly-hidden door that led to a wheelchair ramp. She shouldn't have been surprised such a thing existed – so many of these people were probably just days away from being wheelchair-bound and at least two of them were already there – but the dark, musty and bookshelf-lined passageway had captured her imagination.

"May I sit with you fine folks?"

Mrs. Howard offered Berry a crooked smile.

"Of course, Betty," said Annabelle. She helped the old lady settle into a chair across from Berry and her father.

"It was a lovely service today," said Kenneth.

"Do you think so?" asked Mrs. Howard. "I suppose the sermon was passable, but I thought the hymn selection was positively dreadful. If I have to sing 'In the Garden' one more time I'm going to shoot myself." She started singing, "'And he walks with me, and he talks with me...'"

Annabelle laughed, then placed her hand on Mrs. Howard's. "Betty's not very good at pretending. It's one of the reasons we get along so well."

Berry tilted her head, trying to sort out the relationship between her aunt and people like Mrs. Howard.

"Mrs. Howard..." began Berry's father.

"Betty, please."

"Betty...have you always lived in Morrowton?"

Her laugh sounded like a hawk's screech. "Oh, no one in their right mind *always* lives somewhere. I've lived all over the place. And some of those places I've actually been to." She winked at Berry.

Berry furrowed her brow. "How can you live in places you've never been?" Mrs. Howard just kept smiling and at first Berry wondered if she'd heard her.

"Books, my young friend. Books," she finally said.

Berry smiled back, a little embarrassed. Of course it was books.

"Do you know anything about the wildlife around here?" her father asked. "When I was growing up, I liked to think there were bears, but I had a pretty wild imagination back then."

"Oh, we've had a bear or two. And wolves, too, I think." She turned around, slowly, as if every tiny movement caused great pain. "Edwin!" she called to an old man at a nearby table. He had a square jaw and a mouth that turned down at both ends even when he smiled. Especially then. His rectangular wire-rimmed glasses were too small for his face and did little to hide mischievous eyes. He was dressed in a suit and tie and wore a Red Sox cap on his too-long gray hair. "Edwin, when was the last time we had bears or wolves around here?"

Edwin looked up at the ceiling for a moment, then back at Mrs. Howard. "There was a bear in 1973," he said. "Probably not the same beast that stole those children a hundred years ago, though." He went back to torturing a perfectly innocent butter cookie.

"You mean that story is real?" asked Berry, her eyes suddenly wide.

"Yes, it's true that six children disappeared," said Mrs. Howard. "But that was a long time ago. And don't you mind Edwin. He's always telling ghost stories. There was no beast."

Berry felt her heart racing a little more than it should. She took two deep breaths to relax, then turned to her father. "You would have been...when were you born, Dad?"

"Thirteen. I was born in 1960."

"So maybe it wasn't just your imagination after all," said Mrs. Howard.

Berry's father seemed lost in a thought. "Mrs. Howard...Betty...who owns the forest below Granby Hill? Annabelle thinks it might be public land now. Is that right?"

"Oh heavens, I don't know. I can barely keep track of my car keys. I don't have the space in my little old brain for details like that. I could tell you who won the Preakness in 1963, I could name all the flowers that decorated the casket at my mother's funeral, and I could tell you Gene Vincent's real name, but that's not the kind of information that really helps anybody. Can't you just look it up on a computer or something? Use the Google?"

Berry giggled.

"Tried that already," said Kenneth. "Couldn't find anything specific about the area behind the house."

"Maybe the bears own it now," said Annabelle. Berry thought it was a pretty good attempt at humor, but no one laughed.

"Candy Spots, lilies, red roses, perfectly horrid blue-dyed carnations, and Vincent Eugene Craddock," said Mrs. Howard, a big smile on her face.

"What?" asked Annabelle.

"Those are some of the things I can remember."

"I'm impressed," said Kenneth.

Annabelle seemed less impressed. "All I know is that my property line ends at the stone wall."

Berry let her mind wander to the break in the wall, the stretch of mud and broken stone that spread like open hands toward the woods. Just then Penelope bounded down the stairs and into the fellowship hall. Berry watched her cross the room, smiling at strangers and stopping to talk whenever someone offered a "hello." She was the opposite of all of them – young (if you didn't look too closely at her eyes), energetic, and about as casually dressed as someone could be on a Sunday morning. She wore a denim skirt that was a little too tight, a white, ruffled peasant shirt that hung down to her hips, and sandals. Her hair was a mess of wild curls and split ends. "It has a mind of its own," she had said that morning while they briefly shared the bathroom.

"I'm so sorry about that," she said, looking at Kenneth first, then acknowledging rest of them at the table with a nod. She looked around for an empty chair.

"Sit here," said Annabelle. She stood. "I'm going to make the rounds and catch up on the latest gossip." She offered a polite smile to Penelope, pointed to the chair, then walked away.

Penelope sat down, crossing her leg underneath her in a way that Berry thought certainly would cause the skirt to rip.

"And?" Kenneth asked, looking at his ex-wife.

Penelope sighed. "I still have a husband," she said. Berry expected her to add, "for now," but she just sighed again.

Berry observed the way Mrs. Howard was studying Penelope. What did she see?

165

"Annabelle has told me very little about you," she said to Penelope.

"I'm sure she shared all the relevant bits."

"Oh yes, I know the relevant bits." She reached over and placed her age-spotted hand on Penelope's freckled arm. Berry saw her mother's future in that wrinkled, bony hand.

Her father began to cough. When he couldn't seem to shake it, even after drinking tea from his plastic cup, Penelope stood, apologized to Mrs. Howard, and decided it was time for them to go. She waved at Annabelle, who was already watching them from across the room.

"I'll show you the way," said Berry. She grabbed the handlebars and started pushing her father toward the secret door.

"Be good to each another," said Mrs. Howard as they weaved between the tables. "And stay away from bears."

Berry let Penelope push the wheelchair once they started heading up the first ramp. She waited for Annabelle to join them, then fell in behind. She slowed at the landing and watched the trio become silhouettes against the sunlight that shouted through the open door at the top of the second ramp.

"Oh, Berry, I'm so sorry," said Penelope.

Berry looked at the blood-soaked tangle of fur on the back deck.

"She's been torn to pieces."

"So sad," said her father. He had ambled over to his chair and practically fallen into it. Berry could hear his labored breathing over the whimper coming from her own mouth.

"Was it a bear?"

Annabelle walked out onto the deck. "I've called a friend of mine from town. He knows a thing or two about the area. He's a hunter. He'll be able to tell us what did this."

Berry bent down and stroked the only part of Red's fur that wasn't painted with congealing blood. "We should say something," she said. "Something for Red."

"Is it safe to be out here?" asked Penelope. "Whatever did this…it could still be nearby."

Berry stood and looked down the hill. The wind had picked up and the wild grass was swaying gently back and forth like the fur of a cat.

"Can bears climb trees?" she asked.

"I think so," said Penelope.

Berry started crying. "Please, God, let her be okay," she mumbled through the tears.

"Oh sweetheart, Red's gone. She's not going to be okay," said Penelope.

Berry looked up at her mother, fear in her eyes, then turned away quickly and ran back into the house. She tripped on her way up to the landing, felt the sharp pain of what would certainly be a substantial bruise on her shin and hobbled the rest of the way to the bathroom. She closed the door and locked it and curled up on the floor against the bathtub.

A minute later there was a knock on the door.

"Berry?"

She didn't answer.

"Berry, can I come in?" It was Penelope.

Berry sniffled for a moment more, crawled over and unlocked the door, then shuffled back to the tub. The knob turned and her mother entered. She closed the door, locked it, and sat down on the floor next to Berry.

"It's awful, isn't it," said Penelope.

Berry wrapped her arms around her legs, rubbed at the throbbing shin and buried her face in them.

"To lose something you love so much, I mean."

"I barely knew that stupid cat," said Berry.

"Oh sweet Raspberry. I'm not talking about the cat."

Berry looked up into her mother's eyes. She saw the years of regret in them, and a sadness she couldn't fully understand just beneath the regret. She thought of the awful things the characters did to each other in *Tender Is the Night*. The betrayals, the lies, the cheating. The abandonment.

"I'm sorry," she whispered. "I'm sorry I wasn't what you wanted."

"Berry…"

"Mom, let me say these things." She swiped at her tears. "I don't know what I did wrong. I don't know why you didn't love me then. I don't know so many things…"

"Please don't…"

"Just be quiet and listen to me!" Berry slapped her hand against the tub. It made almost no sound, but the action was enough to make her mother jump. "I hate that you left. I hate that you never…that you didn't reach out to me. But you're reaching out now. You're here. And I think you want to love me."

"Oh Berry…I never stopped loving you. I just got it all wrong. I loved myself more."

"Tell me why I should believe that you've changed," said Berry.

Her mother reached for Berry's hand. It was colder than the tile floor, but Berry didn't push it away.

"I wanted to come back sooner, but I was afraid that you would reject me. And you have every right to. But then I realized that was just another way of being selfish. I was worrying about how reaching out to you would affect me. When I got that call about your father… It was well beyond time for me to grow up and face the truth. To tell the truth. Not because I wanted to erase my own guilt. I'll always feel that. But because I wanted to make things right. Whatever 'right' means."

"Even if it means I never want to see you again."

Her mother's breath caught, but then she nodded.

Berry rubbed her eyes again. They sat like that in silence for more heartbeats than Berry could count.

"I don't think it means that," Berry said in a whisper. Then, before her mother could add yet another apology to the teetering pile, she spoke again. "There's a girl in the forest."

"What?"

"I met a girl in the forest after we moved here. Her name is Antonia. She lives...somewhere else. I don't know where. But she plays in the forest all the time and now I'm worried about her."

"Does your father know?"

"No."

"Aunt Annabelle?"

"No. I didn't tell anyone because I wasn't supposed to be there."

"Maybe the man Annabelle called can help."

"I don't think Antonia wants to meet new people," said Berry.

"Why do you say that?"

"I think she's hiding from something."

"Berry, we need to tell someone. She could be in danger from this...from whatever is out there."

"Will you come with me to warn her?" asked Berry.

"Into the woods? But there's something out there..."

"That's why we need to find her. Maybe she doesn't have anywhere else to go."

"How old is this girl?"

"Maybe eight? Or a hundred. It's hard to tell sometimes."

Penelope pressed her face into a question that she didn't voice out loud.

"It's not safe..." she began.

Berry squeezed her mother's hand and lowered her voice even more. "I know where Aunt Annabelle keeps her gun."

21

W ell that wasn't particularly helpful," said Berry's father. He was back in his hospital bed, the IV drip reattached to his arm.

"What wasn't helpful?" asked Penelope. "The man who didn't have a clue about how Red died, or the nurse who yelled at you to stay in bed?"

"Yes," he coughed. "Both."

"Bert says there haven't been any bear sightings in these woods in years. He said Red could have died of natural causes and that…I'm sorry Berry…birds could have picked at his body. How is that explanation not helpful?" asked Annabelle.

"It's not helpful because it's only a guess."

"And the nurse yelling at you?"

"That's not helpful because I hate this goddamn." He cleared his throat. "Sorry, Berry. I mean this stupid bed."

"It's okay, Dad. I hate it too."

"We all hate it, Ken," said Annabelle. "But what choice do we have?"

He opened his mouth to speak, then shook his head and tried to fold his arms in dramatic fashion, but the drip line interrupted his attempt to make a point without words. He sighed and let his arms fall to his side.

"We'll bury Red in the front yard," said Penelope. "That's okay, isn't it, Anna?"

"Annabelle," she said. "But yes. It's okay."

"We need to say something," said Berry when the final shovel of dirt had been patted down. She looked up to see Penelope nod.

"You knew her best," said Penelope to Annabelle.

"She was just a cat," said Annabelle. She paused.

"Wait, that's it?" asked Penelope.

"No, that's not it. I'm just not as clever as you two."

Berry jumped in. "She was just a cat, and yet much more than that..." she nodded at Penelope.

"She was loved by us all..." Penelope turned to Annabelle.

"And caught lots of rats," she said.

Berry laughed. "Really? Rats?"

"Oh god, no. They were mice. She was a good mouser. But you didn't give me much choice with the rhyme..."

"I didn't know we were rhyming," said Berry.

"No, it's perfect," said Penelope. "Rhyming is nearly always the best way to honor a cat."

Annabelle offered a small smile. "Well, I'm going to head to the grocery store, then. Are you sure you two don't want to join me?"

"Dad might need us."

"Let me give you some money," began Penelope. She started walking to the front door.

"We have plenty of money," said Annabelle. "But you already knew that."

The lightness between them evaporated. "This isn't about money," Penelope said.

Berry watched her mother's smile fade as Annabelle walked away.

Penelope shifted the backpack from her left shoulder to her right.

"What did you tell him?" asked Berry. They were slip-sliding down the hill along the western slope. It was slower going there, but they didn't want to risk being seen if Kenneth happened to defy the nurse and climb out of bed.

"I said we were going to explore more in the garage."

"Did he believe you?"

"Probably not."

They came to the stone wall and stopped. Berry climbed over first, wincing when her trailing leg scraped across the top stone. "Well, at least now I'll have matching bruises," she said.

They jogged up to the line of trees and Berry ran east until she came to the maple that the dirt path pointed most directly to from the top of the hill.

"Bernice, meet Penelope." She brushed her hand against the bark.

"You named the tree?" asked Penelope.

"I named a bunch of them. I don't know if I'll remember them all."

"Try," said her mother. She copied her daughter's action, brushing her fingertips across Bernice, and then followed her daughter to the next one.

"Buttercup."

"Beanpole."

"Snape."

"Rosemary." She hugged Rosemary until her mother got the point and joined in. Their fingers touched briefly as they wrapped their arms around the wide tree.

"Fitzgerald."

"Junie."

"Templeton."

"Zachary."

"Arrietty."

"Henry."

"Me Margaret." She looked at her mother, who had scrunched her face into a question she didn't ask.

"Eloise."

Penelope laughed. "You were so upset that we wouldn't move to the Plaza Hotel."

"Lucy."

"Billiam."

"Billiam?" asked Penelope.

"I meant to say William or maybe Bill, but I screwed up. Turns out his name is Billiam anyway. So I guess maybe I didn't screw up after all."

They kept walking.

"Horatio Christian Kennebunk MacDougal," said Berry. She offered a clumsy curtsey to the tall, thin tree.

"Pleased to make your acquaintance, Horatio Christian Kennebunk MacDougal," her mother said.

They walked a few more yards, over a small hill, then stopped in front of the twisted tree.

"Nicole Driver," said Berry.

Penelope gasped and put her hand to her mouth.

"The twisted tree," Berry added.

"Yes. Yes, this is Nicole. It is so very much Nicole."

Berry approached the tree, extended her arm, and brushed her fingertips against the bark as she walked in a circle around it. Her mother followed her and they circled the tree slowly, quietly.

Listening.

"She's probably fine," Berry said.

"Who?"

"Antonia."

"I'd nearly forgotten why we came. The forest seems so…pleasant. Should we call out for her?"

Berry bit her lip. "She has a gun."

"Wait, what? An 8-year-old has a gun? Why would she have a gun?" asked her mother.

"It's a pellet gun. Or a BB gun, maybe. She said it was in case of monsters."

"Why didn't you tell me this before?"

Berry shrugged and started circling Nicole Diver again, heading counter-clockwise this time. She didn't feel any sense of worry or alarm. Antonia would be just fine.

"Berry…is there really a girl named Antonia?"

"Of course there is! She's my friend. Well, mostly she's annoying, but you can still be friends with annoying people."

"Why did you bring me out here, Berry?"

Berry stopped walking around the tree and sat down, leaning against it. Her mother carefully slipped off the backpack and sat down next to her.

"What's your husband's name?" asked Berry.

"John."

"That's a boring name."

"It fits."

Berry picked up a stick and poked it at the dirt next to her. She drew a circle, added eyes and a nose and a mouth, and then erased the face with a swipe of her hand. She lifted her left hand and studied it, noticing the lines of black dirt in her fingernails. It reminded her of the time she and her father ate half a package of Oreo cookies in one sitting.

"Do you love him?" she said, starting to draw the face in the dirt again.

Her mother sighed. This was a sound Berry had no intention of adding to her list of favorite things. "He's a good man."

"But you don't love him."

"Marriage is…complicated. So is love. Some days I feel like I'm still a beginner at it."

"Are you happy?"

Penelope's shoulders dropped. Berry drew a frown face in the dirt.

"Sometimes."

" 'If you're in love it ought to make you happy. You ought to laugh.' "

"Well, yes. Laughter is good."

"That's from the book. From *Tender Is the Night*. Rosemary's mother says it to her."

"Yes, yes. I think I remember that scene."

"Is it true? Should love make you happy?"

"Your father makes me laugh." She wrapped her arm around Berry and Berry didn't complain or try to wriggle out of it. "*Made* me laugh, I mean." Berry leaned in closer, breathing in her mother's scent. She smelled like raspberries. Not cinnamon. "We laughed a lot together."

"Then why did you leave?"

"I was young and stupid and selfish. I screwed up."

"You're not here just because Dad's sick."

"I meant what I said yesterday, Berry. I'm here to make things right. I just don't know what that means yet."

The tree behind them began to vibrate.

"Do you feel that?" asked Berry.

Penelope jumped to her feet and started looking around, spinning in a slow circle. "What is it?" she asked.

"I felt it once before."

"Could it be an earthquake?"

The wind picked up suddenly, rustling the leaves into applause and bending the branches into nervous waves.

"We should go back," said Berry. "Like right now."

Berry picked up the backpack, then grabbed her mother's hand and tugged at it. She remained steadfast, watching the trees, inclining her ear to the sounds of the forest.

"Listen…do you hear that?" she asked.

"It's the wind. C'mon, Mom. I think a storm is coming."

"I sounds like a song," she said. "But the wind keeps blowing it away."

"Please, Mom. Let's just go back. Antonia will be fine. I know it now. It was silly of me to worry about her." She tugged at her mother's arm again, then they both began jogging back the way they came. Berry didn't stop to name the trees, though she thought each name as she passed. They emerged from the forest just before the first raindrops fell.

"What is it with all this rain?" shouted Penelope as she walked through the opening of the stone wall and began to climb the hill.

"Maybe God is trying to tell us something," said Berry.

"Or drown us."

"Do you believe in God?" asked Berry. The rain began to fall in sheets. They were both totally soaked when they were only halfway up the hill.

"I might if I thought it would help your father."

"Me, too."

They walked around to the front door, then sneaked in and down the hall to the second bedroom without waking Kenneth. After changing into dry clothes, they both came back to the living room and sat on the couch. Berry heard the sound of a car pulling up the gravel driveway.

"The gun," she whispered. "You need to put it back."

Penelope fumbled through the backpack, then hid the gun under her t-shirt and raced to Annabelle's room. Berry met her aunt at the door and distracted her by offering to carry the groceries from the door to the kitchen. When she went back for the second bag, Penelope had exited Annabelle's room. She climbed over the railing and dropped down into the living room, then gave Berry the thumbs-up.

Berry had heard the singing too. But it wasn't Antonia's voice.

22

G et out of my house!"
Annabelle's words were blistering and brutal.

"Aunt Annabelle, I was the one who told her about the gun..."

"That was a stupid, stupid, stupid thing to do," she said, pointing her finger, quite like a gun, right at her to underline the repeated word.

"We were worried about the girl in the forest..." began Penelope.

"Mom!"

"I think everyone needs to know, Berry. Weren't you the one saying we all had to be honest with each other?"

"What is she talking about, Berry?" her father asked. "What girl?" He was holding tight to the blankets covering his hospital bed and still he seemed to be trembling.

"Nothing. It's nothing," said Berry. She gave her mother an imploring look.

"It's not nothing to take someone's gun without asking," said Annabelle.

"How did you know?" asked Penelope.

"I know where I put my things," said Annabelle. "I'm careful. I keep track. I am a responsible woman. And I saw you leaving my room..."

"It was just sitting there in your bedside table. Anyone could have taken it," said Penelope.

"Really? Anyone?"

"Please stop fighting!" shouted Berry. She got up from the couch and walked over to the hospital bed. She reached for her father's hand. He was reluctant to give it to her at first, but she was pretty sure that was because he was so cold. "I told her to get the gun because I had to go into the forest. I thought it would make us safe."

"You went into the forest?" asked her father. He let go of her hand, fumbled for the bed remote, then pushed the button to bend the bed into a sitting position. Berry could practically hear his bones crying out as the metal frame ground upward.

"There's something I haven't told you yet," she said. He didn't reach to take her hand and the absence of touch frightened her far more than any forest monster could. He hid his hands beneath the covers. She looked over at her aunt, who was standing by the sliding door, fidgeting and fuming. She looked at her mother, who was sitting on the end of the couch, but clearly didn't want to be there.

"Tell me," said her father.

"I met a friend in the forest. Her name is Antonia. She's just a little girl. Like maybe seven or eight. I don't know where she lives – I've only ever met her in the woods. That's why I keep going back – to spend time with her. She's not very nice sometimes, but she's my friend and I don't know if any of you have noticed, but I kind of need a friend right now and living on a hill a million miles from everyone I used to know makes it kind of hard to find one."

"You were worried about her," said her father, his gaze softening.

"I was."

"Did you find her?"

"Stop it, Ken," said Annabelle. "Stop coddling her. She did something wrong. Probably lots of things wrong." She glared at Berry. "What she needs is some good old-fashioned discipline, like we had growing up."

"You want me to spank her?" asked Kenneth.

"Don't people spank their children anymore? Time-out then. Or restrictions. Whatever. It's clear she needs some kind of punishment, though. For god's sake, Ken, she was walking around a forest with a gun!"

"I carried the gun..." began Penelope.

"Have you ever fired a gun before?"

"Well...no...but..."

"I think you probably ought to shut up, Penny," said Kenneth. "You're not doing yourself any favors." He turned to Annabelle. "I'm not Mom."

Annabelle rolled her eyes.

"Look, I'll just go," said Penelope. "I can stay at a hotel or a bed and breakfast until..."

"Until what?" yelled Annabelle. "Until your ex-husband dies? Or until your current husband finds you? What the hell is your game, Penelope? What's your real reason for showing up? You know you won't get any of Ken's money, right? Not a cent."

"I've told you why I came..."

"No. You told us what you thought we wanted to hear."

"It's the truth, Annabelle. I came to apologize. I came to be here for Ken, for Berry." She bent forward and covered her eyes with her hands.

"Oh, save the tears. Just...just leave. We don't want you here." Annabelle folded her arms in front of her chest. "We don't *need* you." She gave an icy look to Kenneth. He closed his eyes and sighed.

"Penny, maybe it's best you find another place to stay...at least until we can sort things out here," he said.

"But I don't want her to go!" Berry plopped herself on the couch next to Penelope and wrapped her arms around her. "She didn't do anything wrong. *I* did. But even if she was wrong, she's sorry. She's really sorry. Aren't you?"

Berry felt her mother's chest expand as she took a deep breath, then shrink again as she exhaled. "Yes. I am." She stood, escaping Berry's embrace, then walked in silence through the living room, up the stairs, and down the landing to the bedroom. A few minutes later, she emerged with her suitcase in one hand, her cell phone in the other. She paused at the front door, looked at Annabelle, then Kenneth, before her gaze rested on Berry.

"I won't be far," she said. She opened the door.

The rain had come and gone. It was far too beautiful outside for such a dark moment, thought Berry.

"You can wait here for a cab," said Kenneth.

"I told him to meet me at the bottom of the hill. A little walk will give me more time to clear my head." She looked again at Berry, offered a sad smile, then exited, pulling the door closed softly behind her.

Kenneth pressed a button on his remote and the bed began to lie flat. When it clicked into the horizontal position, he turned his head to look at his sister.

"Sometimes you can be a real ass," he said. Then he closed his eyes.

Annabelle seemed thrown by her brother's words. She opened and closed her mouth like a dying fish. Berry thought her father was being a bit harsh. It's not like she and her mother hadn't done anything wrong. They had. And the more Berry thought about it, the more it bothered her how easy it had been to orchestrate the plan.

The house phone rang. Annabelle stopped trying to form a response for her brother and walked into the kitchen to answer it.

"Hello?...Yes...Oh, really? That's interesting...Do you think...uh-huh...uh-huh...okay. Thanks Bert. I'll let them know."

Berry listened for the familiar click of a phone being placed back into its holster. It was the same sound she'd heard hundreds of times at her old home in Nashua. She remembered the excitement of the house phone ringing, and the pleasant sort of uncertainty that she felt as she reached for it, wondering in that first touch of cold plastic it was one of her friends or someone calling for her father. Just before they'd moved, most of the calls had been for her father. He stopped answering them after a while, letting the message machine collect all the "Is there anything I can do to help?" requests that for some reason made him feel lonely instead of loved.

"Someone over on the Merton property shot a Lynx."

"Is it dead?" asked Berry.

"Yes. That's what guns do, Berry. They kill things."

"Anna..." started Kenneth.

"Mertons aren't that far from here," continued Annabelle. "Maybe a mile. Bert said it was likely Red was killed by the lynx."

"But that doesn't make any sense. A lynx is a cat," said Berry. "Why would one cat hurt another cat?"

"A lynx is a wildcat. They don't play by the same rules as domestic cats," said her father. His voice had gotten so scratchy while speaking, Berry walked over and handed him his cup even though it was easily within his reach.

"So the forest is safe again," said Berry.

"Oh, I wouldn't say that," said Annabelle. "There could be more than one. And you heard what Bert said earlier – they haven't had bear sightings in a long time, but there certainly are plenty of bears in Maine. One might have found his way to our little woods..."

"We don't own the woods," said Berry. "They're just woods."

"...and there's still the matter of the person who shot Red before." She shook her head. "That poor, poor cat," she mumbled.

"Berry, tell me more about this girl you met," said her father. He sipped at his water, holding the cup with both trembling hands.

"Antonia? There's nothing else to say. She's a little girl who's mostly a pain in the butt but also kind of interesting and spends a lot of time playing in the forest."

"But where does she live?" he asked.

"Once she said she lived on the other side of the woods, and another time she said she lived *in* the woods. She's always making things up, though, so I don't know."

Berry's father looked over at Annabelle. "Do you know if any families around here have young children?"

"I don't keep track of the neighbors. My friends all live on the other side of town..."

"You have friends?" Berry asked. Of course she knew about the people at church, but Annabelle didn't seem to have any contact with other people outside of Sundays. Maybe she had before Berry and her father moved in.

"...so who knows? She's probably just someone's granddaughter who's come to visit for the summer."

"Perhaps you should invite her to dinner, next time you see her," said her father.

"Really? I can see her again?"

"I'm reasonably sure you'll find a way," he said. "But it would be okay, wouldn't it Anna?"

Annabelle looked up at the ceiling. Berry looked up, too. There was no answer there that she could see, but there were plenty of cobwebs.

"Is that how you deal with lies and deceit now Ken? Just pretend it didn't happen or that it doesn't matter? Your daughter has just admitted to you that she's been lying. Suddenly it's all okay? I just don't understand you sometimes." She threw up her arms in dramatic fashion, then offered a world-class sigh. It must run in the family. "Fine, then. Send your daughter into the forest to play with all the monsters and forest girls. But don't come crying to me if she gets eaten."

Berry wasn't sure if she should laugh or defend herself. She looked at her father. His expression was impossible to read.

"So is it okay for her to invite the forest girl or not?" he asked.

She shook her head, but then said, "Yes. But let me know when's she's coming so I can have enough food. What do forest girls eat, anyway?"

"The souls of bitter women," said her father.

Annabelle kept shaking her head, but a small smile crept onto her face.

"I'll invite her the next time I see her," said Berry. But she didn't think she would. Antonia would probably just steal the silverware.

That night, Berry reread a few chapters of *Tender Is the Night* – including the one with the conversation between Rosemary and her mother about love. Penelope made her father laugh. A lot, she'd said. Did she make him happy? Why didn't he stick up for her? Why didn't he fight to have her stay?

She watched her aunt going around cleaning a house that was never really dirty to begin with, apart from the cobwebs on the ceiling that were too hard to reach. Annabelle dusted the bookshelves, vacuumed the carpets, swept the kitchen floor, and scrubbed the back deck until there was no visible evidence left of Red's bloody end.

When all the lights were out, and the sounds from the hospital bed settled into a comfortable rhythm, Berry looked outside and wished upon the first four stars she could see. She didn't know if wishes worked that way, but decided it was probably just as helpful as praying.

"First star I see tonight, wish I may, wish I might, have the wish I wish tonight…Fix my dad."

"Second star I see tonight, wish I may, wish I might, have the wish I wish tonight...Let Aunt Annabelle and my mom be friends."

"Third star I see tonight, wish I may, wish I might, have the wish I wish tonight...Keep Antonia safe."

"Fourth star I see tonight, wish I may, wish I might, have the wish I wish tonight...I mean it. Fix my dad."

Then she closed her eyes and waited for sleep.

23

"S he's not as upset now," said Berry into the phone. "I'm going to ask her if she'll let you come back tonight." There was silence on the other end. "Mom? Did you hear..."

"Yes. I'm sorry. I was just trying to figure something out. John called."

"Oh." Berry wondered if her mother could hear the frown in her voice.

"He wants me to come back to New York."

"But you can't go. Not yet."

"Berry..."

"Mom, Dad needs you. You know he does. Since you left yesterday he's been a wreck. Having you around has made him so much better. You need to be here."

"Oh honey..."

"*I* need you."

There was another long pause. Berry waited as patiently as she could, knowing her mother was sifting through a whole bunch of feelings and practical considerations.

"I'll do whatever it takes to stay," her mother said. "I owe you that and so much more..."

"Tell him we really need you. If he's a good man, he'll understand."

Berry heard her mother inhale slowly. "He's a good man."

"I'll tell Annabelle..."

"No, Berry. This isn't on your shoulders. I'll talk to her. We'll sort this out. Is she there now?"

"No. She went into town. I don't know why. I think she just didn't want to be around when I went into the forest. That's on *my* shoulders." Berry paused. "Did I use that saying right?"

"Yes. Perfectly."

"Okay. I'll see you later, then. Maybe you'll get to meet my friend Antonia."

"I'd like that."

"Bye Mom."

"Bye, Berry-girl."

Berry hung up the phone. She collected the last three packages of peanut butter crackers from the pantry and stuffed them into her backpack. She had her book and her repaired flashlight and some origami paper and a pocketknife that her aunt had given her that morning.

"I hope you don't have to use it for anything but carving your initials in a tree," she had said.

"I would never do that to a tree," Berry had answered.

She walked into the great room.

"Maybe I'll find your old cell phone," she said to her father. His bed was in the seated position and he seemed lost in a thought. "Dad? You in there?"

He turned toward her, stretched a smile across his cracked lips.

"Yes, Berrycicle. But I don't care about the cell phone."

She set the backpack down on the carpet. "Maybe I shouldn't go."

"What? Of course you should go. What about all your adventures?"

She pointed to the bookshelf. "I have plenty right here."

"Yes. Books, books, and more books. I'm so glad you're a reader, sweet daughter of mine. But some of the best stories are the ones that you write with your hands and feet."

She walked over and kissed him on the forehead. "I'll go write one now."

"And then you'll tell me about it."

"Yes. I'll tell you about all my adventures from now on, Daddy."

"Promise?"

"Promise."

With obvious great effort, he reached up to tousle her hair. She leaned in a little closer to make it easier for him.

"Berry..." he called out as she gathered up her backpack.

"Yes?"

"Never stop exploring."

"I won't. At least until I get hungry."

He croaked out a half-laugh and waved. Berry hesitated at the open door, then took a deep breath of the warm morning air, slid the screen closed behind her and started scrabbling down the dried-dirt sledding path.

The permission tree looked down at Berry. She looked up into its arms.

"I have a gift for you," she said to the tree.

She placed her hand on the wrinkled skin of the tree and held it there. There were no vibrations, no rumbles or growls. She reached into the front pocket of her khaki shorts and pulled out a blue origami bear. She had made it in the middle of the night when she couldn't get back to sleep after a coughing spell from her father awakened her. Hiding under the uncooperative covers with her flashlight and origami book, she had folded and unfolded and folded again until she finally had something resembling the picture in the book.

She lifted the bear up to the tree like an offering.

"It's supposed to be a bear. I think it looks like one a little. Sorry about the extra wrinkles."

Then she carefully slid the small bear between the folds in the bark until it was nearly invisible to anyone who might be passing by.

"What are you doing?" The voice from behind her should have made Berry jump, but she'd been expecting it.

"Nothing. Just asking permission." She turned around. Antonia was a mess. Her hair was stringy in spots and matted in others and her face was streaked with dirt. Her dress – a frilly white one from another era – was practically brown from all the dried-up mud. "What happened to you?"

"What do you mean?"

"You're a mess…"

"I'm not a mess. I've just been out playing. That's all. It's okay to get dirty when you're out playing."

"Yes. Of course it is," said Berry. Antonia tried to peek around Berry at the tree.

"What's that in the tree?" she asked.

Berry sighed. "That's a gift for the tree. Not for you. Just for the tree."

"What is it?"

"A bear."

"Oh." Antonia seemed satisfied with that and turned her attention to Berry's backpack. "Snacks?"

"I didn't forget." She handed Antonia one of the packages of crackers. Antonia tore off the wrapper and handed it back to Berry while she devoured the snack. With her mouth still full, she asked, "Where'd you get those bruises?" She pointed to Berry's shins.

"Here and there."

"We should go swimming," said Antonia.

"My dad wants to meet you."

"Why?"

"Because he does."

"Maybe I don't want to meet him." Antonia held out her hand. Berry gave her the second package of crackers.

"Fine. Then don't," said Berry.

Antonia tore through the second package of crackers and once again handed Berry the empty wrapper. She took one bite, then started running through the forest toward the tree house.

"You coming?" she shouted back.

Berry spun around to say goodbye to the permission tree. The origami bear was missing. She looked for it on the ground, but couldn't find it.

"Antonia," she said to herself. Then she jogged after her.

When she crested the hill, Antonia was nowhere to be seen. She called out for her. Nothing. All the plugs were in their foot holes. She looked up at the house. Some of the wall boards were broken and the red door was missing. She called again.

"Antonia!"

Still no response. Berry considered climbing up into the tree house anyway, but then decided it was probably hot enough to swim after all. She headed through the forest toward the pond, hoping she was remembering it right.

She heard Antonia before she saw her. She was singing the Dunderbeck song. When Berry walked out of the trees into the small clearing, she could see Antonia lying on her back on the diving rock. Her dress spilled over the edge, painting a triangle of white against the gray.

She dropped her backpack on the shore and made her way to the rock. She sat down next to Antonia, then leaned back to mimic her resting posture.

"You took my paper bear," she said.

"I thought it was the permission tree's bear," said Antonia.

"Well, yes, I gave it to the tree…"

"And the tree gave it to me." She held up her right hand, the paper bear pinched between her thumb and forefinger. "It doesn't look much like a real bear."

"It's the best I could do."

"I bet I could do better."

"I have some origami paper in my backpack. Go right ahead and try."

189

She tossed the bear into the air and tried to catch it, but it bounced off her fingertips and fell into the pond. Berry sat up and watched it float for a moment, before slowly sinking under the glassy surface. It faded from view like a retreating dream.

"I don't want to fold paper bears," said Antonia.

"Well, then I don't want to swim."

Antonia sat up. "I do," she said. She pulled her dress over her head and dropped it on the rock, then stood there in her underwear with her arms folded in front of her. She looked like a miniature Annabelle, so sure of herself.

Berry sat up, twisted her torso to watch as Antonia walked to the edge of the diving rock, then cannonballed into the pond. Berry counted the seconds as she waited for her to surface. When she got to 50, she started to worry. When she got to 100, she started to panic. She stood up and walked to the edge of the rock and looked down, straining to see a ripple or a bubble along the mirrored surface.

"Antonia!"

Minutes passed. Still no sign of her. Berry started to pull her shirt over her head so she could dive in.

"I thought you didn't want to swim." The voice startled her and she nearly lost her balance. It was a man's voice. Berry struggled back into her shirt and spun around. Antonia was standing by Berry's backpack, searching through the contents.

"How did you do that?" asked Berry. She was shivering.

"Do what?" she asked. She had pulled the third package of crackers out of the backpack and was tearing it open.

"I didn't see you surface after you dove in." She must have imagined the voice. Surely she had.

"Maybe you weren't watching closely enough," said Antonia. She finished the crackers and stuffed the wrapper into the backpack, then rifled around in it another moment. She pulled out the white gloves, snorted at them, then stuffed them back into the backpack.

"Ooh...what's this?" She held up her aunt's pocket knife.

"I suppose you're going to steal that, too."

"I don't steal things. Stealing is wrong."

Berry walked over to Antonia. She was still playing with the pocket knife, opening and closing it, weighing it in her hands, jabbing at invisible monsters.

"Can I have it?" she asked.

"No."

"How about if I trade for it?"

"What do you have to trade?"

"Oh, lots of things. You haven't been to Treasure Place yet."

"Is that near your house?" asked Berry.

Antonia laughed, but said nothing else. She kept the knife and bounded up to the diving rock, then pulled the dirty dress over her head. Her hair wasn't wet, but her face and hands were perfectly clean.

"Tell me where you live, first. My dad needs to know."

"Nobody needs to know but me." She hopped down to the shore and started walking around it to the opposite side of the pond. Berry thought about heading back home, but once again she found herself torn between two worlds.

The best stories are those that you write with your hands and feet.

She rubbed her hands together to brush off the dirt and dust, kicked at her sneakers, and followed Antonia.

24

Walking to Antonia's treasure place was like exploring a different forest from the one where her trees lived. Those were grand trees, clever and interesting and diverse trees. But all the trees here were giants. Wide-trunked behemoths that towered over a moss and thicket-covered earth. The land was mostly flat, but the trees were so thick that Berry kept losing Antonia, who was alternately skipping and running between them, around them, and in moments when a sliver of light flashed through the leafy canopies, through them, it seemed. With every step Berry felt more and more lost. She would never be able to find her way back on her own.

She knew she should have felt afraid, but she couldn't quite muster the courage for that.

Up ahead, Antonia had stopped at what appeared to be a small ridge. Berry caught up and found herself on the ledge of a deep, crater-shaped valley, looking down into a junkyard that might as well have been that other world she was daydreaming about. It was at least a hundred yards across, roughly circular in shape. It was as if a giant ladle had scooped away the earth, then someone had dumped a hundred garage sales into the hole. The sun shone down into it like a spotlight and a spray of a thousand points of light dotted the treasure place, bouncing off the dulled edges and broken frames of refrigerators and dryers and swing sets and bedsprings and something that looked like the wing of an airplane.

"This is Treasure Place," said Antonia.

"It's a junkyard," said Berry. But even as she said it, she began to see order in the way the innumerable abandoned objects were stacked and arranged. If she squinted, she could almost imagine it as a distant city.

"It's Treasure Place. And you need to capitalize both words or you're saying it wrong."

Berry looked at Antonia and smiled. "Well, aren't you full of surprises." She realized that statement was true for a dozen reasons as the words spilled out of her mouth. "It looks a little dangerous. All those rusty edges. Don't wild animals like to hide in junkyards?"

"It's not dangerous if you know where everything is."

"You don't know where everything is. There are hundreds of things here..."

"Thousands. Maybe even millions. And I do know where everything is," snapped Antonia. "I spend a lot of time here." She weighed the pocketknife in her hand again, then reared back and threw it.

"Hey!"

It arced through the air, then bounced off the top bar of a rusty swing set and spun away into a cluster of washing machines, pinging, then clinking twice before falling somewhere between them.

"I didn't say you could have it..." began Berry.

"I didn't steal it. I'm trading for it."

"Well I didn't say I wanted to trade for it either."

"You followed me here, didn't you? You're always following me." Antonia shrugged, then started down the side of the steep hill, moving with the grace of a cat, not the clumsiness of a little girl. Berry had no choice, so she followed her down. They came first upon a row of twelve broken refrigerators, six on each side of a small footpath. All but two were missing their doors. Inside each one, bent and broken shelves held all kinds of little treasures, neatly set in rows and layers – springs of various sizes and shapes in one, handles and doorknobs in another.

"Wow," said Berry, as she studied the makeshift display cases.

"I told you I have lots of things to trade," said Antonia.

Berry continued past the refrigerator welcoming committee, then along a winding path that never grew much wider than a couple of feet, but had been carefully carved out of the mess of sharp metal corners and splintering wood and fading plastic. A crowd of garden gnomes, some missing their hats or their heads, welcomed her around one corner. A row of backyard windmills waved their awkward hellos in a breeze around the next. Tires were stacked everywhere by the half-dozen on metal poles like donuts on a dowel. It was a surreal wonderland.

"This is amazing…" said Berry. She brushed her hand across a forest of wind chimes hanging from a metal clothes line. The music they played was sad and beautiful. "How did you find this place?"

"I didn't find it. I made it."

"No you didn't."

"Most of it."

Berry sighed. "I seriously doubt it." But she didn't care if Antonia was lying again. She was far too mesmerized by the seemingly never-ending path through the organized junk. They came to a small clearing, about the size of a four-square court. New paths went off in three other directions, like the points of a compass.

"Which way do we go now?" Berry asked.

Antonia pointed to the path on the right. "I haven't finished that one yet." She pointed to the one on the left. "You can't go that way because I said so." She started off down the path directly in front of them. When Berry hesitated, Antonia reached back and grabbed her hand and dragged her forward. They weaved their way through a sea of rotting mattresses and quivering bedsprings until the path curved around to the land of abandoned washing machines and dryers. At least two dozen dryers were on the right, neatly arranged in rows like an army awaiting orders. A similar number of washing machines filled the left side of the path. But they were haphazardly stacked, upside-down, sideways, dented and broken. Like defeated soldiers.

"The dryers seem to have won the war," said Berry, mostly to herself.

"They don't always," said Antonia. Berry suddenly felt cold.

"How come nobody knows about this place?" asked Berry.

"I know about it."

"A place like this wouldn't go undiscovered for long," said Berry. "Someone, or lots of someones must have brought all this junk here."

Antonia sighed. "You haven't been listening."

"I know. You made this. But there's no way. No possible way."

"Believe whatever you want," said Antonia. She started off down the path again, paused to motion at Berry to follow her. They left the appliance battlefield behind and suddenly Berry was surrounded by discarded electronics. Dozens of tube-style televisions, boxy wooden objects that might have once been record players or radios and a scattering of other devices including old-school phones, computer towers, keyboards and mice. And cell phones. Berry couldn't imagine how many cell phones littered the ground around them. Hundreds? How could anyone collect so many phones?

She stepped carefully around a black plastic box with wires spilling out of it like the entrails of a dead animal and reached down to pick up a particularly new-ish looking cell phone.

"Why would someone throw this away? It looks brand new."

"Sometimes people get tired of things," said Antonia. She sounded more sad than matter-of-fact.

"Hey, maybe my dad's phone is in here…" She started sifting through a pool of cell phones, but it was like Horton looking for his Whos in a field of clover.

"Do you ever get angry?" asked Antonia. Berry stopped searching and looked up. Antonia was straddling two televisions, towering above Berry, her arms on her hips like Peter Pan.

"Yes," said Berry.

"Then I have one more thing to show you." She hopped down off the TVs onto the path, and continued down it, ducking under a trellis made out of bent and torn window screens and door frames tied together with rope and twine and vines. Berry followed her.

The path ended and she stared at the ground before her. It was covered with books. Rain-soaked, muddy books. A flood of books. She bent down to lift one from the muck, brushed the mud away from its bloated cover. *Tales of a Fourth Grade Nothing.*

"I know this one," she said. She smiled at the memory of reading it. But the smile faded as she stared at the lava flow of bookish destruction. "This is so sad," she said.

"I thought you'd like it," said Antonia.

"Why?"

"Because you like books."

"But these books are…they're damaged. They're unreadable." She set *Tales of a Fourth Grade Nothing* down neatly, then picked up the book that was beneath it – a math textbook, by the look of the faded cover. It fell apart in her hands, the pages dripping like oatmeal onto the ground. "So very sad," she repeated.

"This isn't what I wanted to show you," said Antonia. "Come this way."

Antonia bounded across the sea of books, her feet slipping and sliding across pages and dirt. Berry followed much more slowly, trying her best not to disturb the books that looked mostly intact. They walked up to the edge of a hole that was at least twenty feet deep and twice as many across. Soggy books flowed over it like a frozen, literary waterfall. Directly across from them was a rusted truck cab that looked like it was growing out of a cliff wall. Or perhaps like it had been driving underground and got stuck there, half in the hill, half out. Roots from trees at the top of the junkyard crater snaked through broken windows and around the rotting tires. It had been there a while.

"Look down," said Antonia.

The bottom of the hole was littered with broken bottles and cans and bits and pieces of objects she couldn't identify. It was as if someone had crushed an entire houseful of trinkets and poured the junk into this space.

"Here," said Antonia. She handed Berry a cell phone.

"Wait...this is...you did steal it!" It was her father's phone.

"It doesn't work anymore," said Antonia.

Berry flipped it open and tried turning it on. The screen stayed blank.

"Sometimes when you're angry you do bad things, things you don't mean to do." Antonia paused, kicked at the books by her feet. "So I made this place." She spread her arms in front of her. "This is where I come when I'm angry."

"Well, I'm starting to get a little angry myself," said Berry. "You lied to me. Again!"

"Lying is wrong," said Antonia. "So is stealing."

"I think I'm really and truly and seriously done being your friend," said Berry. She turned to leave.

"Throw it," said Antonia. "At the truck. Just whip it as hard as you can."

Berry spun back around. "Why would I do that?"

"Because you're angry."

"At you, yes!"

"That all?"

Berry opened her mouth. Nothing came out. She *was* angry. She was very angry. But not at Antonia. Not really. She was mostly just annoyed with Antonia. No, she was angry at her mother. For running away. For deciding that Berry wasn't important. And for showing up and confusing her heart.

She was angry at her aunt for being hard-headed and stubborn. For not being honest about her feelings.

And she was angry at her father.

Was she? She could never be angry at her father.

She was angry at cancer. At the stupid, stupid cancer that was stealing him from her.

She cocked her arm and let the cell phone fly. It shot through the air like a missile, struck the bumper of the pickup truck, then spun off into the abyss below.

"Here," said Antonia. She handed Berry two more cell phones. When had she picked those up? "Sometimes bad words help."

"I thought you didn't like bad words."

"I only use them when I'm angry."

Berry looks down into the pile of metal and glass and plastic.

"You must be angry a lot."

Antonia scowled.

"Cancer sucks!" Berry threw the second phone. It missed the truck and slapped against the dirt, stuck there for a moment, then dropped to its death on the pile of plastic and metal.

"Be angrier!" Antonia yelled, then began to giggle.

"Fuck cancer!" Berry shouted as the third phone clipped the driver's side mirror, bending it further inward. Antonia's giggle morphed into a guttural laugh, then abruptly stopped.

Berry was breathing heavily. "Show me where you live," said Berry.

"No."

"*Show me.*"

"I won't."

"I think you live here," said Berry. "And I'm going to prove it."

Berry turned and started across the ocean of books, walking briskly, not thinking about the stories she was pressing into pulp, the pages she was bending into oblivion.

"Stop!" said Antonia.

But Berry wouldn't stop. She ducked under the trellis, then ran down the path to the nexus. She looked left, then took off down the right path. The one Antonia had warned her about.

"Berry!" Antonia was on her heels, but Berry kept running, dodging a tangle of rusty pipes, leaping over a snake pit of coiled hoses, squeezing between stacks of bent and broken chairs, until the path ended abruptly at the base of the rocky cliff. Antonia joined her a moment later. Berry looked up. They were at least twenty feet below the surface of the forest. Directly ahead of her was a deep, dark hole carved out of rock.

A cave.

"Don't go in there," said Antonia.

"Why not?" Berry asked.

"Because of bears." Antonia said it so matter-of-factly Berry felt another chill down her spine. She turned to face her tiny forest friend.

"Antonia. Do you live here? Don't lie."

She looked down at her feet, and for the first time since Berry had met her, Antonia looked like a lost girl. "Sometimes," she said.

"You don't have a regular home?"

"Who wants a regular home?" The sass was back just as quickly as it had disappeared.

"How do you eat? How do you stay warm in winter? Where do you...go to the bathroom?"

"I don't need to tell you any of that," said Antonia.

"No. You don't. But I'm going to have to tell someone about you. About this. I have to, now."

"Please...don't." Antonia grabbed Berry's arm, squeezed hard.

"Antonia, you can't live out here by yourself. It's not safe."

"It's safer than you think."

"You're hurting my arm," said Berry. She shook free and took a step toward the cave.

"You could live here with me..." began Antonia. The ground began to rumble and shake. The whole of Treasure Place seemed to rattle and hum. A growl joined the cacophony.

"No!" yelled Antonia. Except it wasn't her voice. It was a man's voice. That deep, gravelly voice she'd heard before and tried to deny. Berry spun around and looked up into the face of a bearded giant. He tilted his huge head and the sun behind him briefly blinded her. She squinted and screamed and ran past him as fast as she could back along the path. At the nexus, she got confused, and continued straight ahead, following a path she quickly realized wasn't the way out. She slowed as the path came to an end, her feet crunching on a bed of sun-bleached shells. A huge object loomed in front of her.

A ten-foot tall bear stood mostly hidden under the shadow of a gray tarp that flapped in the suddenly howling wind. She froze, waiting for it to lunge for her. But it didn't move. She stared and stared at it – then realized it was a sculpture of a bear. A strange and beautiful sculpture of a bear formed out of metal and plastic and rope and wood. Out of junk.

She leaned to the right to look behind the bear. There, on the bottom shelf of a scratched and scarred china cabinet were six skulls. Six human skulls lined up like trophies. Children's skulls.

She looked down at the ground. Not bleached shells. Bones.

She spun around and began to run back the way she'd come. She stepped on something round, twisted her ankle and fell. The last thing she saw before she blacked out was the boot of a giant.

200

25

Berry choked on a mouthful of water and fumbled to find purchase for her arms, her legs. She sat up in the shallows of the pond, the muck sucking her deeper as she struggled. She jerked her head around to see if that monster of a man was near. She listened for footsteps or heavy breathing or the rustling of leaves, but all she could hear was quiet groan of the forest.

She felt for a knot on her forehead, but there was none. She stood up and looked down at her shins. Most of the scrapes and bruises were gone. She tested her ankle. It seemed fine.

"Antonia?" she whispered.

There was no reply. She ran her fingers through wet, stringy hair and sloshed to the shore. Her backpack was leaning against a rock. She grabbed it and started running through the forest, once again praying that she was going the right way. When she saw the tree house, she took a wide arc around it, then avoided every other landmark she could as she wound her way through the trees back to the stone wall. She hurried through the opening and up the hill, stopping halfway to catch her breath. The sun had nearly set when she reached the deck. She sat down on the top step and pried her muddy shoes off, then peeled away her soaked socks. She could hear activity inside, but wasn't ready to face her aunt or her father.

Berry opened her backpack and reached inside. She removed her book, her flashlight, and...her aunt's pocketknife.

"What?" she said aloud.

The screen door slid open. "There you are."

It was her aunt's voice. Berry didn't turn around.

"I'm sorry," she said. "I lost track of time." It wasn't a lie. It was never a lie where the forest was concerned.

"You got caught in the storm?" said her aunt.

"The storm?"

"It was pouring here. Wasn't it pouring where you were?"

Berry couldn't remember any rain. "Oh, yes. It's why I'm so late. I waited out the storm in the tree house."

"You should come in and dry off. And…well…your father needs to talk to you."

Berry turned around and looked in through the door. "Is he okay?" Her heart, which was already beating fast, found a new gear and sped up even more.

"He's…he's tired, Berry. So hurry on in and I'll make you some hot peppermint tea."

Berry nodded. Did Aunt Annabelle know that was her favorite? She stood up and held out the pocketknife.

"Thanks for letting me borrow it," she said. "I didn't need it after all."

"Oh, you keep that. It's yours now." Annabelle closed Berry's hands over the knife, then held them for a long moment.

"Has my…has Penelope come back? Did she call you?" Berry asked.

"No." Annabelle's response was firm and final. Berry wouldn't ask her again.

Berry grabbed the backpack and carried it into the house, she paused to look at her father. The bed was bent into a partially reclined position but he had his face turned away from her so she couldn't see if he was awake. She hurried up the steps and down the hall, stealing glances at him, watching to make sure his chest was rising and falling. It was. She quickly changed into dry clothes, stopped in the bathroom to brush the knots out of her still-wet hair, then returned to the living room and sat down on the couch. Her father opened his eyes.

"Hey, Raspberry," he said. His voice was little more than a whisper.

"Hey, Dad."

"How was your adventure?"

"You aren't going to believe it…" she began, then stopped. "Aunt Annabelle said you wanted to talk to me."

"Tell me about the adventure first," he said.

She told him everything, except the part about the giant man who might or might not have tried to drown her.

"Antonia the forest girl," her father said after she had finished. "Well, you're right. That is quite a story." He paused. "Can I ask how much of it is true?"

"Yes you can."

When he smiled, Berry could see a sliver of blood appear on his chapped lips. "How much of it is true?"

"All of it."

"Really?"

"Most of it," she corrected herself, even though all of it was absolutely true. She grabbed a tissue and gently wiped the blood from his lip.

Berry looked up to see her aunt standing in the kitchen doorway. When she saw Berry look at her, she shrank back, like she was embarrassed she'd been caught eavesdropping. It wasn't like there was enough space in the house for true privacy, but Berry still thought it odd.

"Your turn, Dad," said Berry. "Tell me about your adventure." She scooted forward on the couch and reached for his hand. She nearly recoiled when she felt the cold clamminess of his skin.

He cleared his throat. "I want to talk a little about your next adventure," he began.

"No," said Berry. "No, no, no."

"Berry…"

"You're going to get better, Dad. I just know it."

"Berry, I'm not…"

"I'll call Mom. She'll come back and you'll start smiling again and the cancer will be so frustrated with your happiness that it will

203

run away and everything will be like it used to be. Well, not like it used to be when she left us, but a new kind of used to be..."

"She's married, Berry..."

"...but she still loves you. I can tell she does. You make her laugh. I've seen it."

"Berry..."

"And she makes *you* laugh."

He slid his hand out from under hers and placed it on top. She repeated his action, and they played a brief round of the slap-happy game they'd named "top hand" when she was seven. Berry won, her hand resting on her father's in the end. But then she slid it under his anyway.

"I know you have important stuff to tell me," said Berry. "But you can tell me tomorrow."

"You know we can't delay this conversation forever..."

"Tomorrow, Dad. I promise." She lifted a cup of water to his lips. He sipped some through the pink bendy straw.

"Okay. Tomorrow," he said.

Berry had climbed onto the couch and was leaning over the back of it, trying to see the titles of the books hidden behind it.

"What are you looking for?" Berry turned her head to see her aunt adjusting the pillow under her father's leg cast.

"Do you have any Judy Blume books? Like *Tales of a Fourth Grade Nothing*, for example?"

"Oh, I must have at one time. But...hang on a second..." She walked over and helped Berry pull the couch away from the bookshelf. "Check in the cabinet," she said, pointing to the two closed doors in the lower middle section of the bookshelf.

Berry climbed over the couch and squeezed into the space there. She pulled open the doors. Books were stacked front to back in the small space.

"I'll have to pull them all out," said Berry.

"Do it. I'd like to see what I hid in there."

Berry started removing the books, stacking them on the back of the couch. There wasn't much of a ledge, so the books fell onto the cushions. Like a waterfall, thought Berry. The Treasure Place memory troubled her because it wasn't nearly as vivid as she expected it should be.

"Do you ever forget stuff?" she asked Annabelle as she continued to remove the books and drop them onto the couch.

"Well, I think so. But how would I know?"

Berry looked up at her aunt. She was trying to smile.

"Oh, that's a joke. Right?"

"I guess. I'm not that good at jokes. But it's also kind of true, don't you think? I mean, if we forget things, then that means we don't know about them anymore. So how would we know we're forgetting them?"

Berry pulled the final stack of books from the cabinet, closed the doors, and stood up, setting the books gently onto the couch cushion. "Maybe we don't forget everything…just enough to know that something's missing."

"That sounds about right."

"What's something you wish you could forget?"

Annabelle took a breath, then pursed her lips and exhaled slowly. "My almost-marriage."

Berry laughed. Her aunt wasn't laughing. "That's not a joke, is it."

"Nope," said Annabelle.

"What happened?"

"I left him at the altar."

"No you didn't," said Berry. She looked up from the stack of books.

"Well, not literally. I left him a few days before the wedding. Right after your grandmother died."

"What was his name?"

205

"Morris." His name sounded exactly like a sigh.

"Why did you leave?"

She took another deep breath. "He was a really good man."

"That doesn't sound like a very good reason to leave," said Berry.

"I suppose I just didn't feel...worthy. Well, that, and I was scared."

"Of what?"

"Becoming my mother," she said.

A buzzer rang out from the kitchen. Both of them jumped and even her sleeping father seemed to startle. "Oh, that's funny timing." She laughed. "Cookies are ready."

She walked briskly across the living room floor toward the kitchen.

Berry started going through the books that had taken over the couch. Most were unfamiliar to her, but there were a bunch of children's and young adult books in this mix, so she was at least a little hopeful.

"You read *The Boxcar Children?*" she called out to her aunt. Her father stirred again. "Oops," she said. Annabelle walked back into the living room, came over to look at the books with Berry.

"Yes," she said. "And more than my share of Hardy Boys books." She pointed to a half dozen of them.

"Hardy Boys? Not Nancy Drew?"

"Oh, some of those, too, but I preferred the boys."

"So did Dad," said Kenneth from behind them.

"You're awake?" asked Berry. "Sorry about that."

"Wait. What do you mean, 'so did Dad'?" asked Annabelle.

"Berry and Penelope found some letters in Mom's old trunk. They were love letters..."

"So?" said Annabelle. She had stopped sorting through the books and was looking at her brother.

"Love letters from a man named Benjamin. To Dad."

"Ben? Ben wrote love letters to Dad?" she gasped.

"You knew this…Ben?"

Annabelle sat down on the couch, knocking a few books to the floor in the process. "I called him Uncle Ben because he was always over at the house. Don't you remember? He hated it when I called him that. He said, 'I ain't no box of rice.'"

"No. I don't remember."

"Oh Kenneth, do you think Mom knew?"

"The letters were right there with all her stuff." He nodded at Berry.

"Her wedding dress was in there, too," she said.

"She must have known," said Annabelle. "I'm pretty sure she put that trunk together herself. She might have mentioned something about it to me before she died, but I was tuning her out in the last days. She was just so hard to listen to. Oh, I don't know how to process this. I mean, I might have suspected if I'd thought about it. And…yes, it makes sense. A whole lot of sense. But why wouldn't she tell me? Us?"

"Maybe she was embarrassed," said Berry.

"Or maybe it didn't matter," said her father.

"What do you mean?" asked Annabelle.

"I mean maybe it was just who they were and how they related each other and there wasn't any reason to say anything to anyone because what would be the point? Further judgment from people who already thought them a bit mad? And besides, secrets aren't something new. They've been around as long as people have."

"Oh, I know that," said Annabelle. She reached down to pick up the fallen books. "Oh Berry…here it is! I do have it."

Tales of a Fourth Grade Nothing. Berry took it and opened the book to the title page. She looked down at the publication date.

"Aunt Annabelle…how old were you in 1972?"

"Oh…let's see…fifteen?"

"Then why do you have this book? It's for little kids."

Annabelle looked over at her brother, then back to Berry.

"I was a late bloomer," she said.

"What does that mean?"

"Well, it can mean lots of things. But in this case, it means I wasn't a very good reader early on. I didn't do very well in elementary school or junior high. It wasn't until I got to high school..." She let the words trail off into silence.

"Your Aunt Annabelle was a little preoccupied during those early years."

"Doing what?"

"Making sure your grandmother didn't burn the house down, for one," she said.

"I thought the house *did* burn down?"

"Well yes, but that was entirely coincidental. Unless Mom called down that lightning strike from the grave." Annabelle looked over at her brother and smiled.

Berry pondered that for a moment, then nodded. "Well, you like books now, and that's what matters," she said. She held up the Judy Blume book. "I'm going to read this one again. I liked it the first two times, so I'll probably like it again."

"Do you read all books more than once?" asked Annabelle.

"No. Just some of them." She looked at the pile of books. "Should I put these back?"

Annabelle pointed. "Just set them on the floor there next to the couch. I might want to re-read one or two myself." She smiled at Berry and Berry thought it was the nicest one she'd offered yet. A shared love of books must bring out the best in people, she decided.

"I know Mom will show up soon," she said, hoping to take advantage of the swirl of kindness in the room.

"That would be nice," said her father.

"I think she might have gone back to New York," said Annabelle.

"Why do you say that?" asked Berry's father.

"I might have spoken with Jeanette down at the B&B," she said with obvious embarrassment.

"You called to check on her?"

"No. I called to *talk* to her, but Jeanette said she'd checked out this afternoon. Jeanette only mentioned it because Penelope had asked specifically if she could stay an indeterminate number of nights. Jeanette says they never keep a booking open like that. It's just not good business. But she agreed. I suspect Penelope offered money. Did you see the designer tags on her clothes? Maybe I was wrong about her motives. Anyway, she checked out late this afternoon."

"Maybe there was an emergency," said Berry.

"Maybe there was," said Annabelle.

"But that doesn't mean she won't be back."

"I don't know what it means, Berry," said her father.

He started coughing and Berry turned her attention to him, handing him his cup of water and wishing she could just push a button like the ones on the bed that would set the cancer and the cold and the chills and the dehydration and the broken bones straight.

Annabelle started to leave, then stopped and turned back to face Berry. She began to leave again, then repeated the spin.

"What is it?" said Berry's father after catching a breath. "What is it that you want to say? You're fidgeting again."

"Am I? Well, it's nothing," she cleared her throat. "Okay, it's something. I told Sheriff Noonan about the forest girl."

"Why?" cried Berry.

"Because if it's true that there's an eight-year-old girl living out there in a junkyard, someone needs to do something about that. It's not safe. And it's not right. What if she's a runaway and her parents are worried sick about her?"

"She's not a runaway," said Berry. "She's an orphan. I think."

"Even more reason to find her. She needs a home – a real home."

"So you eavesdropped on my story," said Berry.

"Yes, I did."

"And you believed it?"

"Yes...yes. I did."

Berry smiled. "Well, that's something." She tilted her head in thought. "What did they say? Are they going to look for her?"

"They said they'd search the woods tomorrow."

"I don't think they'll find her," said Berry.

"Why not?"

"Because she's really good at hiding."

The sound of her father's raspy breathing woke Berry around seven. He seemed to be gasping for air. She stumbled out from under her covers and walked over to him. His eyes were open, and he looked panicked.

"Annabelle!" Berry shouted. A moment later, her aunt came bounding out of her bedroom wearing a floor-length nightie. Her hair was pressed against the side of her face.

"What is it? What's the matter?"

"Dad's having trouble breathing," she said. "We need to do something."

"Press the button," Annabelle said. "Help him to sit up."

"Will that help?"

"I hope so."

Berry pressed the button and the bed moved much too slowly into a partially upright position. Her father's hand reached out and grabbed her shoulder. He choked away some phlegm and, after a long sip of water, found his voice. Annabelle had run down the hall and was holding the kitchen phone in her hand.

"Should I call 911?" she asked.

"Yes," said Berry.

"No," said her father. "I'm okay. It's just some congestion."

There's no such thing as 'just' anything at this stage, thought Berry.

"Are you sure?"

"I'm okay," he rasped. "I'm okay." He ran his fingers through Berry's hair. "Sorry to scare you like that."

Annabelle started dialing a number on the phone. But it wasn't 911, thought Berry. Too many numbers.

"I'm calling the hospital anyway. I'll have them send that nurse over later today to make sure you're...comfortable."

"Not the mean nurse." He looked at Berry and rolled his eyes. She tried to smile.

"No, the nice one."

"There isn't a nice one," he said.

Annabelle disappeared into the kitchen to talk on the phone. When she was finished, she hung up and wandered back into the living room.

"Who does your hair?" said her brother.

"Donald Trump," she answered without missing a beat. Berry didn't know who Donald Trump was, but by the way her father started laughing, she figured it must be a really good joke.

"I'm going to get dressed..." began Annabelle, but her words were interrupted by the ringing of the phone.

Berry listened in as Annabelle answered.

"Hello?...Ah, well, we were wondering where you were...Why don't you just come here?...Okay, I can do that. Give me...fifteen minutes or so to get dressed and fix my hair...make it thirty...see you there."

She walked into the living room.

"Who was that?" asked Berry's father.

"Your ex-wife."

"Mom?" said Berry. "Where is she?"

"She's still in town. Says she spent the night in the bus station. I didn't even know we had a bus station. She wants to talk."

"You invited her over, right?" said Berry.

"She wants to talk to me. Alone. I have no idea why."

"I'm sure you have some idea," said Berry'.

"We're meeting for breakfast."

"Will you bring her back after?" asked Berry.

"I think that all depends on what she has to say."

"What about what you have to say? Will you invite her back?" he asked. The answer he was hoping for was pretty clear in the way he said it.

"We'll see."

26

How are you feeling, Dad?" asked Berry. Her aunt had been gone for just a few minutes, and Berry knew she didn't have much time to put her plan into action. She had decided it when she saw the new bruises on her father's legs.

"A little weak," he said.

"I think you need to write a story with your hands and feet."

"What? When?"

"Now?"

"I don't think I can go very far…"

"Dad. I think the pond is a healing pool. Look at my legs. No bruises. Well, mostly none. And you saw how my rash disappeared that one time."

"Oh Berry, I don't think I can walk all that way. I can barely shuffle to the bathroom."

"You don't have to walk."

"Are you planning on carrying me?"

"No…but there's the wheelchair…"

"And how are you going to get that down the hill?"

"With ropes?"

"Berry, that chair weighs almost as much as I do."

"You don't weigh very much," she said.

"It sounds like a grand adventure, Berry, but…"

"Wait…I can lower you down on one of the sleds."

"And then what?"

"We'll go slow. You can lean on my shoulder. It might take a while but that's okay. It would be worth it. It could make you better…"

"Don't go raising your hopes now, sweet Raspberry. Okay?"

"I know. I might be wrong. And it could all go very badly. But…"

"But what?"

"Even if it did, it would be *our* adventure…"

"One last grand adventure together."

"Or maybe not the last one…" Berry started to feel those nasty tears growing in her eyes. She swiped at them and wiped her hands on her shorts. "And…" She stuffed her hands in her pockets.

"And what?"

"I'll let you tell me the things you need to tell me…you know…before you go."

He took a deep breath, then slowly let it out. He began shaking his head and Berry's heart sank. But when he spoke his voice was as sure as it had been in days.

"Let's go on an adventure."

With her father's guidance, Berry attached the long rope from the garage to the two-man sled she had wrestled from the garage wall. Then she wrapped the rope around a beam that was supporting the deck. Just once, to give her more leverage, her father said. She pushed the sled to just over the edge of the hill and tested to see if it would slide down on its own. It just sat there in the dirt.

"Maybe if you sit on it?" she said.

"Why don't we use the wagon?" he said.

"But I lost the wagon…"

"Isn't that it?" She looked where he was pointing at the edge of the woods. Sure enough, there was a wagon.

Berry slid down the hill, then jogged over to the wagon. It was the one Antonia had claimed as her own. That meant it was her grandfather's, for sure. She pulled it up the hill slowly, worried that she might expend all of her energy before she really needed it.

When she got to the top of the hill, her father had already untied the sled. He tied a new knot to the wagon handle, then tied it again. A double knot.

"It looks much different than I remember. Did you paint it?"

"I think Antonia did."

"Well, that makes me even more eager to meet this forest girl."

Berry tested the wagon on the hill and, as expected, it rolled just fine.

"With me in it, it's going to roll a lot faster," said her father. Put your gloves on. That will prevent rope burn."

Berry put on her white gloves.

Her father looked over and laughed. "This might be the craziest thing we've ever done," he said.

"So far," she said. She held tight to the rope. The wagon was just over the edge of the hill. "Climb in and see if I can hold you."

He sat in the wagon, with his left foot dug into the dirt for purchase, and his right lying across the front, his cast looking like a cannon on the front of a warship. She turned to face the deck, giving her full attention to the rope. She felt the weight pulling her toward the deck, but dug in her feet. It was more than she had anticipated, but she adjusted her footing and held fast. "I'm going to lower you down now," she said. "Hold tight."

"You, too."

She started to let the rope out little by little. She could hear the wagon roll slowly down the side of the hill.

"How are you doing," she called out.

"Fine so far," he answered. But she could hear a little trepidation in his voice. "Only a few million feet to go."

Berry let another foot out. Then another. A bee started buzzing by her face.

"Dad, there's a bee..." she said. She wrinkled her nose, shook her head to get it to leave.

"Don't let go, Berry."

She tried to ignore it. She batted at it with her elbow and the rope started sliding through her hands. She gripped it tight, felt it burn through the gloves.

"Dad!" She couldn't hold on any longer and the rope flew out of her hands. She turned to see her father racing down the hill in the wagon, jarring left and right, threatening to tip with every bump. But somehow it stayed upright, and flew straight. It rolled to a stop just a few feet beyond the gap in the wall. Her father was grunting or howling or screaming. Berry hurried down the hill.

"Dad! I'm sorry…I couldn't hold on…are you…?"

When she got to the bottom of the hill, she saw that he was holding his chest, fighting for breath.

"Are you okay?"

He let out a gasp and started laughing.

"Oh. My. Goodness." He said. "That was…awesome!"

His laugh quickly turned into a wheezy cough, and Berry grabbed the water bottle and handed it to him. A few very long moments later, he seemed to have caught his breath.

"You sure you're okay?" she asked.

"Better than okay. I mean, apart from the heart attack I nearly had."

"I'm sorry I let go."

"Sometimes you have to, Berry," he said. He reached out for her hand and she helped him out of the wagon. He placed his hand on her shoulder. "Sometimes you have to," he repeated.

They walked slowly and silently toward the forest, her father limping along while holding tight to Berry's shoulder. She felt every ounce of his weight in that shoulder, but she didn't care. It was a blessed pain and a holy touch.

"I'm not sure…I can talk much…while we're…walking," he said as they approached Bernice.

"That's okay. I'll do the talking for now. I have some introductions to make, anyway."

"You mean...the forest girl?"

"No. I mean the trees."

She named the trees as she approached them, and her father insisted on stopping to touch each one. She was thankful for the breaks. He leaned against the trees like they were old friends. If he weren't so tired from walking, Berry was certain he would have carried on a conversations with them. Instead, he played a guessing game with Berry.

"Bernice," said Berry.

"After the school librarian?" said her father.

"You remembered."

"Hard to forget. She looked like my mother."

"Buttercup."

"The Princess Bride."

"Beanpole."

"The Tripods books?" he said.

"Snape."

"It looks just like him."

"Rosemary."

"Oh...*Tender Is the Night.*"

"Fitzgerald."

"F. Scott."

"Junie."

"...B. Jones."

"Templeton."

"Hmm...oh, I know...Charlotte's Web," he said.

"Zachary."

"Got me there."

"I just like the name."

"Arrietty."

"The Borrowers?"

"Henry."

"Huggins, or is it Higgins? No, that's from My Fair Lady. It's Huggins."

"Me Margaret."

He laughed. "The Judy Blume book. You thought that was her full name."

Berry smiled.

"Eloise," she said at the next tree.

"Picture books?"

"Yeah."

They kept walking.

"Lucy."

"Narnia?"

"Yep."

They took an extra long pause at Lucy.

"Billiam."

"No clue."

"I made it up."

"Horatio Christian Kennebunk MacDougal."

"You made that one up, too. Well, some of it, anyway."

"The first name is after the dog, of course. But yeah. The rest is made up."

"You should write a story about him."

"Maybe I will."

They approached the twisted tree. Berry could feel her father's lumbering gait falter. She held tighter to his waist and they stopped short of the tree.

"Nicole Diver," said Berry.

"The twisted tree."

"Yes."

He let go of her shoulder and walked up to the tree, dragging his cast-wrapped leg like a pirate's peg leg. He ran his fingertips across the sticky bark.

"Hello old friend," he said.

They rested there for a few minutes, sipping water and sharing an energy bar Berry had found in the cupboard.

"Better than chalk soup," he said. She thought it tasted like cardboard, and she worried that her father might choke on it, but he managed to eat nearly half without incident.

They continued on in silence, apart from her father's wheeze and frequent grunts. They stopped again in the middle of the baseball field, and in that pause Berry saw their adventure through her father's eyes. He stood there and stared down a memory that Berry imagined involved lots of shouting and running and balls flying through the air. As she watched him remember, she thought of the movie they'd watched together when she was eight. He said it was his very favorite movie because it reminded him about the best parts of growing up.

The Sandlot.

They continued on, ever more slowly until they reached the permission tree.

"You didn't know about this tree," said Berry.

"No."

"Antonia told me it was a permission tree. But now I'm not so sure. Maybe it's not a special tree after all. She makes up stuff a lot."

He took a long sip of water. "Maybe it's special to her," he said.

"I'm going to ask permission anyway." She danced around the tree, stroking it with her fingertips, whispering her request to the leaves. After a moment, she stopped. She looked at her father. He didn't look well at all. He was sitting on the ground, breathing heavily. His skin was pale.

"This was a bad idea," said Berry. "This was a terrible, horrible, awful idea."

"I just need to rest a moment more," he said.

She sat next to him. He lay back against the ground. She did the same, then reached for his hand and held it.

"Listen," he said.

"To what?"

"Everything."

She breathed in the scent of the earth, stared up through the leaves at the patches of blue, and listened.

"Is that singing?" her father asked. He sat up. "I hear singing."

Berry listened harder. "I think it's Antonia."

"Help me up. We have miles to go before we sleep…"

She scrunched her face into a puzzle.

"It's from a poem by Robert Frost."

"Read it to me when we get back," said Berry.

"I'd quote it for you now, but my brain is a little fuzzy."

They lumbered on until they came to the tree house. Berry noticed that more of the wall boards were broken or missing. The porthole was nowhere to be seen. In its place was an irregular, gaping hole. Some, but not all of the foot hole plugs in the tree were gone, too, and she couldn't see them near the base of the tree.

"It wasn't this broken before," she said.

"It's perfect," said her father. He was crying. "So perfect."

They stood there for another long moment, then her father nodded and Berry led him through the deeper forest to the pond. When they finally reached it, the sun was almost directly overhead.

27

W e've been gone a long time," said Berry. She helped her father around the rocks to the only place where they could wade in, just the other side of the diving rock.

"Worth every minute," said her father. She helped him remove the shoe from his left foot.

"Is it okay for the cast to get wet?"

"Actually, it's a very bad idea. Especially if the water isn't clean." Then he shrugged, stood up awkwardly, and waded into the pond. Berry kicked off her sandals and chased after him. They stopped in knee-deep water.

"Now what?" asked Berry.

"Help me sit down," he said. "Or you can baptize me like they do in the movies."

"You mean like in church."

"No, like in the movies. It's more dramatic in the movies."

"I don't think I have enough strength left to do that."

"Then just help me sit."

She did, then sat down next to him. The cool water came up to her chest.

"How do you feel, Dad?"

"Exhausted," he laughed. "But the good kind. The relaxing kind of exhausted."

"But do you feel any...different?"

"Berry...remember what I said about getting your hopes up."

"I know. I just..." she drew circles in the surface of the water with her fingers. "Never mind. Either it works or it doesn't."

"Exactly," he said. "But I can tell you this: It feels good, Berrycicle. Really good."

They soaked in the pond for a long quiet moment. Her father bent forward and splashed water on his face. She did the same.

"It's not fair that you're going to miss all my best moments," said Berry.

"I'm not missing this one," he said.

"I know, but...who's going to be there to cheer for me when I do important things?"

"I'll be there, if there's any way I can be, Berry. You'll just have to feel it in your heart. I know that sounds cheesy, but..."

"Like in E.T."

"I'll be right here," he said in a voice that was naturally like E.T.'s these days. He pointed to her heart. She grabbed his index finger, then lifted his hand to her lips and kissed the back of it.

"Who's going to teach me all the becoming a woman stuff?" said Berry when she'd let go of his hand.

"Well, let's see. There's Annabelle and Penny. Pick one."

"Was Annabelle ever my age? I don't think so. And Penelope, Penny...Mom acts younger than I do sometimes."

"I guess you're screwed then," he said.

"Yeah. I suppose I am."

Berry closed her eyes and leaned back on her hands, feeling the mud sift through her fingers and the sun bear down on her face.

"Okay, I'm ready. Tell me the stuff you have to tell me."

"Are you sure?"

"Yes."

"Well, the most important thing is something you already know: I love you Raspberry Lynette Granby. You won't forget that will you?"

"Don't think I ever could," she said. She kept her eyes closed tightly, fighting the tears, but they began to seep out anyway. "Do you think Mom really is sorry? She has apologized like a thousand times."

"Yes."

"What did you talk with her about?" asked Berry.

"You. The future. And a little about the past."

"But not too much."

"No," he said. "Not too much about the past. Can't change it, you know."

"Nope," said Berry. She swatted at a fly. The first she'd seen in all of her visits to the pond.

"Annabelle has agreed to adopt you if that's what the three of you decide."

"What three of us?"

"You, Annabelle and Penelope."

"Wait…so you do trust her. Mom, I mean."

"I knew her once and I trusted her implicitly then. She's not that person now, of course. But I trust this version of her. I know it's not much to go on, this brief re-introduction into our lives. I do know she loves you, terribly."

"That sounds like the right way to describe it. Terribly."

He laughed. "I also know she thinks it will take a miracle for you to love her back. But she's willing to wait for that."

"I suppose I might be able to love her at least as much as I hated her. Did you talk about her marriage?"

"Only enough to know that it's going through some tough times. But John seems like a good man."

"How do you know?"

"Because Penny chose him. Because he misses her."

"She hasn't said much about him. I don't think she likes him."

"I don't know. But this isn't just her story, you know? He has his own stuff – his own battles. She didn't say exactly what they were, but there are no small battles when you're fighting to stay together."

"You didn't get a chance to fight."

"Oh, but I did. And I fought like hell. You were so young then, I thought it best to keep it from you. It took me weeks, but

I eventually found out where she was. We traded some really heated words then. We both said things we later regretted."

"I thought she just left and we never heard from her again."

"She had fallen in love with someone else, Berry. And that made me so angry. It was…a complicated situation. I fought for her, pleaded with her. I tried everything, but when she said she couldn't promise me she could find her way back, I told her I didn't want to see her ever again."

"You said that?"

"I did."

"But why? You could have shared…what's that word?"

"Custody."

"Yes, custody. I could have visited her…maybe on weekends like some of my friends back in Nashua…"

"I was a stubborn man, Berry. Sometimes I take after my sister. And I thought I knew what was best. She was hundreds of miles away, and I couldn't stand the thought of seeing her once a week or once a month or even once a year to hand you off."

"Because you hated her?"

"Yes. And because I loved her. I still do."

"I don't understand," said Berry.

"I don't really either," said her father. He lifted his hand out of the water, ran his wet fingers through her hair. "And that's probably the most important thing I wanted to tell you."

"That you don't understand?"

"That love is complicated. That it doesn't always make sense. That it makes you do stupid things. And that sometimes…sometimes those stupid things end up being the right things. And even when they're not, you can't give up. You have to keep moving. Just keep going forward, even when your life feels like it's stuck, or going backward. "

"But you didn't date much."

"I tried. But there's no one quite like Penny."

A hawk flew across the sky in front of them. Berry watched it disappear over the trees. She listened to the gurgle of the pond and the whisper of birdsong.

"Do you wish she could take care of me when you're gone?"

"I think Annabelle would do just fine, but..."

"But..."

"Maybe it's not just a coincidence that she got that phone call. She told me she'd been praying for a chance to see you again."

"She prays?"

"Well, not in the churchy way. She's not very religious. She made that abundantly clear. But she's quite spiritual...it was one of the myriad things that made me fall in love with her."

"What does 'myriad' mean?"

"Many, varied."

Berry took a deep breath. "This is a lot of stuff to think about."

"I'm sorry, Berry."

"It's not your fault. And I know it's not my fault either. Sometimes things just happen."

"Sometimes they do," he said.

Berry pinched her nose and leaned back to submerge herself in the water. She wanted to wash away the clutter that was collecting in her head and her heart.

When she sat back up, the sky was dark and she was alone.

28

"Dad!" she shouted.

"Shh…" he said. She turned around and saw his silhouette on the diving rock. He was sitting there, his legs dangling over the edge. "I think I hear voices."

Berry sloshed out of the pond and started to shiver.

"We were talking," she began, "and then I ducked my head underwater and when I came up it was night. It's just like when…"

"There's something out there in the forest. It's been watching us."

"I was underwater…"

"What? I…I thought you were sitting next to me," he said. She climbed onto the rock and sat next to him. "My brain is scrambled. I don't know…" He hugged her. "You're shivering. We need to get you back home. Warm you up by the fire."

"There's no fireplace at Aunt Annabelle's."

"Annabelle's?"

"Dad…what's going on? Are you feeling okay?"

"I…feel…I don't know…"

"We need to get you home," said Berry. She helped her father stand and led him down off the rock. She pulled the flashlight from her backpack, then slipped the backpack onto her shoulders. "Are you okay to walk?" she asked. He wrapped his arm around her shoulder and they started through the forest.

"Listen," he said again. She stopped. "Do you hear it?"

"I hear the wind," she said.

"There's something out there."

"Dad, you're scaring me."

"Berry…you're soaking wet." He looked at her as if just noticing.

"We were in the pond…"

"There it is again!" She felt his body jerk around to the left, then the right.

"Daddy…it's okay. I'm going to take you back to the house. It's all going to be fine…" she said, but the sobs had stolen the last words. She urged him forward, one small step at a time. He wouldn't stop fidgeting, twisting this way and that to seek out the source of sounds Berry couldn't hear.

They made it as far as the tree house before her father collapsed onto the ground. His breathing had been loud and raspy, but now it was thin, barely audible.

"Dad," said Berry. "Dad…you need to get up. We have to get you home." She tried to lift him. He was too heavy. "Please Dad…"

A growl froze Berry in place. She didn't move. Another growl made her spin around in a circle. She waved the flashlight like a sword, but it found no enemy. Still another growl. A deep, throaty growl like that of a bear.

"Antonia?" she said, her own voice reduced to a croak. "Is that you? I need help. My Dad needs help. Please…"

Berry shined the light up at the tree house. The walls and roof had been torn away and there were deep scars on the boards that remained. There were gouges on the tree. Claw marks. Another growl came from behind her. She spun around again and pointed her flashlight at the source of the noise. There, standing just ten feet away, was the giant bearded man. He wore torn brown rags for clothes and smelled like rotten eggs. He must have been seven feet tall.

"Who are you?" asked Berry. She sounded more confident than she felt.

"I am Anton," he said, his voice heavily accented. "I will help."

He took a step toward her. "Don't come any closer!" Berry waved the flashlight at him, pulled off the backpack and fumbled through it looking for the pocketknife. But before she could grab it, the beast of a man had lifted her father off the ground and thrown him over his shoulders. Her father grunted, but didn't speak.

"He's sick," Berry said. She finally grabbed the knife. She threw the backpack over her shoulders again and started after the giant. "Where are you taking him..."

"Keep up," he said.

He moved quickly, dodging around branches and stepping over logs without slowing. Berry had to jog to catch up, and even with the flashlight guiding her, she couldn't keep from stumbling.

He stopped for a moment at the permission tree, brushed his hand across it. Berry followed him at a safe distance and shined the light where his hand had been. There, stuck in the folds of the trunk was her blue origami bear. She pointed the light at his head as he walked away. He turned to look at her with his bright green eyes, nodded, and kept walking.

When they got to Bernice, the giant stopped. He set Berry's father on the ground.

"No more," he said. He pointed toward the hill.

She looked ahead and saw dancing lights bouncing down it like a waterfall of fireflies. She heard the shouts.

"I see something!"

"There, in the trees!"

"It's the girl!"

The monster...Anton...walked up to Berry. He placed his giant hand on her head and held it there. "I am sorry," he said. "I miss parents, too." Then he lifted his hand and started running back into the forest. He paused, turned back to her and called back in a child's voice, "Thanks for the snacks." Then his footsteps faded into the blackness.

The rescuers arrived less than a minute later. Two of them lifted her father onto a gurney and carried him up the hill. Another placed a blanket around Berry's shoulders. She pointed her flashlight at the upturned wagon by the stone wall. It was rusted and dented and old. She refused the insistent help of the strangers with flashlights and crawled up the hill by herself. Annabelle and Penelope were both standing at the top, waiting. Annabelle took a step toward Berry, then stopped. She looked at Penelope and nodded. Berry fell into her mother's arms and sobbed.

29

Berry woke with a start, confused and lost and stiff and sore. She squinted at the bright sunlight pouring in through the unfamiliar picture window.

Her aunt was curled up next to her on a rollaway bed under a hospital blanket that didn't quite reach her ankles. A monster of a hospital bed sat directly in front of them. It was nearly hidden by a wall of machines and wires and tubes. Berry briefly thought of Treasure Place, then wiped the thought from her sleep-addled mind.

"Dad?"

She slid off the boxy chair onto the cold floor, stretched, then walked up to the hospital bed. Her father was hooked up to a dozen different machines, each of them beeping and wheezing away in a complex rhythm. But it was a song without a melody.

"Dad?"

Behind her, Annabelle stirred.

"Berry, you're awake."

"Yes. Dad isn't though."

"No."

Berry walked back to the chair and picked up a blanket that had fallen off of it. She wrapped herself in it and sat down.

"Is he ever going to wake up?"

"Berry...I'm sorry. No."

"But he might..."

"His body has shut down. It's just the machines keeping him alive, now."

A nurse walked into the room. She came directly over to Annabelle and Berry, not even bothering to look at any of the machines that surrounded her father like soldiers. Or mourners.

"Dr. Magnussen had to go into surgery, so he won't be able to stop by until later today. I wouldn't expect him until after lunch," she said.

"Isn't there anything you can do?" asked Berry. She felt like she had asked this same question a hundred times. Perhaps she had. Her head was still foggy.

The nurse looked over at Annabelle. "It might be good to take a break. Get some fresh air. Nothing is likely to change in the next few hours."

"I don't want to leave," said Annabelle. She looked past the nurse to the door.

Berry followed her gaze. Penelope was standing there. She was wearing her business suit again – the one she'd arrived in, but her hair wasn't confined to a bun this time and she wore sneakers on her feet. She brushed a wayward strand of hair from her face and Berry could see that she wasn't wearing makeup.

"I could take Berry for a while," she said.

Annabelle nodded.

"But what if Dad wakes up while I'm gone?"

"Berry..." began Annabelle.

"Then he'll be happy to see you when you get back," interrupted Penelope. Berry knew she was lying. She knew her father wasn't going to wake up again. But this was the right time for a lie.

"Is it windy outside?" asked Berry.

"Windy? Um...I don't know. Why?"

"I want to fly the kite Dad and I made."

"Really?" asked Annabelle.

"It's at your house," said Berry. "Can Mom borrow your car?"

Berry and her mother sat at a picnic table near the small parking lot at Moose Run Park, putting the finishing touches on the kite's tail. They hadn't said a dozen words to each other except to coordinate the plan to fly the kite.

Penelope finished tying a knot in the string and tugged at it.

"There," she said. Now all we need is a little wind.

"I think maybe it's better to fly kites in the afternoon," said Berry. "But I don't know. This is my first kite."

"Really? Ken…your father never took you kite flying before?"

"Nope. But he took me bowling. And skating. And sledding. And he took me to the zoo and baseball games and movies and even the opera once…" She paused. "Sorry. I'm not trying to be mean."

"I know." Penelope laid her hand on Berry's. Berry didn't flinch. "He really took you to the opera?"

"Yeah. Just before we moved here. It was weird. I think it was about love and lying and murder and death and stuff like that. Kind of like *Tender Is the Night*, I suppose. But I didn't understand the language so I'm not really sure. The singing was good, though. Or maybe it wasn't. How can you tell if opera singing is good?"

Penelope laughed. "Do you remember the name of the opera?"

"Carmen?"

"Ah, Carmen. The gypsy. Of course he would choose Carmen."

Berry lifted the kite, studied its shape – a diamond; considered the balsa wood frame shadowed under the fragile paper – a cross. She ran her fingers across its tail, feeling the knots in the thin strip of cloth and pausing at each of the seventeen crepe paper bows, whispering their names with every touch. It felt a little like praying, but what did she really know about prayer? When she was done, she set the kite back on the table.

"I had a long talk with my husband, with John," said her mother.

Berry didn't respond. She was watching the trees, looking for evidence of a breeze.

"He wants to meet you," she continued.

"So he's a good man after all."

"Yes. Of course we've had our share of challenges. All relationships do."

"Not the one my dad and I have. Had."

"Oh, sweet Raspberry. Your father is the best of his kind. I know that now. I probably knew it eight years ago, too. But even that relationship would eventually have challenges. You're almost a teenager..."

"He won't be here for that."

"No. He won't. So all of your memories will be good, then. That's not the worst thing in the world, is it?"

"Maybe it is."

Penelope sighed. "You're right. Maybe it is."

They sat in silence for a while. When her mother was looking away, Berry studied her profile, looking for traces of herself. She saw clues in her mother's freckles, of course. And a little bit in her eyes. But not so much in the cheeks or the nose. Her mother turned back and smiled. And there it was. She had seen the same smile in the mirror. Back when she smiled.

"What do you think will happen to Antonia?" asked Berry.

"Annabelle said they searched the woods for hours last night. Didn't find anyone. They were at it again this morning, but I haven't heard an update." The wind started to pick up. "Ooh...do you feel that?"

Berry grabbed the kite and jumped off the picnic table and started walking to the open field. Her mother jogged after her.

"Here," said Penelope, pointing to the string. "Hold the kite by the end, and the string in your other hand right about here and start running. When I say 'let go' let go of the kite and then keep running until the kite rises into the air."

"How do you know how to fly kites?" Berry asked.

"My father taught me," she said.

"You can tell me more about him later," said Berry. She took off running.

"Let go!" shouted Penelope.

The kite flew up into the air, then immediately bounced down to the grass, then up into the air again.

"Keep running!" shouted her mother. She came up alongside Berry, urging her on.

Berry lifted the string as high as she could and ran as fast as she'd ever run. The wind caught the kite again and it lifted into the air. It rose up, up, up. Berry felt a hand on her arm. She slowed to a walk, then stopped. The kite was as high as the treetops. It tugged at the string, dipping and dancing in the sudden strong wind. Her mother walked up behind her and reached around to help her hold the roll of string. Slowly, they let the string out further, until the kite was a tiny pink diamond against the deep blue of the late morning sky.

Berry felt her mother's heartbeat pressed against her back. She inhaled the smell of the park – the grass, the dirt, a hint of bacon from someone's breakfast picnic. She breathed in her mother's scent, cinnamon again. And for a moment, only a moment, it was like her mother had never left.

"I know you're tired of me saying this, but I want to make everything right, Berry," she said.

"It's too late to make *everything* right," said Berry.

"Then how about everything that hasn't happened yet?"

Berry leaned her head back against her mother's shoulder.

"Hi Dad, it's me. Your Raspberry."

The machines kept wheezing and pumping. Her father's chest kept rising and falling. But he didn't wake nor speak.

"I flew a kite today. Mom was there. I wish you could have seen it…"

She bent down and kissed the back of his hand, then the tears came. She turned around and hugged her aunt. Annabelle's arms wrapped around Berry.

"When the machines are turned off, it might take just a little while…" the doctor stopped. "You can step out of the room if you like," he said.

"No," said Annabelle.

"No," said Penelope.

Berry shook her head.

"Goodbye Kenneth," said Annabelle.

"Goodbye, sweet man," said Penelope.

"Goodbye, Daddy," said Berry. Her voice broke in the middle of "goodbye". Berry thought about that and it made her smile through the tears. *Good Daddy*. Yes. That was exactly the right thing to say.

30

Berry had insisted that everyone wear their best adventure clothes for the funeral. She wore her khaki cargo shorts and a light blue button-down shirt with pockets. Annabelle had found a fedora in the church's lost-and-found box that was only just a little big too big. It made Berry feel like Indiana Jones.

Annabelle wore a navy blue skirt and a white blouse and a leather jacket that Berry was surprised to learn had come from her closet. It wasn't quite the right kind of adventure clothing – it seemed more like something for riding a motorcycle, but it was leaps and bounds better than the black dress she had wanted to wear. Penelope wore faded jeans and a t-shirt and a vest that had more pockets than Berry could count. A flashlight and a compass hung from her belt, and she wore dark sunglasses. Probably to hide teary eyes, thought Berry. But the look fit the theme, so she didn't mind.

Most of the people were dressed up for a regular funeral, though. The note about requested funeral attire hadn't made the rounds quite as successfully as the news about the discovery of the junkyard and the skulls. Six children, gone missing a hundred years earlier. Finally there could be some rest for their families, said Annabelle.

Berry wondered if any of their family members were still alive. A hundred years is a long time. Nevertheless, she didn't think they'd rest any easier once the other stories got out. Rumors of a forest girl and a giant. No one would get it completely right. Even she didn't know how it all tied together. But that wouldn't stop people from telling their versions of the stories to their children. And to their children's children. The stories would grow into something new with each telling.

That's how books are, too, thought Berry. No matter who writes them, they always become the reader's story. *Tender Is the Night. Tales of a Fourth Grade Nothing.* Those were her stories now. *Horatio Christian Kennebunk MacDougal.*

Her father said she should write a story about him. She would write lots of stories. Maybe one day she would write a story about Antonia.

Or maybe not. *I already wrote that story. With my hands and feet.*

The sky darkened, and Berry recognized the moment as something her father would have called a cliché. The threat of a storm during a funeral. A heavy sky moment for a heavy earth moment.

Except it wasn't a heavy moment for Berry. She felt the sadness, of course. Mostly she felt it in her stomach. She expected it would eventually move to her heart. But she would always feel it somewhere.

But to see her aunt and her mother standing next to each other in their adventure clothes brought Berry strange joy. Her father would have loved this moment. The man beside Penelope hadn't gotten the message, though. John Parker was sweating in a charcoal gray three-piece suit. At least he had agreed to give up the tie.

Berry reached into the biggest pocket on her cargo shorts and touched the silk of it. John was a quiet man. But quiet wasn't always bad. She would call him John, though. Not "Dad." It was a small enough name not to feel too awkward. She had tried it out a few times already. He smiled each time.

The pastor talked about a future time when they would all be reunited with Kenneth William Granby. Berry didn't know what to think about most of the churchy talk these past few days, but she liked that part. In the meanwhile, she decided she would see him everywhere. At bowling alleys. Zoos. At baseball games and on sledding hills and maybe even at the opera. But mostly in trees and books.

The people bowed their heads to pray. Berry didn't close her eyes; they were drawn instead to movement far across the cemetery. She sneaked away from the crowd and stepped around a tree to get a better view. Antonia was standing near a row of six identical gravestones. Everyone knew whose graves these were by now. Antonia waved at Berry.

Berry looked over her shoulder to see if anyone else was watching. They still had their heads bowed. When she turned back, it was the giant, Anton, kneeling by the graves. He lifted a flower, smelled it, and set it back down. He looked up and held a finger to his lips, then stood and walked toward the woods. Just before he faded into the shadow of the trees, he turned into a bear.

Berry's eyes grew wide, her lips curled into a curious smile.

Tonne, she whispered.

After

Raspberry Lynette Granby-Higgens is standing at the front of the garage. Like the rest of the property, it is nearly empty. There are no stacks of gardening tools, no car parts, no boxes or bins or trunks. There is only a single sled hanging on the far wall. *Rosebud.* She wonders if the auction company left it on purpose. Perhaps one of the men knows about the sledding history of the property.

She pulls her coat tight around her, brushes the melting snow from her cheeks, her nose.

Annabelle's service was perfect, she thinks as she walks over to the sled. Just the right blend of somber and irreverent. She had been lucid to the end. Seventy-seven long years, she'd said. That was plenty. She didn't seem angry at God about her cancer, though she had often yelled at Him about her brother's.

"Your father would have been so proud of you," she had said. Her last words to Berry.

She sighs a puff of condensation into the bleak space.

"He is, Aunt Annabelle," she says to the empty garage. "And he's proud of you, too."

She runs a mental movie through the years, beginning with the day she moved to Morrowton. She sees Antonia as clear as day, wearing a century-old dress, skipping through the forest singing songs and making snide comments. She walks through Treasure Place with Antonia, but stops short of going down the wrong path. She wants to remember it differently. Better.

She sees Anton, though not as clearly. Perhaps he was a little blurry in real life.

And then she sees her father. He is sitting next to her in the pond, his hands folded in front of him, hidden beneath the surface. The water is drawing a line just above his stomach. His gray Led Zeppelin t-shirt is spotted black by the splash and spray of the water. He has just run his hands through his thin hair and it is wild. His smile is even wilder. Like all of her forest memories, it is a moment she can't be certain really happened. But it feels real enough, so she holds onto it.

She fast-forwards to the park – to the first kite she ever flew. Far from the last. To her mother's scent. It was cinnamon that day. Now it's something more complex, harder to identify. Earthy, and a little bit floral, but thankfully not half as pungent as her aunt's last obsession.

"Twenty-one years is a long time," she says to the sled as she lifts it from the hook. She sets it on the muddy floor of the garage, tests its sturdiness with the press of her foot. It still has a few hills left in it, she thinks.

She finds it difficult to believe this is her first winter at Annabelle's. All the Christmases they might have spent here, and yet none of those plans worked out. Of course she spent many summers here. Penelope and John insisted. Not because they didn't want her around all the time (they truly did), but because they learned to love Annabelle, too. Nine summers, she thinks.

No, ten.

And not one sign of Antonia.

Without Antonia, the forest had lost most of its magic. Treasure Place had become a junk yard. The tree house had fallen into disrepair. Then there was the logging. She didn't notice it much the first couple of summers, but by the third, she could see the far edge of the forest from the top of the hill. And each year after, that forest shrank more and more.

She flew a kite at Moose Run Park each time she lost a tree friend.

Berry grabs the fraying rope and starts to drag the sled out of the garage. Her husband is sitting in the idling truck on the un-shoveled driveway. They had barely made it up the hill. She waves to him. He waves back. Paul is a good man. He came all this way without complaint, despite the sudden snowstorm.

He will be a good father, too. Maybe not the best father in the history of life. But surely the second best. She will tell him the news next week. On Christmas morning. It will be his favorite gift.

"You ready?" he calls out to her through the open window.

"Nearly."

She looks at the house one more time. It is a greeting card in twilight under the falling snow. It had never been home, but it was always a safe place. Annabelle made sure of that.

"I'll just be a few minutes," she calls to Paul. "Maybe you should join me?"

He pauses, then turns off the ignition and climbs out of the truck. He crunches across the snow to her with a curious look on his face.

"You aren't thinking what I think you're thinking...are you?"

She laughs. "Maybe I am."

She takes his gloved hand in hers, dragging the sled behind them as they walk around to the back of the house. The deck is weathered and worn, the awning lists to one side. It looks naked without Annabelle's old leather chair. The one her father had claimed for just three short weeks.

Three weeks. Was that all it was?

"It looks so different," she says aloud. The ocean of trees is completely gone now, swept away by giant machines and a hunger for houses and books, though not nearly enough of the latter.

Bernice is still there. She is standing tall, queen of the last line of defense between Granby Hill and what has become a ribbon of empty hills. They are painted white with snow, like shallow scoops of ice cream. It's better to see it that way, she tells herself, than to see what it once was. Too many ghosts.

"Logging," her husband says, then simply shakes his head. She adds this moment to her very long list of "Reasons I Love Paul."

Then she thinks back to the vibrations she felt in the forest during the Summer of Antonia. Had they started clearing the forest then?

The Summer of Antonia. That would be a good book title, she thinks.

"I hope you're okay," she whispers.

"You're talking to the forest girl," says Paul.

She nods.

"Still think she was a shape-shifter? You had a name for it..."

"Leshii. But that's always just been a guess. Some kind of magical creature, anyway."

"Magic," he says, in exhale. "Tell me again about the wall."

"It's what kept the magic in," she says. "Well, that's just one of my many brilliant theories anyway. Aren't you tired of hearing my silly stories?"

"I love all of your stories," he says. "But I'm still puzzled about Antonia. If she really was a hundred years old, why didn't anyone else find her? Why did she stay silent for so long?"

"Maybe she was waiting for a friend. Who knows? Monsters are as fickle as people."

Paul laughs.

"For years I believed Antonia was just a lost little girl and all I could do was hope she eventually found a happy home. But I couldn't shake that scene at the funeral."

"It could have been a trick of the light," says Paul.

"Or maybe it was all in my head," says Berry. She pauses, sighs. "Probably that."

"I'd like to believe it all happened just as you remember."

Berry studies her husband's face, sees only sincerity and kindness.

"Oh, I almost forgot," he says. "There was a bear sighting in the news last night."

"Really? Where?" Berry holds her breath.

"Up near Presque Isle."

"That's almost Canada!" She sighs. "But there are still plenty of bears in Maine…aren't there?"

"More than a few. But not so many with green eyes," he adds.

"A green-eyed bear? Someone saw a green-eyed bear?" He nods. Berry closes her eyes and smiles and inhales the icy air through her nose.

"Well?" Paul says. She opens her eyes. He is looking down at the sled.

"It's not the first snow," she answers. "The hill will be extra fast."

"I'm not afraid of extra fast," he says.

"What are you afraid of?"

"Monsters," he says.

She laughs again.

They point the sled toward the gap in the stone wall and climb aboard. He pulls them just over the edge of the hill, digging in with the heels of his work boots. She holds tight to the reins. He wraps his arms around her.

"This might be the craziest thing we've ever done," says Berry.

"Just another in our endless succession of magnificent possibilities," says Paul.

Berry closes her eyes to see the forest as it was. She begins humming a forgotten song.

And Paul lifts his feet.

Acknowledgments

A book is only a solitary act while it sits in the writer's head. Here are some of the people who showed up to make this one better. Let's start with the early readers: Sarah Elwell, Amber Butler, Kelly Sauer, Kristin Russell, Dylan Hearn, some people I'm forgetting, and a few random family members (see also, below). These are people who tell you with a friendly smile what they loved and a forced smile what they didn't. Patrick Rothfuss, a generous soul who was a slightly-later-than-early reader, gets a nod here, too. His comments were, in a word, invaluable. Thank you all.

Then there are family members (told you), who, in my case anyway, didn't just say kind things, but also offered helpful advice. This would include my mom and dad (heroes for many reasons, including being rabid readers and skilled storytellers), my brothers Mark and Tim, my sister Martha, my children, Topher and Scot, Scot's uber-talented wife, Abbie (thanks for the origami illustrations), and my brilliant, perfect granddaughters, Harper and Luna. Many thanks to each of you.

There are hosts of others who don't know they mattered, but did: Neil Gaiman, Wil Wheaton, Carol Rifka Brunt, John Green, Maureen Johnson, Lois Lowry, Craig Ferguson, Zach Braff, and Imogen Heap. You don't know me, but you helped. Thanks.

There are a few others who deserve thanks, but won't be named here because secrets make things magical. So if your name isn't listed, it's magic. Or forgetfulness. It could also be that.

One final thanks goes to Jenny Lawson. Jenny is not only brilliant and insane and hilarious, she's the kind of friend who can make you believe you have created something worth sharing. Thanks Jenny. (And Hailey. Okay, Victor, too.) I may not yet be furiously happy, but if I ever figure that out, I'm blaming you.

About the Author

Stephen Parolini is a full-time freelance editor and writer who shares his small Colorado apartment with an assortment of imaginary characters and the occasional misguided spider. He is the author of the novella, *Duck*, which isn't about a duck at all, but you know that already because you read it, right? You didn't? Well, maybe you should.

You can find Stephen on the web in two locations at once. While this sounds like alchemy, it's really just technology. He has a small collection of short stories (the absolutely free-to-read kind at www.countingonrain.com. And you can find information about his day job (freelance editor) at www.noveldoctor.com.

CPSIA information can be obtained
at www.ICGtesting.com
Printed in the USA
LVOW04s0346120816
500068LV00014B/159/P